THE BABY

by
Alan Levy

HARNIX PUBLISHING

www.harnixpublishing.com

For my parents, my heroes.
Who told me anything was possible,
and were right.

BOOK 1
GENESIS

IF THERE'S ONE thing I've learned, it's this: only through our lies do we find our truth. Sounds like some metaphysical mumbo jumbo, right? Well, it's not. It's my way of warning you. Sending up a flare. Preparing you for what's to come. Because trust me when I say you are not prepared.

Me, I'm a shoo-in for eternal damnation. I'll fit nicely in Hell. But on the slim chance I could still sneak into Heaven, I'm sharing my story as a penance, one last-ditch effort to claw my way out of Hades under the heading "mitigating circumstances." No, "temporary insanity"—that's better. All I ask is when you trip over the lies, the ruse, the severed hand of a two-week-old in a box, maybe you will consider that it wasn't entirely my fault. In fact, if you want to blame anyone, I'd say why not start with *that man?* Or the Sisters, or the money. And if you still can't forgive, even after that, just go ahead and ask yourself, "What would Jesus do?"

CHAPTER 1

Veritas liberabit vos
"AND THE TRUTH shall set you free."

No doubt Jesus, being *Jesus*, when coining that phrase, *had* to know two thousand years later it would be silk-screened (in gothic letters no less) on the back of an oh-so-snug T-shirt donned by a pimpled hipster who I'm pretty sure couldn't translate the sentiment if the Second Coming itself depended on it. The Lord certainly does work in mysterious ways. That's what we get for flying commercial: sweat and slogans.

Okay, so maybe the truth *will* set you free, but bending it a little just might set you apart. Besides, maybe it isn't freedom you want. Some of us want more.

I contemplate this as we walk through airport security, London. We are flying first class, of course, but not private. That means a regular airline at a regular airport— Heathrow, to be exact— which also means we have to suffer the indignity of a security checkpoint. We're late and in a hurry. They won't hold the flight, not even for the young (40 is the new 30, don't you know), handsome, recently retired US Ambassador (John) and his wife (me,

Amanda – 28 years old, 5'9", 110 lbs., all-American goddess, Terminal 5's latest star attraction, who looks like she just stepped off the runway in Milan. Conceited? Not at all. You just haven't seen me yet).

I feel like a first-time drug runner, fidgety and on edge. My birth control pills, the object of my paranoia, are right there in my Hermès bag, nestled ever-so-delicately in their matte-pink plastic wheel with the days of the week clearly marked, nearly a month's supply. The night before, I considered taking them out and putting them in a nondescript bottle instead. Then, in my first-gear paranoia, I imagined the ethnically ambiguous TSA officers eyeing me—no, eye-fucking me—lingering in their ill-fitting uniforms behind overpriced X-ray apparatuses and surgical masks.

"Excuse me, ma'am. Could you and your husband come 'ere, please?" They would like nothing more than to pry me open and inspect me, but dumping out the contents of my Hermès is as close as they'll ever get. They pick out the bottle, feigning shock, exchanging disapproving glances. "What do we 'ave 'ere, luv? Little pills then? Could you show us the prescription? Um, no, we will not go somewhere private where you can explain out of earshot of your husband, and no, we don't actually care that he would swan dive off the Tower of London if he knew you were on the pill." For obvious reasons, that can't happen. I consider just tossing the pills and keeping my legs crossed instead, freezing John's precious little swimmers in their starting blocks until I get a chance to fill another prescription back in LA. "No rumpy-pumpy for you, Johnny-boy." (G-d, I love British slang!) "The Chunnel is officially closed for business."

"I need to piss," I say instead. I like how crass it sounds.

My frigid words spray the chilly London air, provoking a heated temper tantrum.

"Why do you always have to wait till the last minute?" John fumes. "I swear this is what traveling with a child must be like (not that I will ever know). Just hurry it up, okay? If we miss the flight (and the champagne service), I'll literally kill you—"

I slip into the ladies' room and toss the pills in the bin ("trash cans" are a uniquely American convention). I pause for the appropriate tinkle-time, check my face and hair (*Damn*, I'm gorgeous—did I mention that?), and then I'm back with John, apologizing for my "wee little bladder." Suddenly we're lovers again, bounding down the concourse hand-in-hand like a couple of eloping teenagers, drawing less-than-admiring looks from the hoi polloi. In hindsight, my *couture* micro-mini and four-inch Christian Louboutins were probably not the best idea.

The security detail, of course, doesn't even glance at our bags, which makes me feel like an idiot. Already I pine for my pills. Abstinence is only a temporary solution; I'm going to need a refill, and quick. Unfortunately, this will involve going to see Dr. Goldman, OB-GYN, in person—no way would he call in a prescription, not three and a half years since my last stateside appointment, especially with my history. A small price to pay, I suppose, considering the alternative.

The next thirteen hours are a blur of premixed Bloody Marys, rubbery airline food, and some unapologetic eavesdropping on a couple of old gray-beard geezers seated behind us—"It was so much faster on the Concorde." "Three and a half hours." "When first class meant something." "And you could leave your bottle-blonde mistress in Essex where you found her." "Keep it down, Walter; they're not deaf, you know."

John pats my hand to stop me from turning around and saying something, which—he should know by now—I would never do. I may have been born in a barn, but I'm not an ass. If there is one thing marrying up has taught me, it's that discretion is indeed the better part of valor, or more succinctly: *Amanda, keep your big fucking mouth shut.*

"I'm so sorry to bother you, Ambassador, but the captain has asked me to make sure everything is to your liking. If there's anything I can do for you, just press my little button." The flight attendant is dark and curvy and leaning just a little too far in. Her intentions are so transparent she might as well dangle her moist panties under my husband's nose. Of course, she ignores me entirely. I'm used to it by now—the effect John has on women. The funny thing about John is he *looks* interesting, but he's really *not*. He could have been an actor. All he needs to do is stand there and stare and people think he's thinking deep thoughts, or is sincerely moved, or contemplative, or thrilled—whatever you want. But the truth (which takes some time to learn) is that *nothing* is going on in that head of his. He's not acting; he's not even pretending; he's simply absent. If he endorsed a cologne, it would be called "Vapid & Beautiful—the scent that isn't."

It's homecoming. We've been in London for just short of four years, where John was the US Ambassador to the UK, and now he isn't, having given millions to the wrong candidate this time. Oops. Such is politics. This morning we moved out of Winfield House, a *real* mansion with 35 rooms, the official British residence of the US ambassadorial family (formerly us and now "some Democrat libtards," as John so eloquently puts it). Looking back, it's actually more of a palace, twelve-and-a-half acres in Regent's Park, with the second-largest private garden in central London after Buckingham, sold to Uncle Sam for a dollar back when a buck was worth something.

Talk about your art of the deal. This evening we'll be sleeping in a different mansion, in Bel-Air, heart of Los Angeles, just as snooty, though a different kind of snoot. In Europe, "old money" is measured in centuries; in LA, it's weeks. This goes a long way toward explaining why our new abode, 16 Oak, looks more like a military compound (complete with gaudy warrior statues) than actual architecture. I don't care; it's temporary anyway. John Speedy will soon become *Senator* John Speedy (D-CA) (after switching parties—it's complicated) and we will end up in Georgetown somewhere (or Virginia or Maryland), wielding power and influence like feudal lords and ladies. This might sound "half-baked" as my suburban-simpleton mother would say, but what do I care? I follow the money.

The chauffeur, a card-carrying member of the double-digit IQ club, doesn't even know what we look like (they don't teach Google at community college?), so he stands there at the Bradley International Terminal at LAX with a homemade sign (piece of cardboard pasted to the front of an iPad), "Speedy," our unfortunate name, scribbled in green ink and underlined twice. It's only slightly less embarrassing than taking the bus. On the plus side, it's a short drive, no time for chatter, just a "did you have a good flight?" and "no, it was awful," before the window goes up and chauffeur whoever gets his first lesson in Speedy transportation.

Too tired to check out the new digs except to confirm they're massive, expensive, and tasteless, I go straight to bed. Baring the standard California earthquake, mudslide, or forest fire, I assume the house will still be there in the morning.

Which it is, and I'm blissfully in bed, waking, before I realize to my horror that it's Tuesday, aka "fornication day," and John is already in the shower, no doubt polishing his joystick and contemplating an unscheduled approach and landing, ETA any second. I bolt from the sheets, wrap myself in the nearest robe, and charge downstairs, rolling through the impressive square footage like a tumbleweed, eventually discovering the dining room, where a copy of the *LA Times* beckons. I flip to the only page of consequence, the society page:

"Kayla Smithe-Beckworth is pregnant."

Jesus, kill me now.

Of all the people who could have been blessed with offspring, why her? Or more to the point, why not me? Stunned, I take a seat at the dining table. Confirmation of the news, along with a breakfast of Greek yogurt and assorted pastries, is immediately served up warm by Valeria, our long-serving chef, who has weathered the journey from England in good form as well, it seems.

"I see you happy today, Missus Amanda. I see on my Instagram the Queen Bee she is having a baby." *Thank you, social media; what would we do without you?* "Me, I am loving babies very much. Maybe you can also be having one now, Missus."

(Make that our long-serving-but-soon-to-be-dismissed chef.)

"Yes, yes, she told me last week," I fib, dismissing the news. "We've all been very excited, but no one's talking about that anymore. By the way, Val, your croissants are especially fluffy this morning. You should really make them more often."

My first interaction of the day, and I already have five little white lies under my belt. I'd like to see Kayla Smithe-Beckworth pull that off. Now *that* would be a newsworthy accomplishment, more significant even than Kyle managing to insert his pathetic little member (yes, *of course* I have firsthand knowledge) into Kayla far enough and with sufficient frequency to produce a result. Kayla and Kyle: if procreation required a minimum combined IQ, the conception would have been deemed illegal, *ab initio.*

"Congratulations, babes," John breezes in, taking a seat at the table. "I guess your friend's finally knocked up."

My husband's callous word choice confirms that he's either totally oblivious to my true feelings on the matter or has grown balls the size of coconuts overnight.

"Yeah, I think I saw that on Facebook this morning," I reply, feigning indifference. I wonder if he buys it. More fundamentally, I wonder if he can perceive I'm tempted to remove his tongue with the antique ivory letter opener next to the mail. Either way, he continues his morning routine of cappuccino and Fox News relatively unaffected. His inadvertent nonchalance is infuriating. I have an urge to start an argument but immediately think better of it. (He's going to suffer enough.)

On the kitchen's second monitor, a polished black and silver Mercedes-Maybach creeps into view. The vanity plate, "SPEEDY 4," could easily be misconstrued as creative wordplay, but actually it's a statement of fact, the fourth in an annually updated collection of bespoke automobiles, all owned by my mother-in-law, Mary-Elizabeth Speedy, and all driven by dedicated, full-time chauffeurs. It amuses me to note that if she'd married Dr. Lipshitz (her cosmetic surgeon) instead of Charles Speedy, then "Shitty 4" would be pulling up to the house right now. I quickly dismiss the idea; Mary-Elizabeth would never marry a Jew.

"So, did you hear?" Mary-Elizabeth says as she breezes in. (Everybody's breezing this morning; I'm getting windburn.) "The announcement in *The Times*," she crows, tapping the very same newspaper sitting there on the table. "What wonderful news."

"Yes, it is," Valerie chimes in, coming in from the kitchen to offer Mary-Elizabeth breakfast. "Just a cold iced tea, please, Sally," Mary-Elizabeth answers. Why Mary-Elizabeth never gets

Valerie's name right? I can't explain. Why Val doesn't correct her? *That* I get.

"Now that's what I would call a good wife," Mary-Elizabeth drones on. "Staying so active on the church committee and now giving her husband a little one. Their parents must be bursting with pride, don't you think? Every family needs an heir, you know."

I mimic her faux-English accent under my breath: *"Every family needs an heir, you know."*

You don't have to work in cryptography at the CIA to decode that message. Now mind you, John and I have our own British-infused accents, picked up legitimately from our three-and-a-half-year stint in London, an enviable appointment granted as a courtesy by a president grateful for the mouse (John) who removed a couple of sharp thorns from the president's claw during his re-election campaign, mostly with cash. You may have read about it—it involved a sex worker, a golf resort, and a three-wood.

But enough sports; time for the weather.

Hot and stormy, that's Mary-Elizabeth Speedy, my mother-in-law, the quintessential matriarch, a caricature of the oedipal parent, tanned, toned, sculpted, terrible with names, surgically enhanced. At this stage, it's almost impossible to discern DNA from scalpel; but as much as I hate to admit it, she still looks virtually flawless—not a hint of gray, and wrinkles conspicuous only by their absence. There's no denying that her proprietary beauty regimen of collagen, Botox, and spite presents the world with a blue-eyed, blonde-haired Grandma Barbie (complete with DreamHouse and hard plastic shell).

For the past six-or-so decades, Mrs. Speedy has used her lineage, money, cunning, and world-class body to ascend the social ladder, where, having reached the pinnacle, she now presides as the undisputed HBIC (Head Bitch In Charge). Her children, three boys and a girl, have by proxy more than their fair share of influence, which Mary-Elizabeth has taught them to (ab)use ever so well. Secretly, I've always wondered how much alcohol was required for Mr. Charles Speedy, G-d bless him, to fertilize her overprivileged icebox on four separate occasions (assuming, of course, he *is* the father). Whatever the answer, I'm relatively certain my husband and his siblings owe their very lives to a Mr. Johnnie Walker (Blue Label, of course).

Speaking of intercourse, I remind myself that it's Tuesday, so John will expect sex—*poker night* ("poke 'er" night)—the droll euphemism the overeducated, under-fellated men of the Harvard Club use in reference to their wives' obligatory performance of spousal duties.

(Glad to see that half-million dollars of Ivy League tuition didn't entirely go to waste.) It means John will certainly arrive home from the local chapter of his weekly men-and-members-only club ready for *action*.

I remind myself to call Dr. Goldman, OB-GYN. I need the pills. Now.

I'd almost forgotten how entertaining navigating the west side of LA could be. The sidewalks are a show unto themselves. Upmarket restaurants overflow with the rich and wannabe-famous. Self-designated "agents" talk too loudly into their cell phones while eyeing the long-legged future waitresses posing as starlets-on-the-rise. From the comfort of my brand-new, custom-built Bentley SUV, a homecoming present, license XBH476, which means *nothing*, I rise above it all. Chauffeur-whoever has been fired and I'm driving again, the way I like it, in control, on the right side of the street. The new car smell blends nicely with my Chanel. I inhale deeply.

For the moment, despite the tempest I suspect is coming, I'm perfectly at peace. I have yet to make my decision, but when I do, I'm certain it will be the right one, and I'll live with the consequences, one way or another.

"Babes, don't forget I have my club tonight."

The message appears on a plasma touchscreen accompanied by a robotic voice completely devoid of both commas and inflection: "Jonathan Speedy Office has sent you an attachment. Do you want to open it now?"

I nod my head. The attachment—a picture of John and me—pops into view. I'm not sure whether to be impressed by the motion-sensitive operation or genuinely frightened by the technological intrusion. Either way, I can't help but grin.

The photo: John and I in matching Armani *couture*, smiling and looking ever so slightly off-camera, taken by a world-famous cinematographer with several Oscars on his shelf. John looks particularly dashing. I remember the first time I saw him in a tuxedo. With his perpetually tan skin, quaffed hair, and square jawline, he reminded me of James Bond—not any of the movie actors who played the character but rather *the spy himself*, from the novels, with toned abs, broad shoulders, and a heart-melting smile. I would have liked to have imagined he had a huge penis as well, but by then I already knew better. Nevertheless, it was obvious that (otherwise) John was genetically blessed, a nearly perfect specimen (a girl can't have everything) proving what generations of pedigreed breeding could produce. Standing next to John in the photo makes me appear shorter than I am. Even with my mandatory four-inch Zanotti heels, he still appears to be a good head taller than me. For some reason, the Academy Award-winning director of photography has me placed a half-step behind John, quite literally in his shadow. The thoughtless composition makes my green eyes appear gray, dull even. My blonde hair looks muted, and my dimples are all but invisible. Figures—the cameraman knows who's paying his fee. To me, it's our *American Gothic* painting, sad and disturbing. To John, it's captivating. It makes me wish John and I were closer, or at least more aligned. *If he only knew what I was thinking . . .*

Like a slap in the face with a cold mackerel, there's Kayla Smithe-Beckworth in Sunflowers Beauty Salon, her wafer-thin, five-foot-ten frame perched next to the neon-white "Beauty is Life" sign like a praying mantis: wide eyes and impossibly full lips. Her perpetual pout gives her a deceptively innocent quality. Looking at her, it's easy to understand why ever since I can remember she's always been the center of attention. Yes, if I were that way inclined I'd fuck her (and enjoy it, too). When she sees me, her eyes light up. Either she's orchestrated this "impromptu" encounter or it's a coincidence of cosmic proportions. In retrospect, it makes sense: Queen Bee frequents Sunflowers—I should have seen that coming. Now I'm the victim of a sadistic new game show: "*Face Your Frenemies,* the only show where you enjoy cash and prizes for tolerating the intolerable. Let's welcome our first contestant to *F-Y-F*: Amanda Speedy!"

My stomach churns. With a hard-to-get appointment booked months in advance and nowhere to run or hide, I brace myself for the impending exchange, starting with her squeal of recognition, followed by obligatory air-kisses, and before I know it, I'm trapped and talking "girl-girl."

I'm going to throw up.

"O-M-G. What are you doing here?" she spews like Mount Etna.

It's a waxing salon, you imbecile—I'm here to play tennis.

I often wish my alter ego was in charge, tearing off loose, blunt, face-whitening sentences at will. I'd be the Don Rickles of social interaction, the insult comic of friendships. Instead, I flash my most disingenuous smile.

"Poker night prep," I say simply. She knows exactly what I'm talking about: the plucking, preening, washing, and waxing, readying ourselves to give our husbands their weekly succulent taste of our forbidden flesh. "You?"

Kayla licks her lips, savoring the moment. Her eyes narrow, twinkling with anticipation, like a lioness sizing up her prey, a Prada-clad sociopath ready to pounce. She doesn't intend to merely deliver the news; she means to drill it in. Employing her most dramatic drawl, she twists the words, boring them slowly and deliberately into my psyche:

"So" (pause), "I guess you heard" (pause), "Kyle and I are" (pause)—

She's waited too long. I shoot the gap, whitewater rafting right through her unnecessarily protracted delivery.

"Yes, yes, we're so happy for you," I dismiss it all, feeling the bile rise up in my throat.

"Isn't it amazing? A little miracle growing right here inside Mommy." For emphasis, she rubs her still perfectly sculpted stomach. Adding insult to injury, she offers: "I have a feeling you're going to be the next one." That is true but in a different way. On the list of women who will punch her squarely in the mouth for referring to herself as "Mommy" after only two months of pregnancy, I am all too eager to be "the next one."

I call the doctor's office. As expected, I can't get a prescription without a checkup—*id est*, Dr. Michael Goldman, OB-GYN, wants to fondle my pussy again. The birth control pills are merely the bait in his little amateur cop-a-feel extortion racket, plain and simple. But he's playing hard-to-get: "No open appointments for the next six weeks—vacation, medical conference, he's really slammed right now," the receptionist tells me. I take the first appointment, six weeks off, then heave the phone away.

CHAPTER 2

THAT MAN THINKS it's hilarious. I meet him that afternoon at his mid-Wilshire condo. It's not *entirely* the danger of our meetings that excites me. In fact, part of me wishes I'd never met him. How different my life would have been. We sit on his balcony "afterward," drinking iced tea and looking out on the fastidiously manicured garden courtyard of the complex. There's a tennis court in the distance, two basketball courts, and a swimming pool. Nobody's using any of it in the middle of the day. How that man affords this, I'll never know, but I suspect things. He doesn't have a job; he doesn't work. He does *scheme*, I know that much, and if that knock on the door comes, LAPD or FBI or CIA or some other form of organized crime, I won't be surprised.

He easily made the trip to London several times a year. He said he had business there; I didn't ask what. Maybe *I* was his business. I certainly am now.

Directly below, three stories down, in a pentagon-shaped playground area, a young Latinx mother sits in a swing and rocks a three-month-old to sleep in her arms. It's a Hallmark card or a Norman Rockwell painting with a touch of Diego Rivera. For a moment, I'm almost taken in by it.

"Hey, Maria," that man calls down in a gentle voice. She looks up, smiles, and waves one delicate hand like a homecoming queen. She's even younger (17 at most) and more beautiful than I first thought. She touches one finger to her ruby-red lips to indicate she can't speak lest she wake the infant, an endearing gesture. That man taps his lips back at her, showing he understands, with the suggestion of a kiss at the same time.

"That's Maria," he tells me.

"I heard," I retort, refraining from asking how he knows her, and how much. "She seems pleasant, and that baby of hers is beautiful," I add to be polite, though all babies that age are pretty much indistinguishable, everybody admits.

So, she's got a baby, my mind mutters. Why's everybody so baby-crazy all of a sudden?

"It's not her baby," that man corrects me.

"It's not?"

"She's just the nanny."

"Oh."

"The baby's name is Janice. Her parents work for Pixar Animation, I believe. Mom and Dad went back to work almost right away. Crazy to think that parents would be away from their baby for weeks at a time, right? I guess that's Hollywood for you. The show must go on. Fortunately, they have the resources to hire someone full time; otherwise, there's no way they could do this— have a kid, have a family, I mean."

I admit it; I have no idea why that man is sharing all this information with me out of the blue about people I don't know or care about, or the teenager below, whose nubile young body I'm now certain he's had his way with. But like everything about that man, he has his reasons.

On closer inspection, the baby can't be Maria's. Maria has beautiful, olive-dark skin; the baby's as pasty-white as they come. In fact, at that very moment, Maria is slathering the kid with sunscreen.

"They want to have another child," that man mentions.

CHAPTER 3

SHE'S PROBABLY TOO goddamn crazy to get away with it—but she's gonna try anyway. I know that. And no matter how nuts, that doesn't mean I'm not willing to tag along for the ride. Or is it her who's getting taken for a ride? Am I playing her, or is she playing me? "Time will tell"—isn't that what they say, which means "I don't know jackshit," right? "Partners" is what we're telling each other, but nobody ever believes that. It's every man/woman for himself after all, right?

Which is all by the wayside because I love her (I shouldn't be writing this down), up to and including her face, body, and those perfect tits, plus the way she knows how to use 'em.

Superficial, sure, but that's just the part I can talk about. Our connection, going way back and way deep—that's beyond words. Needless to say, anything she wants, she can have as far as I'm concerned, even if it comes out of my hide, which I'm sure it will, and you can quote me on that. I know I have to share her. That was the deal from the very first. That's the way she is. That's not the problem. It's this baby thing that's got everybody's panties in *a bunch. Some of it's my fault—I admit that. Stirring the pot. I can't help it. The Devil finds work for idle hands, she once told me. Question is, am I the Devil or the hands?*

CHAPTER 4

WHEN YOU'RE CERTAIN you have everything under control, that's usually a good time to worry. For the sake of my sanity, I need to remind myself I'm no longer the young girl who would lie in bed with the lights off, teasing Aaron, my first boyfriend, daring him to send yet another full Monty photo of his impressive physique, at which I would swoon, then dutifully reply with carefully edited—face blurred or offscreen—naked photos of my own. I was infatuated with Aaron, desperate for his approval, producing what I now realize was essentially child pornography. *That girl*—the wide-eyed, willing nymphet—died a long time ago, at least that's what I try to tell myself. But when that man buzzes my phone, it sends the same thrill up my midsection and I'm compelled to go to him. The distance between adolescence and adulthood is measured in experience—sounds logical, right? But what the mind hears, the heart ignores, and I probably should be worried."

"Torturous. And yours?" is all I can think to offer when I arrive home and John greets me with the obligatory, "Hey, babes, how's your day?" He's watching YouTube on the giant big- screen, "smart" TV in the cavernous viewing grotto. The grin on his face matches the size of the room.

"Um, yeah, pretty good, thanks," he says, oblivious to my reply. "Come check this out. It's like a prank video show."

"Interesting," I lie, sinking into the cushion next to him.

"Eight million views," he enthuses. "I can't believe how much planning goes into these things. The poor schmucks never see it coming. They just fall right into it. It's really insane how easy it is to fool people."

Is it, John? Is it *insane*? Or is watching other people getting duped and humiliated the last bastion of sanity we all cling to in a desperate attempt to make our own self-loathing slightly more bearable? *Jesus, what's the matter with me?*

"You're so right," I play along, and he believes it—*talk about getting duped*. I stop there, wary of his bullshit detector. (Yes, he has one.) I regroup, kiss his forehead, and begin to decant the wine.

"Dr. Goldman called," John mentions—

I drop the wine. It hits the table and rolls, spewing red all over the white carpet. *Why couldn't it have been a Chardonnay?*

"Babes?" John yelps, grabbing the bottle, surveying the damage. "You okay?"

"The rug . . . " I stutter.

"I don't like shag anyway," he says, forgiving me, generosity overflowing, the bastard.

"So, what did the quack want?" I manage through the terror . . . *aside from revealing the innermost secrets of my womb . . .*

I barely hear the answer, something about how "he's going to fire his receptionist because she didn't know who you were and of course he'll fit you in—is three weeks okay—?"

"Three weeks?" I interrupt, outraged. "I wrote it on the calendar—"

"He called *you?*" I respond again, doubly outraged.

"Sure," John replies. "He's an old friend of the family, after all. He wanted me to know he hadn't dissed you. He's also very aware of how much we want to get pregnant."

He is? I refrain from asking.

"I made sure he knew that," John states, oblivious.

That night, *Poke 'er Night,* John makes the fatal mistake of not locking the bathroom door. I wait, listening outside for the appropriate moment, then sneak in on little Norman Bates feet.

"Babes," he says, both stunned and delighted as I slip in naked next to him.

"I couldn't wait," I explain, grabbing my weapon of choice, an overpriced, cruelty-free brand of body wash, "extra moisturizing," sudsing up both hands, leaving nothing to chance, seizing both the moment and his equipment at the same time. He's there in a hurry (and I'm pretty good at this—practice makes perfect); a dozen strokes later, his seed is twirling harmlessly down the drain, disaster averted, Bernard Herrmann violin-screeches playing in my head. A quick rinse and dry, and I'm back in bed; he's helpless to stop me. He's also grinning, happy and grateful, and since I appear to be asleep (I'm good at that, too), he manages to drop off to Dreamland without reminding me again of that "we're trying to get pregnant" crap.

CHAPTER 5

AS A YOUNG girl, I dreamed of living in a big house. Not that my childhood home (the one after the orphanage) was in any way modest. Quite the contrary. Big Brian Stafford, my adoptive father, worked hard at the airlines repairing planes and kissing corporate butt—local boy made good. Our five-bedroom architectural in a gated community was the physical manifestation of his twenty years of loyal service. But even in my youth, I had grander dreams.

"When I'm married," I told my friend Melissa, "I'll live in a castle. It will have too many rooms to count, secret passages and gardens, maybe even a dungeon or a pet tiger." The majestic narrative made her giggle.

"I hope you're right, and I hope I'm there to see it," Melissa said sincerely. Then, endowed with wisdom far beyond her years, she added a warning: "Just be careful what you wish for because maybe one day you'll get it."

Winfield House in London, where the US Ambassador lives, and where John and I "resided," was commissioned in 1936 for the American heiress, Barbara Hutton, aka "The Poor Little Rich Girl," which about sums me up as well, ha ha. It's named for Frank Winfield Woolworth, Hutton's grandfather, the five-and-dime man. Barbara Hutton was only twenty-four years old when she and her husband, Count Haugwitz-Reventlow, bought the property because of kidnapping threats against their son, Lance, at their midtown London digs. A couple of years later, with the marriage ending and WWII just starting, the Count himself was forced to "strenuously deny any attempt or threat to kidnap my own son." Inside job or not, Lance was never taken and went on to live a short but colorful life as a race car driver. Winfield House's rich history continues, visited by kings, queens, world leaders, and movie stars. I could give you the whole tour, as I did many times for chosen dignitaries, dropping names like raindrops through its thirty-five rooms.

"The Oaks" isn't quite the same: 11,000 square feet of "Tuscan-style" faux marble, slapped on the side of a steep hill in Bel-Air, advertised as "big and fancy" in the original listing, once owned by the guy who popularized ripped jeans or something, recently inhabited by a couple of Iranian reality show stars who "prefer to be called Persian, thank you so much." When the TV show went bust, so did their marriage and their jumbo bank loan.

"Got it for a song," was whispered around, which in Hollywood is considered a good thing, but in our world and the world we planned to become part of as "Mr. and Mrs. Senator Speedy (D-CA)," price was no object and certainly not to be discussed. The concrete colossus boasts high, thick hedges and a dense forest of trees, possibly oaks—what am I, an arborist? There's a tennis court and a pool and a fireplace and the requisite Chihuly chandelier. There's also a wood-paneled library with—you guessed it—another fireplace. Never mind that burning wood in the fire is illegal in LA (or should be), the equivalent to driving a diesel truck to Orlando and back in terms of carbon output—I'm not Al Gore either.

The point is we're rich as shit and the world knows it, which makes us a target for all kinds of schemes, like Barbara Hutton and her kid. You wouldn't believe it. Just watch. You'll see.

CHAPTER 6

AT FIRST, IT was a game. Truth or Dare. Me and Aaron (my "crush," I told Melissa) would sneak, giggly and dewy, into his father's study. The lockable door afforded us precious seconds to buffer any unwanted interruptions. Later, I would sit in class and daydream of our extramural activities. While my teachers waxed lyrical about Shakespeare or the periodic table or long- fucking-division (who cared?), I would fantasize about Aaron's hands on my body.

"Promise me you won't tell anyone," I insisted.

"I promise."

"No, pinky swear."

"I swear."

His fingers slid inside me. I bit my lip to stop from crying.

"I dare you to put your hand on my thing," he countered.

"Double dare me?"

CHAPTER 7

JOHN IS HOME early, whisky in hand and already in his gym clothes: a pale-blue Lululemon- for-men shirt and cycling shorts so tight they reveal as much about his endowment as his taste in workout wear. He's had a hard day (I can tell). Running for the US Senate from the State of California is no easy feat; John will need to switch parties and positions on just about everything, and it's been a generation and a half since the Golden State had a male senator.

"You should get a sex change," I suggest.

"Not a bad idea," he answers as if he's already considered it.

Fortunately, he has no opinions and no scruples and believes in nothing except his own unlimited future, with me by his side the whole way. Since there are over twice as many rich, white men named "John" in the US Senate than people of color, he has a good chance.

"Sit," he commands. "Gimme a kiss."

"Are you joking? I could smell you from Sunset Boulevard."

He pulls me to him on the sofa. G-d, he's strong. Resistance is futile. He kisses me. Playfully. He tastes salty and I feel myself wanting more.

"Aaarggghhh. Get off me, you sweaty beast." I push him away and scowl delightfully.

He laughs and half tries to kiss me again, but we both know the game is over. After a while, all married couples develop a kind of intuitive foreplay radar. They know when to push and when, more frequently than not, it's just not going to happen. Sighing simultaneously, we shift to our respective sides of the couch. Game over. I tap on my phone and John floats away down Johnnie Walker River.

"So, I met with the advisors today," John tells me.

"Oh?" I say, pretending interest. "How's the campaign looking?"

"Don't call it a campaign, not yet."

"Okay."

"Not until we've announced."

"Got it."

"All this has to be carefully orchestrated."

"I'm sure."

"It's a hard mountain to climb, babes," John confesses.

"I bet," I chime in. John is not good with mountains. He's a downhill man, a skier, snowboarder, a bobsledder maybe, a coaster. Drifting, not rowing, with the current. I fear for him.

"We talked about you," he tells me, voice lowered. *Serious talk.*

"Oh?" I try again. Despite all evidence to the contrary, I know when to lay low, shut up, and listen.

"They're worried about the timing."

"What timing?"

"The baby, of course."

"What baby?" I protest.

"You . . . having . . . the . . . baby," he intones as if *I'm* the baby he's talking about. "There's still a year before the major campaigning, and if you'd already had the baby, it would be much better. You and the little one could join me on the campaign trail. That would be perfect. But if we wait . . . "

If we wait, I'm a giant, pregnant, Thanksgiving Day Parade blimp teetering on the platform.

" . . . it's apparently not good to be seen with a pregnant woman, candidate-wise, even if she is the most beautiful wife in the world and you love her very much," John manages with a straight face.

I refrain from laughing.

"As Richards tells it, 'it's okay if a candidate's wife has a baby, but nobody wants to know she did some fucking to get it.'" John laughs. I don't. "Richards came up with that one. Can you believe it? Stick-up-his-ass Richards said 'fucking.'"

I'm still not laughing. Richards is his disheveled, stern, trim-bearded, bow-tied "ideology guy," tasked with plausibly orchestrating John Speedy's one-eighty-degree turn from red to convincing blue before November without pissing off the wrong people (too much). *Probably should go for the sex change to be sure.*

"So anyway, the sooner the better, babes," John adds, taking a swig of whisky, chasing it with a hunk of protein bar.

"I don't know what's wrong," I tell John, seizing on the opportunity. "Anyway, you know I'm going to see Dr. Goldman in three weeks."

"That's good," John agrees, skipping the opportunity

to be outraged two nights in a row —"*three weeks? I'll call him immediately! Get you in tomorrow, dammit!*"

"Maybe you need to do the tests again," he says instead, as if he knows what tests I took in the first place, or listened to anything beyond the "good to go" lie I told him Goldman pronounced those many years ago, before England. "Don't you think?"

"Listen, we are in this together," I state for the record. "You know I'll do what it takes." The words sound sweet, but they leave a bitter taste in my mouth.

"I was thinking *I* should get tested," John says out of the blue. I freeze, horrified at the possibilities. "Make sure my little soldiers are ready to invade the fortress. What do you think, babes?"

I think if it turns out he's medically infertile, I'm screwed, is what I think. *How am I going to explain that?*

"Are you fishing for a compliment, you stud, because I think we both know all's good down there. Of course, *I* could go see another doctor maybe," I offer, changing the subject as casually as I can, in a way that gives me plausible deniability in case John is repelled by the idea. *Crazy, of course, Dr. Goldman being almost a member of the family . . .*

"Wow," John remarks, genuinely stunned. "I hadn't thought about that."

I had. A lot. And John walked right into it. Sometimes I amaze myself.

"I could ask around," I suggest, pushing it. "See who some of the wives use. The ones with children, of course." *The ones with giant broods of snot-nosed, designer-clad brats roaming the malls, shuffling off to private schools, bullying weaklings on social media, ridiculing the homeless—*

"That's not a bad idea," John muses. I'm sincerely moved; I can count on one hand the number of "not bad ideas" John has attributed to me over the years. "You could ask Kayla," he adds.

I grit my teeth and prepare to strangle him. He's strong, but I can be stronger, and angrier. It would have to be quick: snap his neck before he knew what hit him. But I stop myself, the model of self-control. Kayla's doctor is Dr. Goldman anyway, I happen to know. That's not going to get me anywhere. I need a quick pill-pusher and that's all—why is this so difficult? The greatest country in the world and a gal can't get a fast supply of fuck-mints?

I'm not naive about the danger I'm in. When it comes to matters concerning my ability to conceive, John is scoping out every angle. It's not an overstatement to say that he's obsessed with being a father. He even suggests adoption again, despite my feelings about it (when Hell freezes over).

I mean, really, what is John thinking? Did he even *ask* if this is what I wanted? To be an ambassador's wife (no) or a senator's wife (nuh-uh) or a mother (un-bloody-likely). I want to be rich, sure, but at what price?

Power, ambition, a square jaw, and a strong chin—all very attractive in a man, along with the money, but it's a double-edged sword, a mixed blessing, two sides of the coin, isn't it? With the ridiculous wealth comes a matching ego, thoughtless narcissism, and casual sociopathy. No, he didn't ask what I wanted. He assumed (making an ass of both you and me) that I wanted *him*, and now that I had *him*, nothing else would matter, including picking up a kid at the orphanage the way you'd pick up a pizza.

"Say, what do you say we go out to eat?" John suggests, sensing either my food analogy or my darkening mood.

"Where?" I ask, though that doesn't matter. I'm a poor girl, an orphan. I live in Bel-Air, in this house, with this man because of hard work and "aesthetic blessings" (perfect tits and an ass like a Swedish gymnast). The payoffs are legendary, but I often have to remind myself to cash in and enjoy the perks.

"Benson's?" John offers.

I like the idea. It's the hottest place on the Westside this week, a "see and be seen" spot with perfect decor, strong drinks, handsome waitstaff, and semi-edible food to boot.

"You'll never get a reservation," I dare him.

"Oh, I'll get a reservation—a booth," John promises with a forthright determination I wish he'd use on Dr. Goldman's new receptionist. He heads for the bedroom to shower and shave and work his seductive magic on the phone.

My delight at being "out" is dashed when Chez Benson's *maître d'*—disgracefully unaware that John Speedy is soon to be Senator Speedy (D-CA)—makes us wait in the bar. I'm further horrified to see Dr. Michael Goldman, OB-GYN, dining at one of the tables. He spots us and comes right over before we've even had a chance to order drinks.

"If he offers us to sit with him and his awful wife, say no," I order John in a fast whisper. "Goldman!" John greets the man. They shake hands.

"John!" the doctor answers. Nobody calls John by his last name, no doubt because "Speedy" is so silly. "So how are you adjusting to The States?"

"Right back in the swing," John says, an attempt at enthusiasm.

"Amanda?" the doctor asks, turning to me.

"Doctor?" I answer. The quintessential geek, Goldman tops out at five-foot-two. His receding hairline and visible paunch help complete the look, but it's his Scotch-taped Oliver Peoples glasses that put him over the top. Kisses and hugs follow. I can play that game, though it's awkward—he's had me naked in his stirrups; he's played with my forbidden chalice (as the Sisters called it).

"So, when are you going to get our girl pregnant?" John blurts out.

Goldman gives me a puzzled, significant look, which I'm sure is going to precede telling John the whole sad story about my birth control regimen in violation of all sorts of physician-patient confidentiality norms and laws, but instead:

"I should think that was *your* job," the doctor quips. I'm eternally grateful.

For his part, John has completely forgotten my "not-such-a-bad-idea" of finding another OB-GYN and is droning on, further bonding us to Goldman, forcing me to launch the whole ploy again at some later date—

"Something about the fog or the rain or the meat pies—I don't know," John complains. "She just couldn't get pregnant over there."

"A little Southern California sunshine might be just what she needs then," the doctor joins in, talking as if I weren't sitting right there. "Would you like to join us at our table?" he inquires of *John*, not me— "It can take so long to get a table here—"

Mercifully the *maître d'* signals us—

"Ah, we're set," John gloats, and we're escorted to a *booth*, better than the doctor's table— significantly better, suitable for a senator.

"Later," Dr. Goldman waves as we walk away. I refrain from sticking my tongue out at him. Goldman knows I'm lying to John. He doesn't know the reason or exactly how serious, but he's spotted the lie there, and now he's complicit in that lie.

When I tell *that man* about it the next day, he (again) just thinks it's funny. Everything's funny to that man, I mean it.

"You should give your husband what he wants," he tells me. I'll never forget it.

"What?" I say, not believing my ears.

"Give him what he wants."

"He wants a baby!" I almost shout.

"Then give him a baby," that man whispers. "He wants a baby, why not give him a baby?"

That's the thing about that man: when you shout, he whispers. When you fall apart, he gets it together. He's yin to your yang, or however that goes. I'd say we were complementary to each other, or "soul mates," or "completed each other," but that's a little too gushy for me. He's opaque, let's put it that way; the opposite of John, who's as transparent as a freshly cleaned glass door, the one you walk right into, shattering it in a million pieces, cutting yourself so severely you bleed to death.

"I'm not 'giving' him anything," I protest again, "least of all a baby."

That man smiles. He already knows what I'm going to do, what I'm going to agree to. He has it figured out ahead of time, and I'm helpless to resist. He just hasn't told me yet.

I'm pretty jumpy anyway. On my way over, I spot Kayla on the road, car-to-car, in the high-rise section of Wilshire just south of UCLA More to the point: Kayla spots *me*.

I don't want to tell that man, but I know I have to.

"Kayla who?"

"The one I hate. My best friend."

He laughs. I love him for that. "Oh, yes—*her*."

"Yes, her."

"So, she saw you driving—"

"Over *here*," I remind him. "She'll ask about it. There's no way to explain this. I've been spotted."

"You're not allowed to drive?"

"Where am I going?" I demand to know.

"You went to a movie in Westwood."

"What movie?"

"You'll have to look that up."

"What am I, a bum," I ask, "going to a movie in the middle of the day?"

"A film buff!" he blurts out, laughing at me. "Or a college student!" which he finds even more hilarious. "You're taking classes!"

"It's not funny," I tell him. I can't think of anything else to say. I hide my face. "We know all the same people; we go to the same shops."

"You were on your way to Rodeo Drive," he suggests, which shows how much he knows about it. Nobody drives down Wilshire through Westwood, not if they can help it, not in the late afternoon, even now after they straightened out the freeway onramps slightly—billions of dollars and still a mess. *Have to speak to Senator Speedy about that.*

"Okay, Rodeo Drive," I agree—that would have to do until I could come up with something better.

"Or you say, 'Where were *you* going?' Turn the tables."

I don't like that idea much, either. That man knows even less about Kayla than he does afternoon traffic patterns. She would have a good answer, which would be the truth—so much easier to remember. She wouldn't cheat on her husband, and she wouldn't lie to a friend, either. She'd have been driving to feed homeless orphan-babies or read to the blind or saving a nun from drowning or something of similarly sickeningly saintly proportions. Fuck, I hate that bitch.

"Fine, going to Rodeo Drive," I say. "I was going to Rodeo Drive to do some shopping." "Now, why didn't I think of that?" that man chuckles all over again.

CHAPTER **8**

AS THE SUMMER days passed, Truth or Dare turned quite naturally into something more, something extraordinary: a transcendent tutorship in the sublime Art of Pleasure. Aaron and I, partially clothed, fully intertwined, learned one another's bodies. I corrected his inept touches over and over until he could navigate my puffy, virgin mound with gynecological precision. He, in turn, coached me, instructing me nervously how to stroke and knead his narrow, pulsing shaft until he spilled, warm and milky white, into my hand or, more often, his pants. Looking back, it was innocent and beautiful, bordering on the ethereal—the tantalizing, sensual first touches that, as adults, we crave, but like youth itself, never again find.

I wish it was a nightmare. Nightmares are safe. Dreams, on the other hand—those are dangerous. In the end, it's only your dreams—the ones you wish for in your heart of hearts—that will ruin you. I open my eyes again and clutch my belly. I feel queasy. Something is *off*. I shake my head, clear my thoughts, and remind myself that I often wake up paranoid these days. I roll over, back to sleep. *This too shall pass . . .*

It's the weight I feel first, pressing down on my chest, stomach, pelvis. It's hard to breathe, yet I hear the intake and exhale. It's not me; it's John. He's on top! On top of *me!* Pressing me into the mattress, holding my knees apart. He's pumped, full, stiff, inside me, all the way up my "Holy of Holies" (as Sister Mary Grace would say). He's poker-faced, rosy-red, the King of Hearts, the way he gets right before he gooshes all over the place. I squawk, outraged, trying to push him off, but it's no use—all those days in the gym, all the machines. How dare he! It isn't even his birthday, or *my* birthday, or Christmas or New Year's, or *Taco Tuesday*, for cryin' out loud! The balls on this fucking guy!

"What the hell?" I half cry, half moan. On the other hand, I can feel him, really feel him now, and it's as good as I've had it, I gotta admit, since Aaron. The next moment I'm drifting over the dam. I try to resist, but the current is strong.

"I need you, babes," he whispers plaintively, magic words, and now I'm thrusting, too, squeezing it out of him even as my brain tells me this is wrong, *all wrong!* The match is lit, the pin is pulled. We explode, me first by a nanosecond, him like a fucking firehose.

What the hell? I want to know.

"Gotcha," he whispers smugly, rolling off me onto his back, one hand still gripping my thigh.

Like one of his g-ddamn YouTube pranks.

Aha, nailed your coffin shut, babes. Good one, eh?

I roll off the bed and crawl to the bathroom, thighs and calves wobbly, threatening to cramp up. Of course we've got the giant, novelty-sized, six-in-one handheld adjustable shower head that can't possibly fit up in there no matter how hard I try. So I do the best I can with body wash and anything else I think might shrivel the Little Johns squirming around in the dark.

But in my heart, I know it's too late.

You're doomed.

I won't tell that man. I'm not sure what he would do. It needs to remain my secret. *So many secrets.* Maybe I'll get lucky.

You make your own luck, Momma Stafford always said.

CHAPTER 9

I GO SEE that man the next day at his insistence. He says it's important. When I arrive, he offers me a little gift box. It's a good size for a ring, maybe a bracelet. I stare. I don't mention that he's already given me the world and hope for the future. I also don't say anything about marriage, which we've discussed fully, discarding the idea. He's not poor, but he's not John Speedy, either, and I need a certain level.

"Open it," he tells me, and by the way he says it—on the couch and not on one knee—I know it's not an engagement ring (my existing marriage wouldn't stop him proposing if he were that way inclined). No, it must be a gag gift, but between us just as important as some Hallmark sentiment embedded with diamonds or pearls.

I flip open the box. I squeal, as shocked and surprised as I would have been at precious stones or a coiled novelty snake. I'm also deeply moved, recognizing it immediately as something I've lost: a little plastic wheel with the days of the week and tiny pink tablets inside—

"My birth control pills!" I blurt out in amazement. How had he gotten hold of them? Had he followed me through Heathrow Airport? Had he slipped into the women's loo? (I'm not an idiot, just temporarily.) "Where did you get these?" I insist.

"I made some calls," he answers mysteriously.

"Are these for real?"

"I'd bet my life on it," that man answers.

"It's my life you're betting here."

"I'd bet *your* life on them," he corrects, "and you know you're worth more to me than life itself."

"Sweet-talker."

He laughs.

"They're your brand. Take 'em till you can get your own."

I don't have the heart to tell him it's too late, that I'd been ambushed already—eternally, internally, thoroughly splooshed—and there could quite possibly be a little something growing

inside me at that very moment. He had gone to so much trouble. It would break his heart. Like that O. Henry story: "The Gift of the Magi." Except I have nothing to give to him except misery and grief.

I'm going to cry.

"Excuse me," I tell him, slipping into the bathroom to pull myself together. I pop one of the pills, then a catchup dose, figuring it won't kill me and might just work.

I can't help wondering what it would be like if that man and I had a baby together. It would look *very* different, of course, than a John/Amanda offspring, which is only one reason I wake in terror some nights.

"Mixed race" is what that man calls himself. He shows me the pictures: white grandmother, Black grandfather on his mother's side. "Before me, that's the only Black blood in the family," he notes, tapping on his grand-father's face in the photo. "My mother has very light-skinned and has almost entirely Caucasian features; same with my sister. Me, I got a big dose of Black—who knows why?"

Some genetic traits are like a light switch, that's why. They can flip off and on, skip generations, show up or not. Other traits are more like dimmers, and you get a mix.

But what am I, a geneticist?

We're both pretty sure if John Speedy's pearl-white wife gave birth to a Black child, it would ruin his chances of winning the Senate seat.

"Still, I'd give my left nut to see the look on his face!" that man crows.

"Me too," I laugh.

Now we're both laughing, the way that man and I used to laugh back then, before all the drama.

It occurs to me this is the only instance where I've heard that man express any animosity toward John, or resentment or ridicule or jealousy. I know it's there, under it all, but he doesn't go there, and I love him all the more for it, exactly the way he is, a mutt like me.

CHAPTER 10

I DON'T FEEL like shaving this morning. The stubble on my face looks unfamiliar—rough, unkempt. Sometimes I hate myself the way I am. There's probably a name for it. It's probably a disease like manic/depression except it's generous/selfish, cynical/idealistic. Sometimes I have to grab what I want, right then and there; other times, I'm able to be patient. I know it's not easy. I want to tell her I care, but I can't. She'd take it the wrong way. She'd see right through me. She's got all the angles, so she figures everybody else must have them, too. What do they call it? Projection?

I'm pretty sure the trigger's been pulled, but the fact that I'm not the one who pulled it irks the hell out of me. It's her call, her play, her game. I'm just the puppet master? Sure, I wish. Behind every good man is a good woman, right? Or is that vice versa?

I may not even go vote. As much as this is about the money, it's also about Senator John Speedy, and who wouldn't have doubts about that? Does the world really need one more rich white guy in a position of power who has no particular qualifications for the job, who claims it solely on the basis of birthright?

Rhetorical question. Of course not.

But there's a bigger picture at play here. Zoom out, look at the whole deal. "Senator John Speedy" is just one aspect of it. Harmless, really, part of the ticket price, "handling charge." All the world's a stage, true, but sometimes we have to stage our world.

CHAPTER 11

"SHE'S *YOUR* PROBLEM now."

That's the last thing I remember hearing before turning around, sticking my tongue out at Sister Mary Grace, and leaving the orphanage behind me once and for all. I was six years old when I was adopted by the Staffords—Brian and Jill—two truly good souls, damn them.

"I have big news for you, little lady," Jill Stafford informed me earlier that day. "Remember what we talked about? About when we picked you, um, well not *picked* you—*chose* you—yes, *chose* you out of all the children here to come join our family. Well, it's all happening today.

We've signed all the papers, and you belong to us now. Um, I don't mean belong to us but belong *with* us. I'm going to be your new mommy, and Brian—you remember Brian, right?" She yanked his hand so forcefully that the six-foot-five ex-linebacker (USC, go Trojans!) almost toppled over. "He's going to be your new daddy. You're going to have a family now. You're going to be a Stafford. Isn't that exciting? Brian, tell her. Tell her how happy we are." After a confirmatory "we're really happy" from Big Brian, the transaction was complete. I was a Stafford. Ironically, it was exactly nine years to the day after that memorable "welcome to the family" address my behavior (no, *misbehavior*) would push those oh-so-saintly Staffords past their limits.

At first, the three of us got along famously. Jill was especially excited about being a parent. From the moment she signed the forms and took delivery of me, she set about molding me into her clone: a cake-baking, penis-pleasing, school-play-attending, executive homemaker. As for Brian, he wanted, admirably, nothing more than for Jill to feel fulfilled. On the second roll of the cosmic dice, I hit the familial jackpot. Then three years later, when Jill told me that I was getting a new brother, I was genuinely delighted, crossing out the days on my pink Hello Kitty calendar, literally marking the time until Devin (named after Brian's boss) was born. Admittedly my enthusiasm had less to do with the new arrival himself and considerably more so with the Stafford's having promised me the glorious bedroom at the bottom of the stairs. From a nine- year-old's perspective, this represented a residential boon of the highest order. The room was bright and spacious and came with a mirrored closet and a four-poster bed. Blue and white clouds covered the ceiling and pixie-print curtains touched the floor. The huge trunk at the foot of the bed would be my hiding place, particularly handy in the event of nuclear attack, unwanted report card, or any level of crisis in between. I was in Heaven. Best of all, while searching for a cool, dark home for my pet silkworms, I stumbled upon a deliciously secret my new room kept just for me: a fortuitously located air vent which, by positioning my adolescent skull just so, allowed me to eavesdrop on upstairs conversions at will. I was constantly entertained by tasty confidential tidbits of information, unsolicited praise, and on (impressively frequent) occasions, the muffled moans of Jill and Brian partaking of the joys of the conjugal bed.

When my brother Devin sprouted like a biological miracle from the family tree, the Staffords' love for their blonde, dimpled, pre-owned daughter never waned. Taking great pains to treat us equally, they shared our interests, encouraged our youthful pursuits, and doted over us like we were the last children in the world. We became their life's work. Until *that night*.

CHAPTER 12

IT'S MONDAY NIGHT and suddenly I'm staring at my reflection gazing back at me from inside the gold-leaf-adorned mirror. I'm pregnant. That's the main thing. With John's baby. Has to be.

"It's John's," the mirror lady whispers. "It's John's." I must believe her; anything else is madness, ruin, a blue-tarp homeless hovel next to the freeway. But I don't look pregnant. "It will come," the mirror lady soothes.

I move to the balcony. From my vantage point, I can see the city of Los Angeles sparkling in the distance: an ocean of lights, flickering, dancing, and ultimately washing up at my feet, lapping at the shores of Bel-Air, soon to be oceanfront property what with global warming and the rise in sea level. That's what I hope anyway. I think about people down there, the dreamers who travel here in search of fame and fortune. They could be looking up right now, wondering who lives in the mansion behind the twelve-foot walls, wondering if they will ever be perched so high—if it will ever happen for them. I know that feeling well. The longing. The hunger. The need. Will it ever happen? Happen for me? While horns blow and neon flashes below, I think how, after all these years, it just might.

What would Gatsby do with all those lights? Not just one green one but thousands in a variety of colors, all burning for him (me), symbolizing hopes and dreams. I burst out into tears. It's 9:20 p.m. and I'm crying. Tears of joy, confusion, guilt. Is this really going to happen to me? For me? For us? I'm deeply moved, or maybe it's the hormones they talk about. I miss my friend Melissa more than ever right now. I wish she could see me now, talk to me. I hold in my hand a pink, thermometer-shaped stick with a magical blue plus sign in the oval window, the single word "PREGNANT" also visible, in five different languages, crystal clear, no doubt in response to any number of comedy skits and movies, and impending legal action—"Tired of all that pink/blue confusion, mothers-to-be? Act now! But wait! There's more!" *What more could there possibly be?* After my hands stop shaking, I position my plastic trophy on the gray Carrara marble countertop and take a series of commemorative pictures with my phone. I should get a newspaper with the current date and hold it with the dingus. Do they do that anymore? With Photoshop, does it still prove anything?

After completing my stint as amateur photographer, I wrap the evidence carefully in velvet, place it neatly in the box, and bury it in my purse, which I hide under the bed. I spend the remainder of the night awake, knowing it's there right beneath me, pulsating, beating a telltale rhythm from a Poe story, keeping me half-awake through the night.

That man is the first one I tell. He has that right. I don't want him hearing secondhand, inferring it, or otherwise being kept out of the loop. I call him on the phone.

"I hope you're ready to hear this. I'm pregnant." Jesus, that feels strange to say out loud. There's a long pause at the other end. I worry I have the wrong number. My mind spins, picturing a strange man at the other end hearing the shocking news, mistaking me for his pudgy mistress, sexy secretary, cleaning lady, *underage babysitter*, then trying to hang himself with a plaid tie and a rusty nail, failing miserably (this being more of a comedy than tragedy)—

"Who *is* this?" that man finally replies, his own little joke, which doubles me over with laughter. "So?" he says when I've recovered.

"Did you hear me?" I ask him.

"I heard," he says, not as surprised as I expected. I wait, curious to hear what he'll say next. I won't let him off the hook this time.

"Get over here," he orders. "My place. Now. STAT." Uncharacteristic urgency. *Is he angry or is he desperate for my body?* Could be both. Can't tell from his voice. I'm suddenly sorry I did this on the phone.

When I arrive, he's not even there. I let myself into his suite and have a couple of drinks.

When he finally shows up, I don't ask him where he's been. Despite his scruffy hair and wrinkled suit, or perhaps because of it, he looks especially attractive. Maybe it's the hormones, ha ha, *his* hormones. He's always smiling and always fidgeting. Even now, when he should be entirely focused on me, his almond eyes dart from side to side. He's a terrible conman; he looks guilty, "up to something." At first glance, you might say he had some type of mild Tourette's syndrome. But if there's one thing I know about that man, it's that despite his distracted disposition, his mind is as keen as a diamond sword (and just as deadly). I once again find myself wondering about us, about how we met again and what we're doing. I wonder how different my life would be if I hadn't walked into that bar. We would never have started talking about marriage. Or life. Sex.

Money. Power. And I wouldn't be here now. Again, I tell that man the news. I need to see his reaction, even if it's his second or third time around. And what *is* his reaction? I still don't know, really. I don't understand. What does he want to do now? I'm terrified, and excited. I did it. Pregnant. That's something, right?

I hand him the note, the one I wrote the night before, when I couldn't sleep, a little after 2 a.m. At first, I wasn't sure why I wrote it. I certainly wasn't planning to show it to anyone, but now it seems like the only logical way to express how I feel. It's short and honest, and he reads it quickly. It begins, *"To you, my man—I have no idea why I'm doing this. The risk is great, but then so is the reward, and not the one you're thinking of."* When he's finished, he leans in, looks at me with wide eyes, and—resting his hands on my thighs—smiles. I wish now, more than ever, that I could read his mind. I want to know exactly what he's thinking about. No—wrong—I want to know exactly what he's thinking about *me*. He squeezes me tightly.

"We have come a long way, you and I," he tells me. "I remember it all, too. Now go home, you. Tell your husband. He needs to know."

CHAPTER 13

WHY CAN'T IT just be simple? She's up to something, which means I'm up to something, too. She suspects I know that she knows that I know that she knows. Who's that artist guy? Escher? Climbing the stairs that become more stairs, never-ending. Half-truths. That's all I ever get. Poor, poor me. Ha! Time for a reality check. I gotta be honest if I expect the same from others. Don't lie to myself. Don't lie to her. Sins of omission don't count. You're allowed to leave things out. That's part of the rules. Nothing works without leaving gaps—that's just the way it is. I didn't invent the world; I just work here.

I know her. I understand she is what I signed up for, but still. Wait, who am I kidding? It's not like I'm telling her everything. Or am I? Does she know? How does she know? Suspect? No. Stop being paranoid. Have a drink. Wash the fears away. Forget that silly Google quiz. "Imposter syndrome." What the fuck do they know? Maybe I don't have that syndrome at all.

Maybe they just never met somebody who's not a perfectionist, but actually is perfect, a genius, who allows others to tag along but never really needs help. Note to *self: delete Google. Only Tor from now on. Once upon a time I would bob and weave, now I Duck-Duck-Go.*

Yours truly,

Superman (the one who eats Kryptonite for break-fast)

CHAPTER 14

MARY-ELIZABETH'S MANSION is just up the road, higher on the hill, three times as large as ours, nothing short of a modern-day palace. The newspapers dubbed it "The Royal Oak," 37,000 square feet of the world's finest building materials exactingly assembled to impress and intimidate, objectives the top-flight architects at Westbum & Krug had unequivocally accomplished. Marble statues, granite fountains, and manicured gardens complement the structure, transforming the property from just another oversized house into "an estate fit for a monarch," so said the real estate listing. Guards jump to attention next to the twelve-foot, monogrammed, electric gates when anyone approaches.

I still love it.

In contrast, our place is a veritable hovel.

Nevertheless, when it was suggested that John and I move into The Royal Oak with "dear Mum" and whoever the boyfriend *du jour* happened to be, I went ballistic, threatening to cut out my own womb with a rusty knife. Melodramatic, sure; inconceivable, not entirely. Hence, The Oaks, our place nearby, "big and fancy, bought for a song."

Yes, I'm profoundly cognizant that without accepting family money we would be living somewhere far more pedestrian. But having tasted real wealth, I won't give it up for the world, and I am not above "doing what it takes" to keep enjoying my slice of the money pie. For the time being, I settle for replacing the shag carpet in the TV grotto with the assistance of our new decorator, the self-described "Andre-the-gay," who tries to upsell me on a plush-white, twelve-seater couch—huge, big enough that no part of John's or my body need ever touch again.

"And soon, my doll," Andre tells me, "you'll have a litter of blonde-haired, blue-eyed kids to worry about, and you'll *need* oversized novelty furniture. I mean that husband of yours looks like he's a stallion, with those muscles and all, and you with that tight little body, I'm sure it won't be long now before this place is overflowing with speedy little Speedies."

I order the couch immediately, strictly as an alibi. Nobody can say I didn't try. Andre will swear to that. Under oath. On the witness stand.

I don't say anything to John that night about the b-a-b-y. Not yet. I'm planning, scheming, looking for the right moment. It's Tuesday again, Tail Tuesday, Diddle Day morning. This time I'm ready. Bring it on, John. Hit me with your best shot; I got nothing left to lose. All the chips are in the pot (there's got to be a country song in there somewhere).

The good morning quickie is spectacular, as good as it gets. Maybe I just get off on the danger; I don't know. Perhaps we should try skydive fucking or bare-ass bungee jumping. Bull riding, that's what it feels like, honestly, when I get him in the right position. Quite a little buckaroo, my cowboy Johnny, when he gets "spurred" on, wink wink. It's a bareback bedroom rodeo, him pounding my *hoo-haw*, me taking it hard. Yeeee ha! He could die this way; wouldn't that be convenient?

Except for the prenup. The Speedies always have a prenup. They're famous for them. In case of divorce, death, you name it, poor Amanda from the other side of the tracks (me) gets a bus ticket, a change of clothes, and a couple bucks "spending money." That man and I studied it six ways from Sunday. We've consulted lawyers, a CPA, even a self-proclaimed "fixer." *Nada.* Ironclad. Airtight. So I let John-boy finish right in there to his not-quite-up-to-size dick's content, then I collapse, too, done as well, two halves of a bagel popping up out of the toaster at the same time. Hubby's full of high praise and appreciation, I'm sure, but he's so breathless it comes out a windy rasp. I never understand it; the man's in GQ cover-model shape, but this is one exercise he can't handle. If I wanted to kill him, I could do it this way, I swear.

That single, homicidal thought buoys my spirit so much that John notices, and at breakfast, he finally asks: "What are you so happy about? You look like the cat that swallowed the canary."

"Oh, I think you already know the answer to that." I find it surprising how easily the lie rolls off my tongue. Practice, I guess.

He blushes, actually blushes.

"So, what happened with your mom's new beau?" I snigger, deliberately changing the subject. That should keep him occupied for a while. He's not even halfway through his "you would think she would know better than to date someone from our club" rant when I signal to the staff to start clearing the dishes. Timing is everything. My news, *our* news can wait. Tonight I will allow him to complain all he wants, and when he's done, I will lead him upstairs and we'll have sex again, it being Poker Night. John will think of the way my naked body feels underneath his; I will think of that man. Or calf-roping.

The next morning, I still haven't told him.

John's mother arrives early, ready and willing to torture us with the details of her new suitor. "He's very, very successful. An industrialist, just like your father was," Mary-Elizabeth declares.

"Like Dad *is*," John corrects. "He's not dead yet."

John and I exchange an "although how he survived *you* is a miracle" glance. Oblivious to the unspoken gibe, Mary-Elizabeth recounts the minutia of the evening, seizing every possible opportunity to emasculate her ex-husband in the process. It's no wonder that (aside from signing alimony checks) Charles Speedy (heir to the Speedy Gas & Paraffin empire and proud ex-husband to a woman twenty-three years his junior) is totally incommunicado.

"He actually pulled the chair out for me. Can you believe that? Your father never did that for me. Not even on our first date. And let me tell you another thing, he held my hand the entire night. Physical affection—that's something else your father could've learned a thing or two about. You understand what I'm telling you, dear. This was a *real* man. The kind of man who knows how to satisfy a woman."

"Dear John, please accept ten more years of therapy. All my love, Mum."

I offer up the weakest of excuses and leave the room.

Fourteen hours later, I'm in the shower getting ready

for bed and John's still going at it: "She's absolutely fucking infuriating, that—"

Between the shower door and my shampoo-logged ears, the rest of John's inglorious tribute to his mother is forever lost.

"Please grab me a towel!" I yell. *In the morning, I vow. I'll tell him in the morning.*

But then I don't. Morning comes and goes and I just don't tell him. You could say I was nervous, but that's not really me. Grew a conscience? Again, no. I just want to do it right.

"Eat out tonight?" I text John as I drive to that man's place.

"Oh," John texts back, which means "no," but I won't let him weasel out of it, not this time.

"Give the chef a break," I insist. *"We must try Uncooked & Uncorked before everybody else does. I'm making reservations."*

I admit it, texting while driving gives me a brief, tingling thrill.

John's not replying. He's coming up with reasons, I'm sure. To emphasize the import of the dinner, I find a picture of a gift-wrapped box with a yellow question mark on the front. *If that doesn't prepare him for life-altering news,* I think, *nothing will.*

But then:

"Sure thing, cute thing," John texts back.

Oh John, you are so eloquent. I send an instant, reciprocal, *"k, gr8"* before he changes his mind.

The picture of the gift stays in my "drafts" box. I will be careful not to send it until I need it.

I will guard it the same way I guard the snapshots of my pregnancy test.

"Jesus, what a day," John declares, coming home a half-hour late. This delay threatens to destroy my credibility at Uncooked & Uncorked, a malfeasance neither they nor I will forgive.

"Our driver will be here at seven," I half-yell down to him from upstairs.

"What?" His tone annoys me.

"Seven," I repeat, louder. Either he's heard me or chosen to ignore me. It makes little difference. From the closed-circuit monitor in the upstairs bedroom I watch as his evening ritual of Scotch and cigars gets underway— that part's good, at least. I want him relaxed. Unguarded.

Not the MBA, Ambassador, Senator, not the heir. Just the man.

The car arrives and for once there isn't much traffic. I run my speech through my mind; I have the little present in my tiny handbag. We're there with two minutes to spare. We are complimented on our promptness and seated immediately.

"It's like we're getting the bum's rush," John commented.

"They do seem in a hurry," I remark, thinking: *They don't even have time to cook the food!*

In a sudden panic, I look around for signs of Dr. Goldman, OB-GYN, certain he has a standing order for "Speedy sightings" with every eatery in town. The coast seems to be clear. I try to relax. Perhaps as a physician, the doctor knows better than to eat raw meat, no matter how trendy.

Drinks arrive at the speed of light, followed by the main course. There's not a moment's pause significant enough for the kind of announcement I had planned.

It's not what I had in mind at all. *"Should have done your research, Amanda"*—that's what that man would say.

John catches and rides the prevailing tempo: "It's not that he's annoying," he babbles, trying hard to remain couth and composed while shoveling mouthfuls of beef tartare down his throat at a comically dangerous velocity, "it's that he's the *most* annoying person in the Western Hemisphere. I mean it, babes, out of the seven billion people on planet Earth, Richards has to be one of the top ten assholes alive—"

Soft lighting, softer jazz, and a slower pace would have made my mission easier. John sticks to politics, something I fear he's starting to actually care about. I'm scrupulously avoiding alcohol, but John's on drink number four, which is good news for me; you do the math. The empty glass, which once contained a golden single malt and an intentionally oversized ice cube, is removed by a white glove, its replacement appearing so deftly I'm certain our waiter moonlights as a magician. The whisky settles, the ice bobs gently, hypnotically. John lifts the glass and I smile.

"I totally agree," I interrupt, no idea what I'm agreeing to. "You've got my vote." John nods, grins, and most importantly, shuts up.

An unusual, awkward silence. This would be the moment. Instinctively he senses that I'm about to say something serious and important. Something that he should pay attention to.

Something *consequential.*

A pause—drive a truck through it if you wanted. I'd rehearsed a speech, a preamble to the news, but I think better of it, and then I freeze. Nothing. The two words I had painstakingly prepared ("We're pregnant!") are like the food itself, intended to be served up quickly, delicious and raw (before it goes bad?). The announcement hovers over the table unsaid, suspended in space and time, a special off-the-menu course for him to savor, consume and digest. *Just blurt it out,* I tell myself. That's what Jill Stafford, my mother-by-adoption would have said. "Don't let the cat get your tongue."

But before I can spill the beans, the waiter reappears.

"I hate to interrupt, sir, but there's a table of ladies over there who insist on buying you a drink."

We turn, and just like that a foursome of high heels, false eyelashes, and miniskirts crush my master plan. Instead of allowing the delicate illusion I have created to expand into the matrix of permanent reality, I simply wimp out.

"Friends of yours?" I ask.

"More like fans," he winks. "But you know I only have eyes for you, sweet-cakes."

Jesus, kill me now.

But the truth is, he means it. One good thing about John—and I give his mother full credit for this—as handsome as he is, he does not expect women to lie down for him. He doesn't assume they're all going to sleep with him, or even that they *want* to sleep with him. Evidence to the contrary is all over the place, but he just doesn't pick up on it—who knows why? He's happy with me and me only, and sweet Tuesdays, even when the entire Westside of the Los Angeles basin (male and female) could be wide open to his touch if he only made the effort. This should endear me towards him, but like eating white bread or vanilla ice cream, I'm bored to tears.

Sometimes I hate myself.

While we're driven home, he somehow dozes off

over the deafening sound of me mentally kicking my-self. I want to call that man and warn him that I haven't done it yet, but I'm too chicken to do even that. I don't want him knowing I'm a coward. I want him to think I'm brave. Maybe I don't even want to go through with this at all. Not that I would ever terminate a pregnancy. I'm opposed to that and so is John, though he would never mention it, not if he wants to be Senator "pro-choice" John Speedy (D-CA). I don't know how that man feels about the issue. I don't dare ask.

Tomorrow, I tell myself, *tomorrow at breakfast, when nothing else is in the way.*

CHAPTER 15

I WEAR A LITTLE jacket thing in the morning, its pocket-size tailor-made for the jewelry box.

John pauses his googling long enough to look up and give me a friendly spousal smile as he sometimes does, taken by my beauty once again. I reveal the small, golden box with the ribbon around it, and slide it ever so dramatically to his side of the table.

"What's this?" he asks, like it is a grenade. I half expect him to dive for cover. Which reminds me:

"We should wait for your mother."

"My mother."

"Please," I plead. *Of course*, I realize, *it's a gift for them both!* It's what was missing before, the reason for all my hesitation.

"Sure, okay, we'll wait for Mother," he says, now *sure* it's a grenade. This is out of character for me, even more than the screwing I'd been giving him—

We both wait and watch the surveillance angle on the driveway as Mary-Elizabeth jumps out of the Rolls (SPEEDY 5) and heads inside. She immediately gives an order to Hilda, the new cook, Val's replacement, though

Mary-Elizabeth doesn't notice, then takes a seat, huffing and puffing as if she has so much to do, she's not sure how she'll ever accomplish it all. But before she can get started outlining each tiny detail, John mercifully intercedes—

"Amanda has a gift for me," he states bravely and proudly (if I do say so).

"Amanda has a gift for you." Mary-Elizabeth's repetition is dripping with implication: *purchased with her own money, of which she has none?*

"Yes, a gift," John states with a smile toward me, more precious than gold, sweeter than diamonds. He opens the box and pulls out the plastic gizmo, unsure of its significance.

Confusion descends over his face. It says "PREGNANT" right there, but he's looking at the wrong side of it, or is totally illiterate and has been faking it all these years.

Mary-Elizabeth gasps—she knows.

"We're pregnant!" she announces, beating me to the punch.

Mary-Elizabeth hurries to her feet in an approximation of joy and comes around to embrace me around the shoulders. For someone who twenty-four hours earlier had extolled the virtues of physical connection, hers was a pretty stony clench.

John's a statue with a furrowed brow. Mary-Elizabeth and I telepathically share the thought that he may be having a heart attack, stroke, or both. Neither of us is sure how we feel about that, but then he explodes:

"I knew it! I knew it! I love you! We're having a baby!"

His outburst is genuine; he's hugging and scurrying around the dining room, then hugging again, a perfect reaction. Staff members, alarmed at the commotion, enter from the kitchen and the rest of the house, some armed with knives—

"We're pregnant!" John tells them all, and hugs them, too, male and female. "Now get back to work." Everybody laughs and does just that, congratulating *him* for the accomplishment mostly, though a few nod in my direction.

"I'm calling Dr. Goldman!" he shouts, looking for his phone in a pocket somewhere.

"What for?" I choke, panic taking my voice on an unplanned nature walk.

"To congratulate him, of course!"

"He doesn't know yet," I inform John.

"He doesn't?" John is clearly confused.

"I'm just going by this," I explain, picking up the pregnancy test gizmo and showing it to John—again.

"It says 'pregnant,'" John correctly reads.

Mary-Elizabeth, sensing a fight, takes a front-row seat.

"It does, but sometimes these things don't take," I speak slowly, as to a toddler.

"What do you mean, 'don't take?'" John asks, stunned, collapsing into a chair.

I'm pretty sure he skipped Sex Ed in school and just looked at the dirty pictures.

Mary-Elizabeth, suddenly fascinated by her eggs and ham and yogurt and fresh fruit, refuses to help me out here—

"Fifty to seventy-five percent of pregnancies end in the first four weeks," I announce authoritatively, with no evidence whatsoever.

"Oh," John replies.

I hate to burst John's balloon, but his quick urge to call Goldman caught me off guard. "When's your appointment with Dr. Goldman?" he asks, a good question—I gotta hand it to him.

"Tomorrow," I tell him. I'm not entirely unprepared; I've timed this and made the announcement just under the wire, too.

"That's great. Let him do the tests. He'll make sure."

"You want me to get it in writing?" I tease.

"Yes!" John answers with energy. "Absolutely." I kick myself. It was an unnecessary joke.

CHAPTER 16

I BELIEVE HER. As far as I can throw her. It took a while, but she finally did the deed. Pregnant. Preggers. Baby on board. One in the oven. Expectant. In the family way. With child. English has a hundred words and phrases for it; the Brits are the best: "up the duff," "brewing a sprog," "up the stick" (where the fuck did that come from?).

I like "fraught." That's what we are: "fraught."

It's her game now; she's on her own. Not much I can do on my end except sit and wait and see what develops. I picture the kid. He looks like me, and he's a "he," of course. I widen my focus. What about twins? That would be a complication, wouldn't it? Cloud the lens a bit.

I desperately want to know what Amanda's up to when she's not with me. I don't dare ask.

She might ask me the same question! I have to pretend sometimes that it's all normal—business as usual. I need to remind her that I support her. It's her game, after all—I already said that, but I'd like her to share the moves with me, open up, let me in. What I'd really like to do is equip her with one of those body cams they're making the cops wear these days. Uploaded in real time to the internet so I could watch along, like our doorbell cam-era. Hours of entertainment. I can imagine her reaction to that.

I laugh. I'm hallucinating. It wouldn't be the first time.

CHAPTER 17

I DRIVE MYSELF to Dr. Goldman's office, a few buildings down from Cedars-Sinai in Beverly Hills. John offers (just for the record), Kayla offers (news travels fast), Mary-Elizabeth offers (no way) to drive me. They say they want to help; I know they just want to keep an eye on me. If John had his way, I'd be bubble-wrapped and kept in a secure location under 24-hour guard until the delivery date.

The office staff and nurses are all suitably "happy to see you again." I tell them the same, though half of them are new, I'm pretty sure. Goldman makes me wait a half hour. I make a note to make him pay for that somehow.

John is waiting breathlessly when I return. "Did you get the letter?"

"What letter?" I ask cruelly.

"The letter from Dr. Goldman," he insists. "The letter that says you're really pregnant."

I don't know why John inserts the word "really" into that sentence. It indicates some suspicion on his part. *I* suspect his mother's doubt has coated the question and deep-fried it to a crisp. Otherwise, I don't know what

I've done to bring this on except give them both hope for the very joyful thing they've so longed for. No good deed goes unpunished—

"No, I don't have a letter from the doctor," I tell him coldly.

"Why not?"

"Because he first has to get the lab result, then verify the pregnancy, then dictate your stupid letter to his office assistant, who will then type it up, get Dr. Goldman's signature, then put it in the mail, a service still in existence, by the way, which you might have been aware of if you'd ever followed one of your secretaries to that big, white building the rest of us refer to as a post office."

I have smashed his lob to the far corner of the court, impossible to return. I expect complete and total surrender. I can be as cruel as the next girl (if the next girl is Lady Macbeth).

"Okay," John says, as close to a white flag as I'm going to get. "But really . . . what did he say?" he begs.

"What did who say?" I ask, making the worm squirm a little longer.

"The Jew doctor, what did he say?"

"Patience," I tell John, patting him on the cheek, walking past, headed for the kitchen—I'm famished. "He counsels patience."

We make love that night. No—face it—we fuck. And it's glorious—all the day's pent-up passive-aggressive role-playing, cruelty, and humiliation bursting forth— and it isn't even Tuesday. I can count on one still-trembling hand the number of times he's taken me like that since we've been married. Whatever the reason for the night's copulatory triumph, I'm not complaining. It's raw and hard, reaching the indefinable and all-too-often elusive space between aggression and intimacy. I'm sore today and sincerely satisfied. I can still smell John's cologne (Tom Ford's Oud Wood) and his sweat. The scent is masculine and bitter and, I admit, makes me wet. I let my hand wander over my thankfully still-flat belly and down between my legs. Closing my eyes and inhaling deeply, I allow myself to remember and dream.

By the time I wake again, John is already in the shower. He's left his pajamas—the ones with the Louis Vuitton logos and the gold buttons—in a crumpled mess next to the bed. Once, a long time ago, I asked him why he wore pajamas at all.

"Because I'm the man of the house," he told me very seriously, "and if there were to be an earthquake or a fire or a mudslide . . . "

You wouldn't want the KTLA chopper to use its super-zoom camera to catch you running around with your little dicky-poo bouncing all over the place, I refrained from saying. He wouldn't appreciate the humor; I knew that much. So he thinks of himself as "the man of the house," does he? Yeah, okay, I'll give him that, for whatever it's worth.

"Currently in Bel-Air it's eighty-one degrees Fahrenheit with clear skies," Alexa is telling me. "Today, you can expect sunny weather with a high of 81 degrees and a low of 80 degrees." As only artificial intelligence can, Alexa announces the absurd LA weather without the slightest hint of irony. I reach over and blind-fumble until, through the inelegant process of trial and error, I manage to press the "wake up" button on the digital panel next to my bed. I feel a disproportionate sense of relief wash over me as the blinds automatically open and a makeshift dawn fills the room. The mixture of sunlight and Sonos-aided-Adele is mildly energizing, providing sufficient incentive for me to unfold my body and roll out of bed. I would usually fix myself up a little before heading to the kitchen, but today for some reason I want to escape the bedroom before John gets out of the shower. It's not because he'll want to fuck again; I wouldn't mind that, but on the other hand, there's just so much a gal (even me) can take.

CHAPTER 18

A STROLL DOWN Memory Lane (corner of Wealth Street between Success Drive and Affluence Way). It's my inaugural dinner at The Royal Oak. The "front-of-house" help greets me first, an actual in-the-flesh French maid.

"Wait here, *s'il vous plait.* You can sit here on the chair and someone will be along to help you very shortly."

"Should I take a number?"

"There are no numbers, *Mademoiselle.* You are the only guest tonight."

I feel the need to explain I was joking, but before I get the opportunity, the butler intervenes. "Please stand up and follow me. Mrs. Speedy is ready to receive you now."

"What a coincidence, I'm ready to be *received.*"

The butler is, of course, just as *sans* humor as the maid. I giggle, entertaining myself, hoping he's going to say "walk this way" so I can parody his tight-assed gait.

"Remember, the Speedies are different," John warns me. Where I come from, "different" means something else, but I don't mention that to John. I understand I'm being appraised— another *objet d'art,* hand-picked and ready to undergo *provenance.* I should consider

myself fortunate. Invitations such as this are a rare and prized commodity. The decision as to whether I'm worthy to don the Speedy mantle rests in the hands of a tight-skinned, thin-lipped, sixty-three-year-old divorcée who, six months earlier, had introduced herself as Mrs. Speedy, and now insists I refer to her as "Liz," which I don't plan on doing.

"So, my son tells me you want to be a lawyer. How ambitious of you. Now how exactly did you and Johnny meet? How old are you? Where else have you lived? What kind of wine do you enjoy? Have you ever traveled to Europe?"

Then she gets nosy.

"John tells me you are adopted? Do you know who your real parents are? Have you ever considered a DNA test? What do you know about your family's religious persuasion? Have you ever visited a psychiatrist to discuss your *special circumstances?"*

The aspiring lawyer in me wants to fight back. Instead, I field the progressively personal questions with superhuman restraint while in the cross-examination of my dreams, I rack up a few counter-queries of my own. *Would you be so kind as to lift your (obviously cosmetically altered) neck so I can choke you into silent submission? Are you always this condescending to your son's dates, or does my "colorful" background warrant particular investigation? More consequentially, are you ever going to let your little Johnny escape your Freudian clutches so he can actually grow a pair?* My rational mind takes hold of the wheel just in time to reassure her that "although I love your son very much, I know no one can never replace you. You will always be a role model for both him and, um, I hope I'm not overstepping my place by saying this, our children as well."

I have delivered the ultimate *coup de grâce*. Breathtaking, I must boast. Having passed the oral exam, "Liz" moves on, taking pains to emphasize that both she and John's "philandering father" are from the finest genetic stock.

"Mother . . . " John warns.

"You and I know what's important," *Liz* confides to me. "If Peter Pan over there ever does decide to make an honest woman of you, I just want you to know you can look forward to some of the bluest blood to be had."

"Mother, please, I asked you not to do this."

"Why not? I'm quite certain this lovely young lady looks to be married one day. After all, you have been courting for some time and I imagine she has her reputation to consider—"

(Spit-take here if you like—no offense taken—but in real life, I manage to choke it back, and so does John.)

"I'm only suggesting, Johnny," she crones on, "that you don't want to be one of those fathers who's too old to enjoy his children, do you?"

I swallow, smile politely, and allow John the opportunity to avoid the question on both our behalfs. Later, when we're alone, John apologizes. "I hope Mother wasn't too presumptuous, babes; she can be a bit much sometimes."

"Not at all, babes. I like 'Liz'," I lie. If she'd already booked our wedding venue and decided on our first song yet, it was okay by me.

"She's just being a mother," John explains. "You'll understand one day. Anyway, it's my decision, not hers."

Oh, it's your decision, is it? Any other man, any *real* man, would feel the pain of disgrace, the discomfort of debasement, but not my John. But I say nothing, and less than a year later, while attending a formal dinner at The Royal Oaks, John proposes. That was that. I was in, with a 10.03 carat round-cut, Ideal, H, VVS2 diamond (so Johnny explains at the moment) on my finger, proof positive.

My phone vibrates, a text:

"Meet now. Hotel A."

Okay, that man is in no danger of winning a Pulitzer.

"I can't wait," I type, followed by a pornographic emoticon (*not* an eggplant BTW, which bears an unfortunate, uncanny resemblance to that man IMHO LOL). I press "send" and almost instantly regret it. What has he done to deserve such a witty, instantaneous, and obedient response? I feel like a teenager again, giddy and unsure, worrying irrationally about how my every action will be perceived. How is it that when it comes to that man, I'm always insecure and perpetually second-guessing myself? I fidget with my Louis Vuitton phone case. *What's the matter with me? Do I really need his validation that badly?* I let the question dissolve, too afraid of the answer. My phone buzzes again. Relief. I grab the keys to the leased BMW (hated the Bentley), adjust my hair one last time, and head for the hotel. I bring a bottle of Versos, intending to share—

"How do you drink this stuff?" he asks, pouring his into my glass, opting instead for his double vodka, rocks.

"It's all the rage," I tell him.

"Rage is right—pisses me off," he quips.

Damn, he's quick.

"Don't let them catch you drinking that, pregnant lady," he warns, getting stern and serious, which both scares and excites me. "Not everyone's as *laissez-faire* as *moi.*"

I fill him in. He knows I've been avoiding him. He understands my lack of nerve. But I've done it, nevertheless, though maybe not perfectly or the way we planned it, fireworks and all.

"But it's done," he states, forgiving me and my absence. "The baby cometh."

"Yes, it does," I agree.

CHAPTER 19

THE MORNING OF my fifteenth birthday, the Staffords are engrossed in *Wheel of Fortune* while I'm supposed to be alone in my room playing with my birthday present: The All-American Girl doll complete with her house, car, and, of course, All-American husband. Instead, I'm in the shed where Big Brian keeps his tools, the place I'm never allowed to enter. Aaron's there, too, *hustling* me, coaxing me into a round of "Truth or Dare," his ultimate intentions thinly disguised. This isn't the first time he's attempted this ploy, with varying degrees of success. This time though, my premeditated answer shocks him:

"How much cash do you have on you?" I hold his gaze. He wants all of me. I know it. He knows I know it. Without breaking eye contact, we begin to negotiate the price, determining the value of my tanned, taut, adolescent body.

CHAPTER 20

THE LETTER IS delivered two mornings later, before I wake up. Georgia, the new cook, Hilda's replacement, puts it on my breakfast tray next to a blueberry muffin and a single white rose.

"I prepare for you the soft egg," Georgia points out, "the one that I only make it special for you. You know you are always loving my food. This is what's making you my best one to cook for."

"Thank you so much," I answer. Georgia aims so sincerely to please I almost believe the sentiment is heartfelt. But I also detect the stench of need, a fragrance I myself used to wear in abundance. She's been with us a week and a half, and she's already trying to make inroads, angling for a permanent, unbreakable connection. I simultaneously admire her and make a note to fire her.

But right then I'm more interested in a formal-looking correspondence from the offices of Dr. Michael Goldman, MD, OB-GYN. Should I open it? Do I even want to? An off-center stamp on the front of the envelope hints at its potentially life-altering contents: "Confidential Medical Information." I try to ignore it and wait until John comes down for breakfast. He needs to break the seal himself.

John bypasses the breakfast table in favor of the TV room, where he sinks into the oversized Fendi recliner, turns on the TV by Crestron remote, and accepts whatever breakfast Georgia rushes in and places before him, along with his usual cup of "rich, white, low-fat coffee" (which still amuses me).

On cable TV, the political fight has gone into extra rounds. Depending on which side of the screen you believe, the country's going right down the toilet, led by a tribe of cerebrally stunted primates, or we're in for a golden era of joy, freedom, and prosperity, "the likes of which will make the slimiest Wall Street hedge fund manager proud to be an American again."

Not having a personal opinion on the subject, I instead wave the envelope in front of John before he starts audibly cheering one side or another, which he *will* do; I've seen it before.

"What's this?" he asks, answering his own question by reading the return address. He *can* read; I will vouch for that. "Should we wait for Mother?" he wonders. I manage to maintain the same smile, the same frozen stare. I won't argue with the TV, and I won't tell John what to do.

"Up to you," I say, generosity overflowing.

He wants to wait, I can tell. But neither his apprehension nor his Freudian-grade subservience is a match for his curiosity. Defying Mama, he rips the envelope open—no ivory letter opener today. I love him for the gesture, then lean in to help him decipher the scrawled confirmation on a page torn from the doctor's prescription pad:

"The test results . . . conclusively . . . confirm . . . the patient is . . . approximately six weeks pregnant."

Anxiety gives way to exhilaration and we both squeal like a couple of just-pinned sorority sisters. There it is, signed by Goldman himself, definitive and indisputable. This is more than just a letter; it's an accreditation. A formal certificate. Proof. Finally, after waiting so long, it's happened. Happened for me. Happened for us.

Spontaneously, I start to cry. Then laugh. Then cry a lot more. John puts his arm around me as if he understands completely what I'm going through, which he doesn't. Has no idea. Not a clue.

"You were wrong," he tells me. "He didn't have the letter typed at all."

I sniffle, accepting the criticism gracefully, secretly angry at myself. A little mistake like that could ruin everything and John is correct to point it out. I stare at the note to be sure everything else checks out. Dr. Goldman's signature is a clichéd scrawl, typical physician's squiggle—

"Do they teach this stuff in medical school?" John jokes. "Illegible Signatures 101."

I chuckle politely.

"I should hit him up for a campaign contribution," John notes. "Is he a Republican or a Democrat?"

"That's not exactly what we discuss when I'm . . . " I let the sentence evaporate, and John leaves it alone, both of us picturing me in the stirrups, affording the "good doctor" unobstructed access—

"Doesn't matter. I won't ask. Not with the baby on the way. We want the doctor totally bipartisan."

"Good thinking," I agree. I'm going to be very agreeable these next seven-and-a-half months, about some things.

"Or is it 'nonpartisan?' I always get those confused. I need to ask Richards about that—" "Listen," I interrupt, "why don't you let me call Dr. Goldman's office and thank him for the note. Maybe I can feel him out about your candidacy. Avoid any awkwardness about his politics. I mean, think about the consequences. We can't be too careful."

Which I repeat, to myself this time.

John thinks about that. This is new territory for him, the deep end, and he's forgotten his water wings and maybe his swimsuit as well. On the one hand, he could drown, but on the other hand, if he gets out now, the girls will laugh and point—

"Mmm, yeah, babes, good idea. Why don't you take care of that," he says. "I've got plenty of other donors to tell anyway."

"You mean plenty of other *friends* to tell anyway."

"Exactly," he chuckles, and I join him.

BOOK 2: CHRONICLES

CHAPTER 21

JOHN, PROUD FATHER-to-be, has been on the phone all morning, spreading the news, talking, texting, posting. It's a minor miracle he hasn't hoisted a "we're pregnant" flag on his erection and paraded it around the town square. The Speedy family tree sprouts a new branch and everybody needs to know. I admit, I do my fair share of public relations work as well. The obligatory "I'm so happy for you," "congratulations" and accompanying memes and Gifs ping my phone with random regularity. Each phonic vibration signals another endorsement of my success, or more accurately, *conformity*. By virtue of this single announcement I am instantly acceptable and accepted.

On his own initiative, without my knowledge or approval, John sees fit to upload and display Dr. Goldman's note—scanned, framed, and afforded pride of place on his much-trafficked social media accounts. Over one hundred and eighty thousand total strangers now know I'm "approximately six weeks pregnant."

I ask John to take it down. He tells me "no." I let it go.

We have sex every night, sometimes in the morning

as well. I'm serving it up hot, and he's devouring it like a starving man. It isn't lost on me that his revved-up virility is directly correlated with my current "condition." The indisputable fact is that John, my husband, is truly, literally, a "motherfucker." I don't mention this revelation to him; I suspect he wouldn't find it amusing. For his part, he makes no comment on our increased activity. I am, however, soon forced to drop the other shoe, or rather, slap him across the face with an Alaïa Python ankle boot.

"I want you to get your fill," I tell him, "while my body's in decent shape because once I get fat and ugly and start drooling and peeing all over the place—"

"You're turning me on," he interrupts, and I realize maybe I am.

This is going to be tougher than I thought—

"You know what I mean," I whimper, threatening to cry. "You know me and my body image issues."

He blinks; he has no idea. I'll explain it to him later—he'll understand, I tell myself, lying.

I speak nothing of this to that man; he doesn't need to know. I don't want to hurt him. I suspect he suspects. We sit on his balcony, one of the last times I've dared to go to his place. Below, Maria relaxes by herself on a bench while her two employers, the couple in the animation business, play with their infant child, Janice, nearby. Maria reads a book, but she's always ready to help out when called upon. She scrupulously avoids looking up at us on the balcony—no waves this time.

"So they're going to have another child," I state, not really a question.

"That's right," he tells me.

"How far along are they?"

"Close enough," is all that man says. "I'll take pictures with my phone." To demonstrate, he pulls out his phone and pretends to take a call, with the thing to his ear first, then he holds it flat in front of his mouth the way people do, except he's not talking; he's lining up the shot, zooming in on the wife, the mother, ignoring the others. The picture snaps, the "before" picture, the control.

CHAPTER 22

I HEAR THE car pull up before I see it on the monitor. It isn't a car I recognize, but it belongs in the neighborhood—German, loud, expensive. Who should step out but Dr. Michael Goldman,

OB-GYN. I am momentarily glad to see him for some reason—an old acquaintance—but then I'm immediately troubled. I hurry to the front door, shooing the servants away. I don't give him a chance to ring the bell. Fortunately, John has gone to the office to scheme with Richards and his cronies; "Mum" is absent as well.

"Dr. Goldman, what a nice surprise," I gush, blocking the door. He looks past me, worried— no, more like scared to death.

"Is John here?"

"No, John's not here."

"Do you expect him back soon?"

"No, I don't think so."

"Good, I need to talk to you," he whispers, looking around the porch for the location of the surveillance cameras. Spotting one overhead, he asks: "Is that on? Does it record?"

"Yes, I suppose it does," I tell him, not mentioning the doorbell camera—"Will John see the tape?"

"He has other things to do, Doctor. Come in. Tell me what's bothering you."

"Come sit in my car," he suggests.

"That would look very suspicious, don't you think? Just come in and have a cup of coffee."

"You're right, you're right," he says.

We go into the living room. I tell somebody to bring us coffee.

"Sit?" I ask him, knowing he'll say no, which he does.

"John just came to see me," Dr. Goldman whispers.

"He did?" I ask, truly surprised.

"He asked me about your pregnancy."

"Oh," I remark. Coffee comes, giving me a chance to get my bearings. "What did you tell him?"

"What *could* I tell him? I *started* to tell him the truth—"

Oh shit, you g-ddamn piece of shit doctor. You'll fuck up the whole thing.

"I'm very hurt, you know," he claims.

Oh yeah, you're the aggrieved party, are you?

"I've found a different doctor, that's all," I tell him.

"What?"

"You're not the only OB-GYN in the world, you know."

"Who?" he demands to know.

"You don't know him."

"You came to me for birth control pills."

"Except I changed my mind," I tell him. "I decided to get pregnant."

"No!" Goldman exclaims, appalled.

"It's what John's always wanted."

"Well now, *that's* true," Dr. Goldman grunts angrily.

"You better go," I tell him.

"What the hell are you doing?" he demands.

"Nothing," I say innocently. "Or rather, none of your business."

"You know how dangerous it would be for you to get pregnant, right?" he squeals.

"It could kill me."

"Not could, *would* kill you—"

"Really, you're so kind to worry."

"We discussed this. I thought you understood. I let you forego the operation," Goldman whines. "You know I don't like unnecessary bloodshed, but maybe we need to go forward with that—"

"My body, my choice," I interrupt.

"Oh, please. Save the bumper stickers," Goldman spits out. "You may not want to hear it, but it's true."

"You understand, when he said you were pregnant, I was at a total loss. I just grinned like an idiot and said 'congratulations,' and that I was sorry, I wouldn't be in-volved. John seemed entirely satisfied with that. He did all the talking, believe me."

Remember that glass door? Well, John walked right through it by going to Goldman, and now the shards fell all over me.

"I promised John I wouldn't tell you he came to see me."

"Yet here you are," I note.

Goldman steps forward. I honestly think he's going to attack me, rape me maybe, exact his revenge for get-ting pregnant on his watch, a thing he truly believes will be fatal for me. He stops before I have to deck him.

"The baby isn't likely to survive, either," he whispers, "if that's what you're thinking."

"My doctor thinks differently."

I can see Dr. Goldman doesn't believe me. He'd like to discuss it.

"There've been some medical advances, I've been told," I say.

"What advances?" he comes back sharply.

"What do I look like—the New England Journal of Medicine? Advances, okay. Anyway, my new physician is very confident," I say, "and I have confidence in him."

Goldman considers that. His face indicates he's reluctantly willing to admit he might be wrong about something for the very first time in his medical career. He shrugs, surrendering apparently, and I have to concede he's almost as good an actor as he is a doctor.

"We'll send your medical records over to him," he offers, a final ploy.

"Thank you so much. I'll call your office," I tell him, playing along with no intention of making that call. I picture him storming into some unsuspecting colleague's office to discuss "the case," me. "Good-bye, Doctor, thank you again for everything." I go to the door, hoping he'll leave. Fortunately, he's a busy man. There are babies to be born, lady-parts to inspect, bills to be sent, and golf rounds to be played.

That night, I give John the news: "Dr. Goldman isn't going to support you for the Senate, I'm afraid."

"Really?"

"He says you're a 'Fascist hypocrite,' his exact words, 'who couldn't even hold down the job his mommy arranged for him in London.'"

"What the . . . ?" John asks, shocked. "Dr. Goldman told you this?"

"Not to me. Not directly to me, the snake," I reply. "Of course not. To a third party—" "Who?"

"It's classified. I could tell you, but then I'd have to kill you."

John, possibly the world's biggest *Top Gun* fan, ignores the *homage* entirely. He really must be distracted, or drunk.

"Kayla," he guesses.

"No!" I insist. The last thing I want is John asking Kayla about this and it getting back to Dr.

Goldman through her. "Not Kayla," I tell him calmly, though I feel more like screaming.

"Wait, when the hell did you hear this?"

From the look on John's face, I see he's replaying his own encounter with Goldman— "Yesterday," I reply.

"And you're just telling me now?"

"I didn't want to see you get hurt," I offer soulfully.

"What else did he say about me?" John inquires, though I don't think he genuinely wants to hear that either.

"'Spoiled little one-percenter, greedy WASP'—you know the drill."

My dearly beloved waves it off, all-too-aware of what the unfair mob thinks and says about its betters when those betters are not around to point out the error of the mob's ways.

"Well, screw him, bald little prick," John states, sipping something brown and alcoholic, his answer to everything.

"Anyway, I think I've found another doctor," I tell John.

"Oh?" he asks hopefully.

CHAPTER **23**

THAT MAN, TRUE to form, keeps his end of the bargain.

"Here you go," he says, handing me a card. It's a foreign name I don't have any idea how to pronounce. "Dr. Anand Prakhid," that man says flawlessly, like he grew up in the Punjab, which I happen to know he did not. "The best in the business."

"I want to meet him," I tell that man.

"He's very, very good," that man assures me.

I don't answer, nor do I budge on meeting him. A woman's relationship with her obstetrician is an important one, and although I trust that man with my life, I need to be sure. I also don't want that man to think I'm his obedient slave. I need him to understand that I'm an intelligent, freethinking individual—that's for when the time comes, too.

It's a nondescript medical building—not too nice, but it'll do. We take the elevator to the fifth floor. The office is almost too clean, as if everything was brand new. Even the sign on the door— Dr. Anand Prakhid, MD, OB-GYN—looks warm from the engraving. The doctor himself, on the other hand, is withered, wise, and clearly experienced. Juxtaposed against his polished maple desk, he looks oddly out of place, the one piece of furniture that doesn't quite fit. His eyes are dim; I'm certain they've seen things they would rather forget. It's the end of the day. Patients and the receptionist are gone. The single exam room is empty and pristine. At Dr. Prakhid's invitation, I look around. The diplomas on his wall say Harvard, Johns Hopkins, and Oxford.

"Undergrad at the University of Colorado," he says quietly. "I don't put that one up, I'm afraid. Bit of a party school. Okay, a *lot* of a party school. I was a Philosophy major, I confess."

His accent is slightly British, his smile disarming. I love him. He's perfect. That man has chosen the right man for the job, an anti-Goldman in every way: brown-skinned, bearded, polite, and perpetually dressed down in denim jeans and T-shirt under a wrinkled, blue-gray lab coat. With his bald head and kind eyes, there is something almost mystical about him. I trust him from the second I meet him, and considering my history, my disappointments, and my singular objective, this is the one aspect of my life where trust is imperative. I sense John will be taken by him, too, and won't be able to say a word against him now that he's joined the "we are all one people" crowd in his quest for DC glory. Dr. Prakhid's qualifications, at least on paper, far exceed Dr. Goldman's, and he has another advantage: he doesn't give me the creeps.

"When can you meet my husband?" I ask.

Dr. Prakhid takes us out to the reception window, where he checks the appointment ledger and finds an opening in the middle of the day, two days off.

"And you are how many weeks pregnant?" he asks.

"Six and a half, I believe," I reply, checking with that man, who concurs. "Give or take."

"Good, good," Dr. Prakhid says. "You came in plenty of time. I'll need a standard medical history, insurance information, inoculations, key to your house, bank vault, the coins in your couch cushions . . . "

We all chuckle politely as the doctor pulls forms from various cubbyholes behind the reception desk and hands them to me.

"Make sure your husband sees these as well," he insists, "and signs them."

"Absolutely."

"Day after tomorrow then," he says, "and at that time, we'll set up a time for a complete physical exam." This last he offers with a wink . . .

Okay, so maybe at that moment, I feel a little creeped out.

CHAPTER 24

I'M ELEVEN YEARS old, and I'm rubbing myself aggressively, hiding under the bunk beds in Devin's room. My breath is frantic. Something restless and desperate needs to be released from my naked, prepubescent body. I'm still sore from the last time, but the thing has stayed inside. I'm moody, incomplete. This time is different. I am literally gasping, squealing, whimpering, not unlike a wet-nosed puppy who's been pulled from its mother's teat. Then, without warning, my body stiffens and quivers. I roll onto my stomach and press my hand firmly into my flesh. *This is good. Very good.*

By the time I turned fifteen, I knew the truth: everyone with a Y-chromosome wanted me.

Well, okay, wanted *it*. My toned physique was at the peak of its adolescent allure: tan skin, golden hair, and piercing green eyes. I was a vision, youthful and powerful, drawing male attention like a carnal magnet. Eight years of dance lessons combined with Southern California's organic eating had sculpted my once chubby frame into an X-rated fantasy, trim and tantalizing, an irresistible balance of burgeoning sexuality and virginal innocence. These, together with wry smiles and girlish giggles, conjured up a singularly beguiling concoction and spawned in me a lifelong addiction, a beautiful burden that would ultimately lead me to this point in my life, feeding what my abandoned orphan soul wanted, needed, and craved more than anything else in the world: *the thrill of being desired.*

"You need to shop," that man tells me.

He's right. We get to work, joyously and meticulously compiling a list, "Baby Shopping," but then the bedroom closet mirror makes a mockery of my plans. It teases and taunts, forcing me to try on half my wardrobe. I agonize for the better part of two hours, eventually settling on a long, nondescript, cream dress, Vivienne Westwood hat (the one Mary-Elizabeth despises), and a pair of fashionably oversized Fendi sunglasses. I call the outfit "Expectant Mother Outfit Number 42" and head out the door, finally feeling equipped to conquer the job at hand.

I drive to a good old-fashioned, brick-and-mortar mall and indulge in what's fast becoming an archaic indulgence: in-store shopping. Or, in my case, "the DIY Mommy Show."

I take the beamer—"Extra-large trunk space in such a compact car," the salesman bragged. "German engineering genius." My retort: "I think that charging over a hundred thousand dollars for a car that the Koreans sell for a third the price—that's the *real* German genius." Check. And mate.

Though today, I'm putting that extra space to optimal use. *Baby stuff.* There is so much of it. My list has proven entirely inadequate. Clothes, diapers, accessories, toys, a Porsche stroller, and a wireless baby monitor are crammed haphazardly into the trunk. This is my reality now. Crib, swing set, and car seat will be delivered. This is the woman I've become. Truth be told, it's who I always knew (feared) I would be.

Breastfeeding. No. Not doing it, which leaves out a whole range of products: bibs, cloths, breast pumps (ugh), bottles, bras, nipple lotion (again, ugh). I call that man. We consult. He vetoes my plan.

"Buy all that," he tells me. "Seriously. You need to buy all that."

"Tit-shit," he calls it. *Seriously,* I want to slap him. I try to argue; he's not having it.

Reluctantly, I give in, though I know it's a horrible waste. I buy it all. I don't care. I refuse to care.

My intuition is to wait to unpack the car. I surprise myself with how percipient I can be sometimes.

"Our mum is on the way," John announces as I enter.

Since the news broke, John's voice has jumped a full octave higher. This, together with his referring to that woman as "our mum," would usually be enough for me to engage him in a level- two domestic dispute. Today, though, he has *carte blanche.* Truth be told, I am actually looking forward to seeing "mum." After all the years of enduring slights, snideness, and jibes, I am finally achieving redemption. As our new butler—name still unlearned—announces mum's entrance, I contemplate how I have inadvertently stumbled on the perfect title for her Lifetime Network Special: *Slights, Snideness, and Jibes, the Mary-Elizabeth Speedy Story.* When she walks in, I am still laughing. Inside.

"There she is, our mother-to-be," she beams, accompanied by the usual no-contact hugs and kisses. Before I know it, she's got my blouse up. Unable to escape without throwing a punch, I'm forced to endure the indignity of Mary-Elizabeth's over-moisturized hands on my bare stomach, the last time I will allow *that* to happen! "I can't believe we're finally pregnant," she crows, as if that excuses the assault. "We have so much to talk about. I'm going to tell you exactly what to do. This really is the best thing you could have done for all of us, you'll see. I just don't know why you waited so long." If delivering backhanded compliments was ever afforded Olympic event status, no doubt Mary-Elizabeth Speedy would bring home the gold.

"I guess John just had to try a little harder than most," I mumble. Before anyone has the opportunity to retort, I clasp my hand over my mouth and, in an Oscar-worthy performance, feign sudden-onset morning sickness. I dash up the stairs with all the grace of a hobbled goose, groaning audibly and grinning silently, charging for the bathroom, leaving John and Mary- Elizabeth alone in the library to busy themselves with a game of self-congratulatory "told you sos." From the upstairs sunroom I listen to them chattering, prognosticating, plotting the academic trajectory of "their" child. When I overhear Mary-Elizabeth ask "Harvard or Yale?" I can't help but cringe. One thing I know for certain is there will be no Ivy League education. *Not in the cards.*

After the appropriate upchuck interlude, I return to apologize and suggest they help me unload the car. When the trunk opens, "Mum" lets out an audible gasp of shock and horror worthy of a Stephen King movie.

CHAPTER **25**

"WE NEED TO talk," I call in a panic.

He picks "Hotel C," an hour's drive from where I live. *Why does he always get to choose the place? It's my body, my risk, my life.* Regrettably, I know the answer all too well and agree to the venue without hesitation. We have to be even more careful now. We've pulled the trigger and now have to look out for the ricochet. He's also punishing me for calling *him* this time, instead of the other way around. I know that.

"They're superstitious that way?" that man asks me, surprised.

"I don't know. They didn't like me buying all those things; I'll tell you that much."

"Huh," he grunts. He won't admit he didn't know. He'll only admit to being surprised that the Speedies cared. My confidence is shaken and so is that man's. It was a stupid mistake, but a horrible one, we both have to admit (though only *I* do any admitting), if we know so little about having a baby as to make that mistake, what other traps are we walking into?

"'It's bad luck to buy things for a baby that isn't born

yet,' they'd said," I inform him, pouring myself a vodka from the bottle he's brought. "Where they got that superstitious nonsense, I don't know but that's what they said and what they think. You'd think I'd just committed infanticide or something."

"No, that comes later," that man smirks.

"Not even a little bit funny," I warn.

"You're taking all the stuff back?"

I shake my head.

"Too late. It's all been put away for later. Hidden. We're not to speak of it again."

"Good," that man concludes. "Don't worry about it then. Oh, and easy on the vodka there, Mommy." He winks. I scowl.

At that moment, I realize he's actually *one of them*. A different flavor, of course, but still part of the same food group, or at least belonging on the same plate.

By the time I return to 16 Oak, all the reminders of my ill-advised shopping spree have been stashed away so the Speedies won't need to be reminded of the bad fortune I've rained down upon their son (or daughter, though they won't concede that). The devil, as they say, is in the details. Fortunately for me, large houses have plenty of wonderful hiding places. Maybe that's why they're so expensive because they keep secrets so well. "Behind every great fortune lies a great crime," I once suggested to John. He wasn't amused. Now, years later, I believe this dark truth to be correct. Maybe that's why I always wanted a big house. Perhaps I craved a big secret.

CHAPTER **26**

THE DEVIL'S IN the details. Whoever made that one up got it right. Unfortunately, I'm a "big picture" man, not one for advance planning, a "wing it" guy, fast on my feet, an ad libber. "Good in the room" is what they call it. I never had a detailed plan with Amanda, just a sketchy outline, a path to take. "Take it as it comes," so to speak. So we took, we came, wink wink. It worked in the past; it'll work in the future, I say. The little stuff gives me headaches.

Amanda? She loves it all, the details, the flashcards, the cramming all night, and the timing and sketching out of the entire road ahead. That's optimism, is what that is, though she'd never admit it. That's thinking what you do today influences what happens the next day and the day after. Ha. Dreamers.

So with us two, you got your oil and water poured over a mixed salad—do we complement each other, or are we like two stable chemical compounds that when touched together cause a massive explosion? Can't say yet. Probably won't know till it happens, and we won't know what hit us anyway. As long as we've known each *other, it seems the wheel still spins; where it stops, nobody knows. Amanda thinks she knows. I know she's wrong.*

It worries me. Everything worries me. People label me as paranoid—I know that. It hurts. Swear to God she's as nervous as I am; she just doesn't show it. She should be nervous. I want her to be nervous. There's no room to let the guard down or laze off or not pay attention. There's too much at stake and too much that can go wrong. I have to remind myself as well. But that's what they say, "a life without risk is the greatest risk of all."

CHAPTER **27**

"NO ONE WILL ever find out, I promise." Aaron knows that inevitably I'm going to say yes. This is just a preliminary dance: two steps forward, one step back. "What have you got to lose? Do you really think you'll ever get an opportunity like this again? I mean, it's not like they're some strangers off the street; they're my brother's best friends." He raises his voice (a good strategy). "Look, if you're not gonna do this, just say so. There are other girls I could ask."

I'm against the ropes and he knows it. For an eighteen-year-old, he's both linguistically skilled and highly persuasive, with an arsenal of psychological and semantic weaponry beyond his years. And he can read me like a book.

"You know what you can do with five thousand dollars? Have you ever even seen that much money in your life?" The final hook is baited. He leans in. Cautious not to startle his trophy, he lowers his voice and whispers, "I mean, we've already done it; what difference will it make? I thought you liked our money game. I thought it made you feel sexy. You are sexy, you know. I think you're sexy. You know that, right? You . . . you know . . . " He's so close to me I can feel his heat. "You know I love you."

I'm hooked. Like a hungry, gullible guppy. I grab his shirt, pull him to me, and without saying a word, kiss him. Before I know it, he has maneuvered his hand into my jeans. I lean back, open my legs, and feel him push two fingers forcefully inside my body. I've surrendered.

CHAPTER **28**

"YOU SURE I'M dressed okay, babes? I want to make a good impression."

"The Harvard tie's a little much. And for Heaven's sake, lose the cufflinks."

I'm taking John to meet my new physician, and he's acting like it's a first date. To his credit, there have been no snide references to "Dr. Prick-head" or other quasi- or blatantly racist sentiments from my dearly beloved since my first mention of the doctor. I am prepared to counter with "he's actually from Greeley or Grand Junction, or somewhere in Colorado," but (to my surprise) it isn't necessary. Perhaps John-the-father is growing up. A girl can hope, can't she?

Unlike the day before, the place is bustling, with a receptionist and a nurse in attendance, and the last patient of the morning just leaving. After escorting us into the doctor's inner office, Dr. Prakhid's staff takes off for lunch. Prakhid slowly and dramatically looks up from my file and is about to speak when John preemptively interrupts:

"So Doc, everything good down there? She still open

for business for the next few months?" His delivery is so upbeat, so well-timed that both the doctor and I burst into spontaneous laughter. Okay, maybe John's not completely grown up, and in that moment, I can't help but love him. Dr. Prakhid reminds John he has yet to assess the situation "down there," but he assures us both that as far as he knows, the pregnancy is coming along "swimmingly."

"I really hope so," John utters. *Are those tears in his eyes?* "We've been disappointed . . . " "Don't worry, please," the doctor assures us, "I have some very clever tricks to help those in your very difficult situation."

"Ah," John cheers a little. "Tricks . . . " He seems to like the idea.

On the drive home, our new, alarmingly stoic chauffeur plays Chopin ("Nocturne Op. 9 #2") while John prattles on about the perils of our eroding educational system. I understand he's sincere, but also practicing a stump speech, and I'm not expected to actually listen. Reclining in the hand-stitched, leather seat, I gaze vacantly through the tinted window where a silver-foil balloon has escaped its grade-school custodian and hovers above the traffic. Printed on its shiny, reflective surface is a family of digitally drawn monkeys in matching outfits holding hands in front of a white picket fence. The primates stare at me, grinning and mirthful, as I float blissfully into an alternate universe, immersed in my role as a suburban housewife.

In this concocted daydream, my mustached husband, a plumber, makes good-natured "wifey" jokes, chugs beer, and works on his boat in the backyard, which will never be finished nor get anywhere near an ocean, lake, or river. Our three pudgy boys eat TV dinners, play video games, and battle for Dad's attention. Melissa lives next door with three kids of her own, all girls. We know my sons and her daughters are going to mess around one day and eventually get pregnant and married to each other and have kids of their own, and that's okay with us. Life is uncomplicated, microwaved, and satisfying. We expect to win the Lotto and be able to afford expensive cars, rich food, and exotic travel. We never lose hope, working hard, putting in the hours, striving to buy the things the TV tells us we should own. Where would we be without our material desires, amusing gadgets, and dull, anesthetizing routines? I know the answer: we'd be exactly here, in the rarified atmosphere of privilege, seeking out ways to complicate our simple lives to the point of absurdity—chauffeured, pampered, indulged, and balancing ever so precariously on the precipice of catastrophe.

My life has now divided into two very distinct hemispheres: BC (Before Child) and AD (After Delivery), and I'm not talking about the delivery of the baby; I'm talking about the delivery of the news, the announcement. I'm at fifteen weeks. Scrolling through the pictures on my phone, it's apparent that I'm starting to show. Or, more accurately, starting "the show." Like most things in life, there are rules to being knocked up, and a specific role every first-time mother is expected to play. The script has been refined over time, condensed into glib sound-bites:

"You're positively glowing. I've never seen you so happy. Your body has hardly changed at all. Have the cravings started yet? I just know you'll be the best mother ever."

My lines: "For the first time, I'm starting to understand what true happiness means. It's like having an alien growing inside me. I just can't wait to hold him in my arms. As long as he's healthy—that's all that matters."

"So it's a boy?"

"Actually, we don't know."

"Why's that?"

"We enjoy surprises . . . ?"

Meanwhile, that man sends periodic spy-cam photos of the pregnant woman downstairs, Maria's employer, so I can "size-up the competition." (It's not enough that I'm forced to compare myself to Kayla, who's exactly two months ahead of me pregnancy-wise.)

Despite the pressure, I have to admit I'm relishing the spotlight and my starring role in my very own soon-to-be-a-mother show. *I'm ready for my close-up now.*

However, some things are becoming unbearable, beginning with Mary-Elizabeth's habitual pop-ins, both longer and more frequent now. Her enthusiasm at the prospect of a grandson gains momentum, casting claustrophobic shadows over my days, making it impossible for me to feel at ease in my own skin. Today, without waiting for an invitation, or even the hint of a welcome, she settles beside me. I perceive the heat of her body; my breathing shallows.

"How's our little mommy today? Did we have another bout of sickness this morning?"

I shrug, avoiding the question.

She continues undeterred:

"Trust me, dear, the first one's always the trickiest. I remember to this day how sick Johnny could make me feel."

"Me too," I'm tempted to respond. But I bite my tongue. *"Pick your moments"*—that's what that man would say.

"Look what we have here. I wonder who's living inside this little belly bump." She's petting me, stroking me steadily over my layered clothing, treating me like Stalin, her absurdly and inappropriately named cat. If I wasn't feeling "a bout of sickness" before, I am now.

Oblivious to my repulsion, Mary-Elizabeth goes on fondling my bulging Prada sweater and talking a mile a minute, frisking me, like the designated "falsy detector" at a middle school with a strict dress code, or a dizzy tweener with a covert crush. She covers her inappropriate fondling with a running commentary on "those people" who have somehow disturbed her, "demanding to be part of our club just because they scraped together a couple of *shekels*. Can you believe the audacity?"

Apparently, I'm expected to answer. "Unbelievable," I say, hoping that's right.

"In my day, we had a name for people with a million dollars."

"Paupers!" I reply, recalling my part.

She laughs.

"I told you that one, didn't I?" she says.

I smile graciously like we're a long-standing and much-beloved comedy team—

But why can't she keep her hands to herself? Does she think if she rubs long enough a genie will pop out and grant her three wishes? I make subtle sideways movements, willing her to stop, but my efforts are in vain.

"You see, dear, money can't buy upbringing. We need to make sure our little one knows that.

The only way to make sure your offspring inherit the character and mettle to make it in this world is to start them on the right foot from day one. I'm sure you, *of all people*, understand."

She's reminding me of my humble beginnings—

"Mother," I stab back. The uncharacteristic moniker out of my mouth catches her off guard — "I was wondering if you had any ideas for the name? After all, he's going to be your first grandchild. You know I really value your opinion on these things. I know you'll guide us in the right direction."

Laying it on a little thick, I know, but when it comes to warm clothing, bug spray, and flattery, I've found you can never put on too much.

Mission accomplished. She's diverted; I slip from her grasp.

Grinning like a mental patient on nitrous oxide, she recites a list of plainly rehearsed and characteristically pedestrian names. Misdirection—it's such a powerful weapon, it should come with a warning label. Sometimes it's just too easy to lead even the most insightful observer astray.

I nod, feigning attention while Mary-Elizabeth recites name after name.

"'Jonathan Junior,' obviously, but let's not discount Adam, Luke, and Blaine. No, scratch that last one; it has to be something Biblical, I'm sure you agree."

"Jehoshaphat" comes to mind, but I say nothing, my eyes catching John, the coward, just outside the room, in earshot the entire time, clearly too much of a wimp to interject himself into the baby-naming Olympiad.

Busted, he sweeps in, grabbing the TV remote—"What's on?"—flipping through channels without waiting for a reply. He's clean-shaven today, well-groomed yet manly. His muscles are firm. I want to feel his weight on top of me. He catches me looking. Since my increase in size, I have, admittedly, been entirely derelict in my marital duties. *No poke' er nights for this gambler.* As can be expected, I've resorted to the tried and true, time-tested list of excuses recruited by pregnant woman throughout history: "not in the mood," "feeling bloated, " "morning sickness," "hormones"—there is no shortage of credible explanations for my frigidity. The truth, as always, is far simpler—I can't let him see my body like this.

Amazingly, Mary-Elizabeth still yaps away.

"You don't want to give our little man a name that could be, um (how can I put this delicately, *honey*), ethnically confusing."

You have to give her credit for her ability to weave racism, sexism, and condescension into a single sentence.

Of course, Mary-Elizabeth sticks strictly with male names, refusing to admit I might give birth to a girl. She's had a girl, of course, her daughter Sylvia. I make a mental note to organize a telethon for the poor thing, or a Go Fund Me page at the least.

While Mary-Elizabeth continues her amateurish anthropological analysis of names versus nurture, and John consumes his daily dose of cable TV conservative propaganda, I check a recently downloaded list of instructions (orders) composed by that man, or as he would say, "guidelines for my protection." But we both know the truth: what he says, goes.

Sometimes I hate that man.

CHAPTER 29

NINE MONTHS IS a hell of a long time. Seriously, I'm not sure I can stand it. How do women do it? Men couldn't, I'm convinced of that. We're built for living life fully—at least I am—seize the day, get it while you can—no clocks, no calendars, no plans, no disappointments, thank you. So how the hell do men manage to be fathers, the exact opposite of all that? Or is it? Do people change? I would have said "no way" before I met Amanda; I would have told you people are exactly what they are from the moment of conception. Okay, they surprise you sometimes, shock the hell out of you even, but it's all there from the beginning. The proverbial leopard that will never change his spots.

Bullshit. There's change. Fundamentally.

CHAPTER 30

JOHN IS AS happy as I can remember him ever being. As for me, the lies are getting easier. When you walk away from the truth, it fades into the distance, disappears over the horizon, and after a while you'll believe it was never there at all. That's pretty much how I'm able to cope. The days pass and I adapt to my new circumstances with the help of maternity books, YouTube tutorials, and, of course, Dr. Prakhid, who I go see every other week, bringing home written results for John's benefit. I'm also informed by the staff that Dr. Prakhid calls John occasionally when I'm not around. I challenge the doctor about this.

"The husbands need to be kept in the loop, my dear," Prakhid admonishes early on.

Nevertheless, the smart doctor knows who his patient is, and sends me text messages between appointments, some of which I share with John.

"Just checking up that all is still being well—Dr. P."

"Now that's a doctor," John exclaims, "not like that Goldman quack."

While the kitchen staff, now augmented with a six-hundred-dollar-an-hour nutritionist, prepares my morning meal and accompanying nutrients, I apply makeup and more makeup. Then hair and nails. Wardrobe selection comes last. By the time I descend the wide staircase leading into the sunroom, I feel as if I'm fit for the cover of *Mommy and Me* magazine. Breakfast with John and Mary-Elizabeth has become standard, followed by a bout of light (non-baby) shopping and heavy, sober socializing. Until now, with alcohol out of the question, I never appreciated quite how mercifully anesthetizing mimosas could be. No matter what, I always make sure to head out for a stroll in the gardens. It's here while roaming invisibly behind the botanical walls that I'll call that man from the other phone, my favorite part of the day. After each maddeningly brief conversion, I hang up, and once the guilt has subsided (yes, I *do* feel guilt), I head back to the safety of the house for dinner. Most nights I make a conscious effort to keep my participation in both the meal and the inevitable pregnancy-centric conversation to a minimum. The world doesn't expect much from the expectant and neither does John. After rebuffing any (increasingly infrequent) advances from him, I'll head to the library where I'll sip on calcium-enriched milk, listen to streaming mood music, and update my growing social media portfolio: pictures, profiles, witty remarks, forwarded memes.

The replies laced with obvious jealousy bring me the most joy: "You look great but are you getting enough sleep? Wow, is that *another* new maternity dress?" and—courtesy of eternal frenemy Kayla Smithe-Beckworth herself: "Hippos forever," accompanied by photos of her own self (though she's more of a whale). If she has twins, I'll kill her. If it's triplets, I'll do it with a rusty knife. But despite my bitterness, simply knowing that my routine updates have somehow bored their way into her warped consciousness is deeply satisfying. A significant victory indeed.

CHAPTER 31

JOHN AND I have words, our first real argument for as long as I can remember. Some would call it a domestic dispute; I call it necessary.

"I just don't get it; I think you look beautiful, why won't you let me touch you? Just once. Please."

John's opening gambit is beyond pitiful. I think about that man, whether he would react the same way? No, of course not—he would never beg.

"That's right, you don't get it!" I counter. "Have you ever been pregnant?"

"But Dr. Prakhid said—"

"Listen, I don't care what Prakhid said," I declare— *time to shut this down once and for all*— "If he wants you to have sex so bad, why don't you just go down to his office and fuck *him* then. This is my body and my life, and I'm saying no."

Stunned, rejected, and fuming, John scares me. *What the hell am I doing? This can't be smart.* I need to stay calm, breathe deeply, and focus on the objective at hand. *And so it was that Jesus showered her with riches, she who was delicate unto her spouse.* I permit myself to apologize, and in so doing, bring the conflict to an in-auspicious end. Wrapping my arms around John's neck, I lean in and whisper, "I'm sorry, baby. It's the hormones. I still love you." Then, before he has the chance to react, I kiss him softly on the lips, squeeze his hands, and push my body firmly against his. "Thanks for being so under-standing. I don't know what I'd do without you." He looks defeated. I know he doesn't deserve this, but what else can I do?

My reluctant decision to rebuff his advances prompts ever-inventive strategies to rekindle "poke 'er nights" on his part, to no avail, the failure of which has dug an un-tenable chasm between us, a Möbius strip of appeal and rejection so callous it borders on humiliating. When I can no longer bear to be the source of rejection, when the circumstance *arises*, I unilaterally (and literally) take mat-ters into my own capable hands. Staying fully clothed, I stroke him tenderly to release, looking directly into his eyes as he whimpers and groans. When he finishes, I tell him I love him and reassure him we will be together again soon. What he will never know is that, secretly, I too want him between my legs (and a drink, too), but rules are rules and, for everybody's good health, I know I have to obey. He wants more, I know, mouth instead of hand, lips instead of fingers, but that's that man's terri-tory in my troubled mind, *his* property, off-limits as far as John's concerned—

Even my XXL maternity clothes are stretching out. Clasps pull and buttons pop. While waiting for Georgia to prepare yet another fresh-fruit juice, I regard the fullness of my frame in the mirror and contemplate "the miracle of childbirth." It's been seven months (DAY 1, AD, "after delivery of announcement"). So much has changed.

The woman I once was has died and been reborn. Resurrected and recreated. Replaced with someone new, someone *different*. As part of this metamorphosis, certain things are expected: the extra two hours it took me to get made-up this morning, for instance. There's no going back now. I changed everything, and everything, in turn, changed me.

I dream I'm back in Dr. Prakhid's office, which seems to get smaller with every appointment. Maybe my perpetually widening girth makes it seem like the world around me is shrinking. More likely, though, it's because of my secret, the one weighing me down and making me ill. Secrets have their own mass, a weight that increases in direct correlation to size. Maybe that's why my secret, my *big* secret, needs more than one person to hold it? Maybe that's why I met that man. I try to imagine, just for a moment, how different I would feel if I held only the truth and nothing extra? Light maybe? No, buoyant. I would float away to nothingness like that AWOL silver-foil balloon hovering over traffic with the monkey family on it. Gatsby had his green light; I have my balloon, flying trash, junk.

Across the waiting room in Dr. Prakhid's office, above the mandatory fern, John and I stare at a vintage poster of a pregnant woman smoking a long blue cigarette juxtaposed against a chrome and white maternity ward. Beneath her protruding belly, a bold, metallic-gray typeface identifies her as a "Bad Mother." The illustration reminds me of the Bobby and Shelly books from kindergarten. "Bobby and Shelly play in the garden. Bobby and Shelly kick the ball. Bobby and Shelly keep secrets from each other. Bobby and Shelly will break each other's hearts, tearing their lives apart." You had Dick and Jane, maybe; we had those two fucks—

"The doctor will see you now." The trainee nurse's high-pitched voice startles me, interrupting my dreamy stroll down Memory Lane.

"You want to come in with me?" I ask John.

"You want me to?" he asks.

"I'd rather not," I tell him. "It's so medical, and embarrassing." I blush for him.

"Okay," he agrees. "I'll wait here for you."

As I walk past the poster and into the office, I swear Bad Mother's eyes follow me in judgment.

CHAPTER 32

IN A DIFFERENT life, back when I'm twenty-three and on top of the world, it's a glorious year to be me, bouncing through classes and boys alike. Life is effortless; I insist on it. Talbord Academy of Law is attended entirely by well-bred and highly privileged individuals, young men and women with enviable aptitudes like Olympic-level skiing, competitive spelling, or surviving birth from a well-to-do vagina.

Except me. I got a scholarship.

From the second I arrive at Talbord, I am determined to claw my way to the top of the fiercely competitive academic landscape and secure my reputation as "the little orphan who could." As Senior Valedictorian, I'm chosen to represent my class in the Debutant Debaters Competition, the most prestigious scholastic event on the calendar.

Colloquially known as "The D," the contest draws a parade of California's academic elite, a who's who of the legal faculty coming together to confirm how relevant they all are. The night is sponsored by "Future Lady Lawyers of America," an all-male super-PAC pretending to promote gender equality throughout the judiciary (a ruse so glaringly artless that it defies explanation).

But with eight-figure donations at stake, everyone in attendance toes the line in their penguin suits and ball gowns, pearls, and Pateks. White-hot gossip is served alongside chilled caviar. Champagne is poured and power is brokered. Law firm recruiters litter the audience—all overweight, balding men telling impressionable young girls how privileged they feel to get this "unique opportunity to see some of America's finest legal minds in action'" and "meet the next generation of female leadership" (and possibly feel them up).

While the band belts out the classics and "The D" gets into full swing, the real agenda (besides the sexual harassment) unfolds quietly behind the scenes, namely to get the invitees to cough up some hard-earned, or more often, easily inherited, dough.

"How much can we *rely on you* to contribute this year?" is about as hard sell as it gets. The *quid pro quo* goes without saying: "Your little-legal-prodigy-in-the-making will graduate from Talbord, join a prestigious law firm, take home a six-figure salary, and most importantly, become *one of us*."

Plus, there's *moi*, a living, breathing testimony of Talbord's ability to sculpt potter's clay into a masterpiece. I am the consummate advertorial with a sharp mind and a tight body.

"You know, she was an orphan," they whisper, "but just look at her now. If Talbord can do that for *her*, imagine what they can do for (insert name) who already shows such enormous potential and comes from such fine stock."

All fine by me; I'm proud of my trajectory, and if they want to show me off, I'm absolutely on board. From my perspective, the night is a triumph, definitive proof that I've left my past, scorched and scalded, behind me once and for all, raised up from the ashes by the fires of my success, or something like that.

From the moment I stride onto the stage the audience is mine. The topic: "Should we negotiate with terrorists?" My opponents: the valedictorians of Yale and Wharton, respectively. The stakes: Talbord's unblemished track record. My position (selected against the advice of my faculty advisor): "Stand our ground—give an inch, they'll take a mile." My closing argument brings the house down (and the donations up). "No deals, no concessions, no compromise, and no negotiations. Ever!"

Everyone is delighted. This is indeed my year. *Cometh the hour, cometh the woman.*

That's the night I met John. He sat quietly in the front row, four seats from the left, dark suit, wrinkle-free, clearly custom-made. His hair looked too good to be real. Even more endearing than his appearance, though, was that when I put the microphone down, he was the first to stand and applaud, holding my eye for a few awkward, exhilarating seconds before Dean Matters himself raised my hand.

"Well said, young lady. I think it's clear we have a winner. I defy anyone to argue against her. She's obviously been well instructed. You see here at Talbord, and dare I say it, here in

America, our liberty is not for sale!" In that moment, with John Speedy cheering me on, I was invincible. Ignorance, it seems, is truly bliss.

I never asked John whether it was my body, delightfully dimpled face, or erudite debating skills that first caught his attention. Maybe it was all three. Whatever his motivation, one week later he asked me out, and by the end of the month, we were going steady. He spoiled me, pampered me, and treated me like royalty. I, in turn, let him. Later, when he invited me to spend Christmas at his family's cabin in Lake Tahoe, it was an easy "yes." It was there in the hot tub I took his virginity, a milestone so long overdue that it bordered on criminal.

"I always knew it would be you, babes. I wanted you from the moment I saw you. You are my . . ." Before he finished, his final groan drifted off into the cool mountain air. The competition was over; he was mine.

Less than twelve months later, our wedding (which made the society pages, but no mention of the jacuzzi) found John at the top of his game, entertaining our 751 closest friends with a tantalizing buffet of anecdotes about his new bride.

"As most of you know, I saw my beautiful wife—wow, I can finally say 'wife' now—for the first time at 'The D,' and let me tell you she was radiant that night. What most of you don't know, however, is what she said." He quoted from memory: "'*Even at the expense of the pain or life of a loved one, I would never open the door and negotiate with terrorists.*' That's my new wife, ladies and gentlemen." He paused for effect. "She would rather see us all tortured and murdered than budge one inch." The room broke into uproarious laughter and John raised his glass "to the most stubborn woman in the world—I will love you forever."

CHAPTER 33

OF ALL THE eateries in all the world, Dr. Goldman walks into the one where John and I have managed to land a reservation, one of only six restaurants in LA (out of 29,000) with more than one Michelin star. John gives the physician a cold "hello" snub, no doubt remembering the "Fascist hypocrite" quote I made up, or maybe it was the "spoiled little one-percenter, greedy WASP" remark I also falsely attributed to the good doctor.

"Excuse me for a moment. I think I see the chairman of the Senate Leadership Fund," John lies, leaving me at the mercy of my former OB-GYN.

"So how is this going?" Goldman asks, reaching for my distended belly. I grab his wrist with an iron grip before his hand can reach its mark. "I'm your doctor," he complains.

"Not anymore," I remind him.

"You're at great risk," he says. "You understand that, right?"

"Thank you for your concern."

Goldman eyes me skeptically.

"Looks a little big to me. Got some extra padding under there, have we? Faking twins, perhaps?"

"What?" I ask, confused. "Go to Hell," I add.

He stares at my belly, puzzled, ashamed that with all his skill and training he can't actually tell. He'd like to test me with his fingers, but I still hold his wrist and he senses correctly that I

am willing to break his arm if I need to. Another idea hits the sick fuck's fantastic imagination. He grins broadly, and I smell some very expensive Scotch.

"Oh, I see. John likes his big mama, does he? It's a game, right?" Dr. Goldman leans in conspiratorially. "A sex game thing. The huge abdomen is a turn on. What do they call it? 'Cosplay?' You still shaving down there or are you letting that grow for extra effect?"

My sudden suspicion is this fancy fetish has occurred to him before, perhaps on "poke 'er night." *Fucking Harvard men.* He reaches for my midsection with his other hand. I seize that wrist, too.

"That's disgusting," I tell him. "Really disgusting." The doctor looks hurt. "I'm going to pretend it's the drinking." He smiles, shit-faced. "But if John comes back right now, he'll beat you to a pulp."

"Really?"

"I'd insist on it."

Goldman looks doubtful. He knows John just about as well as I do, I guess, and although John's not exactly a pacifist, my dear beloved's not what you'd call "quick to rile" either, especially if it comes to something as paltry and inconsequential as a good ol' family friend making a play on his unabashedly sexy wife. Sure, I'd like a husband who'd protect my honor, but Goldman and I both know a paper tiger when we see one. On the other hand, in the interest of civilized behavior, there's nothing much Dr. Goldman can do but shoot me one more provocative glance, say his goodbyes, and stroll back to his own table, a somewhat wiser man than before, perhaps.

CHAPTER 34

"HOTEL B," THE text commands.

"Copy that," I type, followed by a grinning, pornographic (non-eggplant) emoticon. I tell John I'm going out.

"Where?"

"Out," I tell him, like a surly teenager.

Once on the freeway, the cars speed past as Taylor Swift's powerful voice compels the BMW's Sedona-red rearview mirror to dance along to her "End Game." My heart pounds. My internal dialogue is chaotic. Every time I see that man, it's as if I've been absorbed into a cinematic dream sequence, an out-of-body experience where I'm transposed into a passive bystander watching impotently as her (my) story unfolds. The camera tracks me as I touch up my makeup in the elevator. It follows me (full length, in frame) walking down the wallpapered passageway, arriving at his hotel room door on quivering ankles and fluttering knees. Cut to a close-up: his square jaw, his crooked smile. A slightly off-key soundtrack portends a crime of passion. There is no dialogue, only music. The unfiltered lens settles on me again, the star, framing my face and capturing with remarkable artistry my intense emotional state. That man takes my hand and preempts my question—

"Trust me, it's worth it. It will all be over soon."

He pulls me in. I'm morbidly aware that this film, the story of my life, will never be the rom-com I hoped. What I once dreamed would be a love story is more likely to end as tragedy.

"Do you think he suspects anything?"

That man's asking the question, but it could have been me. Either way, I'm lying in bed next to him. His hand caresses my naked belly. Nurturing me. Physically I'm warm and secure, but emotionally I'm raw, exposed, and sensitive to the touch. What's worse is that he knows it, knows how vulnerable I am. *Do you think he suspects?*" he insists, though I know he doesn't really expect an answer, nor do I offer one. Instead I let his question hang precariously over the bed as I roll on top of him. Afterwards, after *it*, I once again feel impossibly satisfied. It's as if I'm incomplete until he's with me again. Inside me. Filling me up. Making me whole.

Years ago, before we were married, I accompany John to an "invitation only'" (read: obscenely large donation only) art exhibit at a private gallery downtown. It's billed as the "masters of the surreal." The *pièce de résistance* is *The Son of Man*, arguably the most famous painting by Belgian artist René Magritte. The work itself could have been unremarkable, a suited man in a bowler hat standing head-on in front of the sea. But in a stroke of inspired genius the artist transcended the normal by suspending a shiny green apple in midair, thereby obscuring the man's face. The result is simultaneously frustrating and mesmerizing. Next to the painting is a direct quote by the artist himself: "Everything we see hides another thing . . . a sort of conflict, one might say, between the visible that is hidden and the visible that is present."

Lying here, next to that man, I finally understand.

CHAPTER 35

"YOU'RE HUGE . . . " the dots to the right of Kayla's text vanish and reappear. She's obviously got something more to share. *How wonderful.* I don't know if her opening gambit is a compliment or a jab. I don't care. The fact is whenever I catch a glimpse of my enormous frame in the mirror, or when my carefully assembled outfits cast ever-widening shadows on the sidewalk, I'm filled with nothing but unadulterated joy, a sense of mischievous victory that carries with it delightfully nostalgic undertones, the rush a liar feels when the lie's so obvious. Dupers delight. That's what my therapist called it.

"You have to understand, young lady," everyone claimed, "you can't hide things from adults."

Bullshit. My teenage self reveled in her ability to *get away with things*, from refilling Big Brian's Scotch with sugar water to sneaking behind the cherry blossoms to smoke. Of course, she'd do the other things as well—the things she loved to do most, with Aaron.

Kayla texts with the speed and ferocity of an adolescent Adderall addict: *" . . . like totally humungous! Any day now and we gonna have ourselves a new mommy.*

Don't worry, hon, I'll show you how it's done. You deserve some help after waiting sooooooo long to join the club." (A strange thing to say since this is her first child as well, as far as I know, scheduled to beat me to it by a whopping two months.) Kayla augments her message with a too-cute-for-words animation of a fuzzy pink kitten peeking out of a stroller, winking and licking its lips, no doubt The Bee's subconscious reminder it's our pussies that started all of this in the first place. I'm onto her little game: far too savvy to launch direct attacks, Kayla sends kitten pictures instead, flanking me with snide references to my weight—the art of war reimagined for the modern housewife. Sun Tzu would have been proud.

Let's see her deal with this, I think, as I press the blue "send" button on a single smiling face emoticon—the undisputed heavyweight champion brush-off of the mobile communication era. If it were anyone else, that would be that. Message received, loud and clear, over and out. Not Kayla. She doesn't just entertain being frenemies; she revels in it. My phone comes alive. An animated stork drops a parachute-harnessed baby into the arms of a confused-looking woman. The pixelated mother looks up as the large bird quips: *"What were you expecting? Amazon fresh?"* Underneath she's added: *"Your best friend misses you. Let's meet up."*

A masterstroke!

I feel obliged to respond, and before my conscious mind can intervene, I've invited her for decaf at the Blue Plate the next day. She accepts with a single letter *"k."* Game over, she wins.

"I dunno why you let her get to you. Just ignore her. Don't give her the satisfaction." John's right and I know it.

"Is she really the kind of person you want living rent-free in your mind?" he asks. I know he's trying to help me, to protect me; nevertheless, listening to him argue on my behalf infuriates me.

If only Apple provided a simple solution to eliminate the Kaylas of our lives, "an app for that," enabling me to erase her with the same self-taught proficiency I use to delete jpeg files. Scroll down to the name of my target, "Kayla Smithe-Beckworth.frnd," then double-click her into oblivion. After the obligatory confirmation request: "Are you certain you would like to remove the highlighted person from your life forever?" I tap the trackpad twice, and a nanosecond later, it's over. She's gone. For safety's sake, I access the aptly named trash file, and after a final, satisfying keystroke (accompanied by a delightfully realistic crunch) any memories of our friendship are permanently erased. We both continue our separate lives as if we'd never met. No calls, no snide remarks, no gossip-laden meals, no pretense. All accidental meetings, joint charity auctions, committee brunches, and breakfast cocktails become nothing more than the ghost of a memory that never quite was.

And Thou shalt choose for yourself a friend, lest you stray, for he (or she) will guide you back toward the path. In my experience, the single most misconstrued element of friendship is the assumption of permanence. Before her (before that night) I was blissfully unaware that friends, like milk, came with expiration dates. One misstep and the person you thought you could trust to protect you and keep your darkest secrets, could become, well, *Kayla*, the wolf in chic clothing. In a way I blame myself.

"I just don't trust her," Melissa warned me. "I dunno why you even like her so much. What you need are real friends, like we are. You know she's the one who told everybody you're adopted. Just be careful, that's all I'm saying. It's not always about being cool."

I ignored Melissa's warning about my burgeoning friendship with the most popular girl in school. And then to repay Melissa, I went behind her back and mocked her, calling her "Ma- loser," which the other girls picked up on, of course. It's one of my biggest regrets. Back then I was certain Melissa was just jealous. Now I know she was right.

CHAPTER **36**

D-DAY APPROACHES. Normandy. Yeah, that's what this is. War. I've chosen my side. Planted my flag. I know the enemy and they are not to be underestimated. That's always how these things unravel, from lack of insight. Not this time, though. I'm expecting the unexpected. While they're thinking one move ahead, I'm thinking two. They're playing checkers, I'm playing chess. I've made my fair share of moves in my life. Chance favors the pre- pared mind. It's not going to be pretty, though. Of that much I'm sure. It never is when she's involved. What is it about her? How far will I go? Simple. All the way.

CHAPTER 37

"I DO KNOW who you are, Mrs. Speedy. Unfortunately, we can't seat you until your entire party has arrived."

I hover at the entrance to the Blue Plate waiting for my "entire party," namely Kayla Smithe- Beckworth, who is nowhere to be seen. I text her. I'll wait for her answer, five minute limit, then call. This was just a bone I tossed her, nothing more, merely coffee, decaf at that, the least I could do, and she doesn't have the courtesy to show up? I won't wait the five minutes. Yes, I will. The lies we tell ourselves. A half-hour later I start to dial. The second I do, the text comes through:

"It's a girl."

A photo is attached, Kayla forcing a grin next to a tiny thing of a baby, name Portia, eyes closed but not asleep, wincing, facing away, clearly sick of her over-bearing mother already. I'm livid. Of course Kayla would have the baby first.

It's not a competition, I tell myself, but I know the truth: *everything's* a competition.

Both mother and child look sweaty and red and ex-hausted. I study that look, guessing I will have it when the time comes. It's a look of unadorned pride and joy, a thing of which I have tasted but never drunk. I vow to study Kayla's every move. I'm going to take notes. She can be the perfect mother—I don't care—as long as she's the perfect *teacher*, too. And that doesn't mean I can't also hate her at the same time.

As the big day approaches, I'm finding it's more and more difficult to avoid attention. My designer maternity gowns, advertised to "minimize girth," are proving comically inadequate at achieving that objective. Dealing with intrusive questions from nosy, disgustingly well- intentioned strangers has become part of my routine.

Still, I confess: I enjoy the attention. I always liked being center stage. There's a certain power that comes with celebrity, or even notoriety. Predictably, most people ask about the due date. I find it fascinating they are more concerned with *when* than *why?* Woman, specifically mothers, are especially curious about "how far along are you?" To satisfy their vicarious appetites I'll offer up tasty morsels from a smorgasbord of delicately prepared comebacks: "It feels like he's kicking the door open in there, so it could be any day now! I'm sure he'll text me when he's ready to pop out!" A quick pat of my midsection, some wry laughter, and the job is done. In many ways I've managed to elevate the science of misdirection to a master craft. I don't let anyone know the truth, that the precise date, time, and location of the big event has previously been set, agreed upon, together with Dr. Prakhid and that man, months ago.

On Friday the 13th (no superstition here) at 9:15 a.m. I will be carefully ushered into Dr. Prakhid's office (or so the story goes), where he will examine me, after which I will be sent to the operating room in the hospital across the street, where I will be prepped. After what Dr. Prakhid has assured me will be a relatively painless few hours, I will be able to leave, holding, for the first time, a bouncy, happy (and G-d willing, healthy) baby boy or girl.

"It's all been arranged," I tell John. "You don't even need to get out of bed. The driver will take me and bring me home."

John is, of course, outraged. He wants to do months of childbirth classes to prepare for "natural waterbirth at home" (over my dead body) or whatever the latest non-sense is, but I regretfully inform him that Dr. Prakhid has already ruled all that out, based on my "precarious, pre-existing condition." (Say that three times real fast.) John whips his phone out of his pants to call the doctor directly. *That's the only thing you're going to be whipping out of your pants for a while,* I think, while aloud I accuse him of not trusting me. He tells me he trusts me completely; it's the doctor he's not so sure about. With no way for me to stop him, John makes the call and Prakhid talks him down with a calm, steady stream of medical jargon John has no chance of understanding. And "no, you can't be in the operating room, either," John is told, "what with infection and all. Besides, the husbands always pass out. This is not a television show; this is real life, I'm afraid, and as routine as a cesarean is these days, we take no chances."

John hangs up, frustrated but convinced.

"At least I'll drive you myself and wait for you," he insists. "I'll bring a book."

I relent; I see no way out of it, and I don't even bother to point out I've never actually seen John read a book. We'll work it out somehow, I figure.

Lately I've found myself wondering if my birth mother was cut open the day I entered the world. I prefer to picture her panting and gasping as my ever-supportive father squeezes her hand. He's nervous and exhilarated, urging her to "push and breathe, push and breathe." When I finally emerge, announcing my arrival into this world with a triumphant cry, they are elated, the proudest moment of their lives. No, *I* am the proudest moment of their lives. They plan to love me forever, and then *it* happens—flood, fire, earthquake, pestilence—so unexpected, so traumatic, it forces them to abandon both their plans and their perfect little girl. To save her from some unspecified evil (does it matter what?), they have no other choice but to put their precious baby in a plastic milk crate and leave her, bruised and bleeding, on the steps of the Our Lady of Mercy Orphanage, where she spends her first Christmas alone, cold and unfed. Her parents, inconsolable, still think about her every day. They miss her, they love her, they wish she were there with them. A box of unmailed birthday cards sits next to their bed, guilt keeping them awake at night. Of course all of this is conjecture dreamed up to quell the tempests of my unquiet mind. Though I've accepted that whatever happened before Sister Mary Grace found me will remain a mystery, I know one thing for certain: as G-d is my witness, I will never be abandoned again! (Or go hungry, either, for that matter.)

It's two weeks later and *of course* she brings the offspring, the greatest sensation ever to hit the Blue Plate. I wonder if my baby will get the same reaction, or is hers just that superior? Or is there something about Kayla herself that elicits the response? As much as I despise her, I acknowledge I have a great deal to learn from her.

After the entire Blue Plate staff and clientele have offered their opinion on how "beautiful" Kayla's little thing is, and Kayla orders *caffeinated* coffee ("the good stuff, just a cup or two, breastfeeding and all"), knowing I'm stuck with pigeon piss in my present condition, we get down to business, how "tired and rundown" I look.

"Don't worry, honey," Kayla assures me. "I'm gonna give you the whole list of foods my nutritionist gave me. They were literally a lifesaver."

I smile and nod, at which point Kayla launches into her inevitable reminiscences of our high school misadventures, anecdotes that have been so dramatically embellished I find it impossible to identify which events inspired the rip-roaring yarns to begin with. True to form, Kayla passes each one off as nostalgic nonfiction. And just when I think boring me to tears with stories of our glory days is her only agenda (after showing off her little bundle of joy), she ups the ante: "So, hon, do ever hear from, um, what were their names, Aaron and your other, um . . . "— a transparently unnecessary hesitation—"*friends?*" Her ability to distend the word is masterfully cruel. She's gone beyond Melissa and the other girls to Aaron and his boys, the ones I would never forget. I recoil, trapped and helpless. Exhaling evenly, she sends a subtle but satisfied sigh hovering my way, a clear proclamation of victory. I have no defense. I'm dead meat. We've never discussed this before. Governed by some unwritten treaty, it had remained entirely sealed in the past, completely off limits. Not forgotten (obviously), but buried forever (I assumed). *Why's she bringing it up now? Here? And in front of her g-ddamn baby, for crying out loud—*

My phone reverberates loudly against the glass table before my rage boils over into homicide.

"Phone 2 now."

Fortunately, the sun reflects directly off the new device's flexible, holographic surface, making the text illegible and out of focus to Kayla's inquisitive eyes. She shields her lids and squints, trying unashamedly to decipher the words in the blue box, a curious expression highlighting my mistake. In hindsight, "Phone 2" is probably the most ill-considered name I could have chosen for my "other" phone, aka my *burner* phone. I make a mental note to keep the alerts but update the descriptor.

"How rude! I didn't catch the name. Who was that?" she asks, her quizzical frown affording me a tiny (but oh-so-desperately needed) counter-victory. That man—even his unintentional interventions are timed to perfection.

"Who knows? Probably a wrong number." I turn the screen face down and use the technological intrusion to catch the waiter's attention and motion, coolly, for the check.

"I saw you with someone," Kayla says, sticking a fork in me. I'm not done, or rather, she's not done with me yet.

"Really?" I ask, the picture of innocence. "Near Westwood. A black man in a silver car." "Must have been the chauffeur."

"Not one that I know," Kayla insists.

"I should have said 'driver,'" I correct myself. "I forget what I was up to."

"You were sitting in the front seat." *She's a bulldog, this girl—once she sinks her teeth into you—*

"I do that. I like to see where I'm going, especially in my condition. Pretty important, don't you think? And the airbags are in front, aren't they? Google it. Depending on the type of crash, it's safer." *I'm making this stuff up on the fly, but it sounds reasonable, right?*

Kayla nods, pretending to agree with me, impressed. We let it go at that.

CHAPTER 38

"WELL, YOU'RE A sight for sore eyes." His charismatic grin and innate nonchalance unnerve me. I can't hold that man's gaze. I look away, reminding myself he's just as culpable as I am, though he somehow wears his wicked deeds better than I do.

"What in the hell are you wearing?" he smirks, amused by my oversized, blue-and-white- striped sundress. It's utterly infuriating for him to mock me like this. If it weren't for him, I wouldn't *be* in this situation in the first place. I'm just the diversion, the garish colossus that draws the gaze of the crowd so the pickpockets can ply their trade. Can he even begin to appreciate the sacrifices I've made? I want to resist, to tell him that I can't do this anymore, to take my life back. But I know it's too late. You can't be slightly pregnant, so they say.

"Don't even start—you know you like it," I tease, lifting my skirt and spinning like some overstuffed piñata waiting to shed its concealed secret. We both giggle like maniacs, and that man seems human again.

I'm breathless. Lying on my back. Curling and uncurling my toes. Trying to stimulate the blood flow and restore the feeling to my extremities. I'm at once conscious of my nakedness and totally unashamed. My skin is wet and glowing, literally, no metaphor here. He's next to me. I can smell him, smell us. His eyes are closed. I'm unsure if he's sleeping or simply spent. Either way he's completely serene, angelic even. It's been a long time. Danger lurks and John hovers like a surveillance drone. That man is temptation personified. I wish I could see into his dreams. See if he dreams about me. Or *us*.

Then, suddenly, wafting in through the paper-thin wall, a familiar voice. Hearing it again after all these years shoots me bolt upright. "Sinner, sinner, sinner." The pronounced southern drawl and accelerated cadence are unmistakable, transporting me back to the orphanage where we spent our Sunday mornings watching *Lessons and Lies: Rediscovering The Good Book*, a three-hour-long TV telethon hosted by Reverend Dr. George Little (who was neither a doctor nor, for that matter, little).

Despite the ominous overtones, we loved TGB. We laughed hysterically when the Reverend worked himself into nothing short of an ambulatory frenzy, reciting *The New Testament* with a fervor so intense that Revelation itself would pale by comparison. Presumably acting in the best interests of both Jesus and his own pocketbook, he bound up and down the TV stage frantically, thick white hair soaked in perspiration, limbs flailing like an electrocuted panda.

"If you succumb to the call of Satan's lascivious seducer," he bellowed, "your body will perish and your soul will rot in torment! Brothers and sisters, this I guarantee. Should you fall prey to the evils of the flesh, the Lord himself will reach out from the Heavens and strike you down. Dead, dead, dead!"

I wasn't concerned. Even before that night, I was

pretty sure our mortal frailties were not so much a choice as a biological imperative, woven into our DNA like an explosive yarn. If Jesus was indeed watching us, he was doing so only out of sense of morbid curiosity and nothing more, acutely aware that, eventually, everyone falls.

That man sleeps on. His body is long and warm, and wraps around me like a second skin, cradling me, protecting me. It's the only time that man is relaxed. The tension doesn't follow him into sleep. I'm grateful for that, for him. As for me, I should be content, blissful even, but paranoid thoughts intrude: "sinner, sinner, sinner." *Are you talking to me?* I gently press my body against that man and mirror his breathing, absorbing his tranquility. It's working. Gradually, as if he's guiding me, I start to unwind, able to remain calm and think rationally: Reverend Little's visit is *not* divine intervention. Instead, royalty-free programming (common to both orphanages and hotels) is to blame.

Yes, I had a religious upbringing. I leave out the "o" in G-d, which is no doubt a dead giveaway. It's not a Jewish thing in my case (thank G-d). Jews are concerned about erasing G-d's name; not for us (Our Lady of Mercy types). For us, it's more of a Ten Commandments thing: "Thou shalt not take the name of the Lord thy G-d in vain"—Commandment Number Two if you're Catholic, Number Three if you're anything else (write your dissertation on *that,* I dare you). But then again, who's counting? The Sisters taught us this. And it's not Catholic, even though Our Lady of Mercy sounds Catholic. It isn't. We are lapsed Baptists, "off-shoot Baptists," "tossed out on our ears" Baptists. Not even Wikipedia tries to explain who we are, or were, in my case. I'm "lapsed lapsed," a scarlet woman, fallen from grace and doomed to suffer

Satan poking my nether regions with a pitchfork for all eternity, or something equally distasteful. Does this bother me? No. Because I'm also an atheist. Why? Simple, because Jesus made me that way, ha ha.

So I leave out the "o" in G-d for the same reason I don't step on cracks—just in case. It's the least I can do, like wearing my pink breast cancer ribbon, even though my own are perfect. To me, religion is little more than a well-constructed boogieman engaged in an extortion racket.

Pay up little children or he'll eat you in your sleep. Cynical? Perhaps. Realistic? Certainly. I refer you to centuries of evidence: if yielding to the temptations of the flesh carried a death sentence, the human race would have gone extinct long ago. In fact, judging by the orphanage's own culpable clergy, their less-than-saintly souls should have been among the first on the existential chopping block.

"And in His name, thou shall abandon thy evil ways. Awake ye non-believers, for He who watches, is watching you."

Together with that man's light snores, it's the last thing I hear.

CHAPTER 39

"I JUST DON'T get you."

"You said it would turn you on," Aaron says, visibly annoyed.

The *it* he's referring to is what he's calling an orgy—group sex with him, his brother, and two of their friends.

"I said the *idea* turned me on."

"Well, uh, I've already told them you'd do it."

"Well, uh," I mimic his slow, deep voice. "I guess you'll just have to *untell* them, won't you?"

"I know what this is about."

"Yeah, what?"

"How much?"

"Excuse me?" I feign outrage, just for the record.

"It's about money, isn't it? That's all it's ever about with you."

He is right, and he is wrong. While money is my preferred method of keeping score, that's all it is. What I only came to realize much later on is that the little abandoned orphan that lives inside me doesn't need money at all. She needs something else entirely. Love.

CHAPTER 40

"FUCKING RICHARDS!"

John tries to highlight his rage by slamming the heavy oak door, but the handcrafted hinge slides the wooden slab snuggly and silently into place, the very embodiment of a first-world solution to a first-world problem: patented "anti-slam technology." It's why they hate us. Nearing boiling point, John finds an alternate outlet for his frustration, namely yelling, "that greedy, self- involved prick. Fuck him. You hear me? Fuck him!"

From my vantage point downstairs in the den I watch as the (full color) monitor scans the entrance hall. Seconds later a scowling, stomping John marches deliberately into view.

Opportunity knocks.

"How was work?" I call half-heartedly, pretending I hadn't heard his rant, provoking him to continue with what has the potential to be a remarkably entertaining diatribe.

"Richards, Richards, Richards . . . son . . . of . . . a . . . bitch!" Although I didn't think it was possible, John's voice elevates in both volume and tone: "He drives me nuts! You don't even know how much I wanna punch that asshole in his fat, bloated mug. I knew he was a snake from the moment I met him. Walking around like a weasel with that oversized chrome dome. Now he wants a majority stake in the company, does he? With what fucking money, that's what I want to know. Over my dead body."

"What was that, babes? You want me to call Richards?" I call in my most melodic voice.

I bite my lip, suppressing a wicked chuckle as he disintegrates into a marvelously entertaining meltdown. Anything that diverts his attention away from how I spend my days helps. Like a mischievous child with a destructive new toy, I just can't resist. I reload and fire again.

"Babes, I can't hear you over the TV. I'm in the den. How was work? All good?" Bull's-eye.

My victim's wounded, stumbling, falling hard.

"Are you fucking joking? You never listen to a word I say. I don't know why the fuck I married you. Just fuck off and leave me alone." There will be no small talk and family time tonight. Instead there will be muttering, cursing, solo dinners, and separate rooms. Perfect.

A day later, with less than forty-eight hours to go, *nothing* is perfect. Everything has changed. I finally realize I'm in over my head. It's all too much. I'm overwhelmed, suffocating, in a panic, like when Aunt Genya (not my aunt any more than the Staffords were my parents) taught me to swim holding my hands as I paddled my way around the shallow end of the pool.

"Yes yes, you making good swimming." Her unfamiliar accent sounded both amusing and sincere. I wanted her to release me, to give me the chance to make it on my own. But instead she forced her outsized hand onto my tiny wet skull and pushed me down. "Good for learn to breathe," she taunted. I never forgot those panic-stricken seconds when I was isolated from the world, underwater and completely alone. I have that same feeling now, desperate for someone to let me go so I can draw precious breath. But who? Who can save me?

"The only people you can rely on in this life are yourself and Jesus, dear," my house-mother (who was eventually escorted out of the orphanage by Child Protective Services) would remind me daily. Could it be that she was actually right? No. Didn't buy it then, don't buy it now. I brush my hand over my Gucci bag, double-checking for my other phone. Its familiar shape provides me temporary relief. I know who's on the other end. He's there for me, *with* me, always just there. No turning back now. I take a deep breath and grab the car keys. If I don't want to drown, I'd better learn to swim. Fast.

Everything that needed to be done is now done. The only thing left is to count the hours.

John and I are, paradoxically, both together and alone, the way only married couples can be. We lounge in the library, a second living room really, my favorite room in the house. The huge windows paint the polished oak floor with sunlight that curls around the carved, majestic stone fireplace. I feel peaceful and powerful here. For John, not so much. He wanders off. I think it's the books; they make him uncomfortable. With him gone I take the opportunity to spread out on the floor, run my hands through the (actual) zebra-skin rug, and daydream. I fantasize that in a past life I was someone quite different, brave, a predator perhaps. I picture myself a she-wolf, sly and strong, stalking my prey, a zebra. The striped creature is lost and alone, separated from her herd. I see and smell her, want her, chasing, pouncing, savoring the satisfying sound of the zebra's neck cracking under the pressure of my canine fangs, vice-like jaws unrelenting. One last high-pitched squeal and it's over. The last embers of life dissipate, leaving only a flaccid carcass. My bloodlust flows. I feast greedily on the still-warm corpse, hunger never satisfied. I look up at the moon and howl. Victorious. I'm aware that I'm no less ruthless in real life. It's why I contacted that man again all those years later, even after I promised myself I wouldn't. It was the hunter in me, the phantom of a past life, she-wolf reincarnated. Or maybe I'm just a selfish, power-hungry bitch.

"Where's my little mommy?" Her voice cuts through me like a scalpel.

"Hi, granny, I'm really not feeling great but if you absolutely have to see me today, I'm in the library," I mentally message Mary-Elizabeth, filling my words with a tasteless, undetectable poison, hoping that when she swallows them illness, vertigo, and death will ensue. Instead, they are well-received and easily digested like some sugar-coated *amuse-bouche.*

"You should really eat more, dear," Mum opens with, striding into the room. "Your face looks particularly gaunt and pale today. I'm going to ask the staff to whip something up. We don't want our baby to go hungry in there, now do we?" She tries to put her hand on my sweater, but I recoil, moving aggressively, dodging the incoming invasion before she has a chance to make contact. Her sour expression leaves little doubt how peeved she is by the slight.

"I need to pee again," I explain, defusing the situation. "It's like the hundredth time today.

I'm sure you remember how that feels."

"I certainly do. That's just our little one making himself known, dear. A healthy sign. Now where's that son of mine? If he leaves you alone again I will wring his bony neck." The only thing more insufferable than her voice is her forced, disingenuous cackle. If she fucks like she laughs, I doubt she's ever had a real orgasm in her life.

CHAPTER 41

WHAT THE HELL are *they* doing here? Our doorbell's faux-orchestral chime, unnecessarily somber and altogether too loud, feels intrusive, even from behind closed doors and distanced by a considerable foyer and passageway.

I check the monitor in the bathroom and feel instantly ill.

"Babes, babes, come downstairs," John calls. Maybe if I ignore him long enough, he will assume I'm sleeping (or better yet, drowned myself in the bathtub). No such luck. "Babes, finish up already—you've been in there forever. You've got to come down. Kayla and Kyle are here, and they brought *the baby*." In what could easily be cited as the most blatant manifestation of our growing dissimilarities, John appears genuinely pleased to see them. Kyle and Kayla Beckworth. The Beckworths. The poster children for inherited wealth. The King and Queen Bees, sobriquets which I'm certain they leaked to the media, not the other way around. The fact that John has temporarily completely abandoned his distaste for these over-privileged misanthropes is rationalization enough for what I'm going to do to him.

I see them gathered below—Beckworths, Mary-Elizabeth, and John—surrounding the baby carrier on the mahogany table, a guest viewing of major import. Mary, Joseph, and a couple of braying Speedy asses gazing upon the baby Jesus, waiting for the messiah (or in my case, the anti-Christ) to show up and stamp the seal of approval on the whole deal. I'm going to throw up. Instead, I could, of course, retreat, or throw myself down the stairs, or jump, but Kayla spots me.

"Here she comes, ladies and gentlemen . . . our new mommy!"

Kayla somehow manages to project her thin, whiny voice across the entrance hall, through the low-hanging chandelier and all the way to the top of the stairs, announcing my triumphal entry as if I were a monarch teleported from the Middle Ages. I make a deliberate effort to quash her affected joviality by pursing my lips and souring my expression. She's overplayed her hand, projecting all honors on me, though it's not me who's had a baby but *her*.

I am clearly *not* playing along. I descend slowly, a mountain of a person now, a pregnant blob incapable of dignity. I lumber past them into the living room without even glancing at the just-born offspring. Feigning disheveled exhaustion, I crash into the cushioned couch like a beached manatee. I'm not going to abide random pop-in's in the future, and I want everyone to know that. To emphasize my indignation, I adopt the defiant posture of a tenth-grade skater girl and continue to ignore the thing they've brought to me for my public blessing (I guess the Blue Plate didn't count). I've deliberately forgotten its name and its sex (the pink might be a giveaway), and I'm not going to ask now. But despite my best efforts to appear uncongenial, Kayla remains undeterred in her mission to show off her latest "accomplishment" and bask in the glory of motherhood, which she graciously plans to share with me in an act of monumental generosity, blah blah. I really am going to throw up.

Drinks are served all around (aged Versos), except for me, who can't have even one. Kayla is now free to drink like a small fish ("breastfeeding, you know, in limited amounts"). Everyone seems comfortable and relaxed, and for once Mary-Elizabeth doesn't seem to need to be the center of attention, which means I'm served up as the main course. My sloth-like movements and vulnerable condition provide the perfect meal.

Then, with a total disregard for social protocol, an unusually intoxicated Kyle launches a surprise attack. His demeanor is strident, and it occurs to me he may be acting under direct marital duress—an epic, passive-aggressive attack-by-proxy, a bank shot as it were, from The Queen Bee herself.

"Well, just look at you!" Kyle gushes, holding his hands wide, indicating a semi-truck. "I think the last time I saw you this happy was after you spent the night with Aaron and the boys." My stomach sinks but my face is a statue. "You've really come a long way since then," he continues, attacking rapid-fire from ambush. "Who'd have thought that someone like you would be getting ready to raise a child of her own." I'm wounded but not dead. He moves in for the kill. "I guess what they say is true, if you live long enough eventually you'll see everything." Kyle's addressing me, but it doesn't take CSI-LA to deduce that this particular bombshell is earmarked for John and his mother, who listen intently, again uncharacteristically willing to let someone else take the floor. The Beckworths—with friends like them, who needs enemies?

I clench my fists, breathe deeply, and count backwards from ten (the way the head-shrink suggested all those years ago), collecting my wits for what I can only assume will be a particularly embarrassing and possibly bloody exchange. We have a deal, Kyle and I, similar but separate from my deal with Kayla, and now he's threatening to blow the whole thing up for some crazy unknown reason. It doesn't make me feel any better that the collateral damage will shred Kyle to pieces, too—I'd make sure of that—but he doesn't seem to care, *the suicidal little prick!* Under no circumstances will I look in Kayla's direction, though I know she's there, the way the rabbit smells the leopard just before it dies. Of course, Kyle wasn't present at "that night with Aaron and the boys." It's hearsay to him and to Kayla, too, and to everyone except the five of us who *were* there, but there's evidence hiding in plain sight all over the internet, and if a certain future senator or his potential voters were to be directed in that direction, there'd be hell to pay. *Where's an open grave and blunt shovel when you need one?*

Kyle won't say his name—Marvin Heffel—but Kayla might, after all these years, emboldened by the baby, with Kyle on her side, and me helpless to fend off the attack. Or am I? Maybe *I'll* be the one to say the name, spit it out like a weapon, scorched Earth—I'm capable of exacting Mutually Assured Destruction, deploying the one secret Kayla is not in on, her blind spot— Meet you in Hell—

Then, as if by magic, the goddess of mercy intervenes on my behalf. In an uncannily fortuitous coincidence, the room's focus is entirely diverted by none other than the little pink bundle itself. Having awoken just seconds earlier, its ear-piercing squeals clearly demand immediate attention. Panicked like only a first-time father can be, Kyle springs to his feet, motions us all to keep quiet, and rushes to the child. How silence will help facilitate diagnosing the source of the trauma, Heaven alone knows. Nevertheless, everyone complies.

"Phone, STAT!" Kyle orders like a TV doctor (phone's in his pocket). It's not to call anyone—instead he summons *Web MD* (First Aid for the Information Age), but before the Harvard Fine Arts graduate has the opportunity to hazard a completely uneducated guess as to the cause of the disruption, the mystery is solved. A telltale odor fills the room and the culpable little infant giggles itself back to sleep.

If I didn't know better I could have sworn that it was a S.D.G.B. (Strategically Deployed Gas Bomb) and that Kayla's baby, already sick of its parent's devious ways, had interceded deliberately on my behalf. The child's pungent intervention works wonders, both souring Kayla's expression and bringing Kyle's defamatory trip down Memory Lane to an inauspicious end. With everyone's efforts now focused on how best to politely ignore the nuclear-fallout-level stench, the conversation quickly returns to its previous trajectory prior to Kyle's verbal bullet whizzing past its target and disintegrating, vanishing forever into the wormhole of unheard words. Kyle glances apologetically at his wife who, with an ever-so-subtle shake of her head, brings the matter to a close. It's over. I'm out of the woods, for the moment at least. With their guerrilla attack having backfired, they are left with no choice but to retreat to the safety of complaining about the gratuitous awarding of Michelin stars, or the lines at our country club's valet parking stand, or proposed increases in the minimum wage, Heaven forbid. The "Aaron card" has been played, and trumped. According to the unwritten rules of backstabbing, it would now, however reluctantly, have to be discarded. *For the moment.*

Before they leave, I make a point of kissing baby-what's-its-name gently on the forehead and telling he/she how we were going to be best friends forever.

CHAPTER 42

THEY THOUGHT THEY were using me—maybe so; I was sure using *them*. Five thousand dollars was the final amount, the same as the opening bid, actually, after lengthy negotiations lasting a little under two hours. The terms: four boys—Aaron, his twenty-year-old brother, Eric, Eric's friend, Wayne, and a "mystery guest," would collectively get to do "anything they wanted" to me, "except anal."

The "mystery guest" intrigued me, prompting a round of "Twenty Questions."

"This isn't some old guy, is it?"

"No comment."

"Somebody's creepy dad?"

Again, they wouldn't say. *Not that I minded—*

"*It's a girl, right?*" I started to ask, then decided not to—*that would be interesting, too—*

"It's not a snake or a gerbil, right?" They laughed.

"You have to answer," I told them, "or the deal's off."

"An animal? Jeez, Amanda, what the hell goes on in that head of yours? You really think we're that sick?" Aaron asked, appearing genuinely hurt.

So I agreed to it, and the event was scheduled for that Saturday in a guesthouse behind a three-bedroom home in Hollywood, set up as a photographer's studio, with black walls and a brushed aluminum lighting grid overhead. Wayne's mother had won the house in a divorce, apparently. "The boys" used it as their clubhouse, but it was equally perfect for an orgy, gang- bang, cluster-fuck, whatever the kids called it in those days. A large white California king mattress sat in the center of the otherwise unfurnished space. In some ways, it was nicer than I expected—clean and brightly lit with large windows to let in the sun. In other ways, I was disappointed—no candlelight, music, booze, cigarettes, or weed. Devoid of atmosphere, the guys called it "The Black Hole." Behind a sliding curtain was a small, clean bathroom and a cooler with sports drinks.

"Gotta stay hydrated," Wayne commented.

A big bag of energy bars, chips, and chocolate completed the picture.

Okay . . . I said to myself, *all business with these guys*. I tingled, already halfway up the ladder to some nirvana I'd only guessed at. The transactional nature of the thing was a definite turn-on. Aaron, Eric, and Wayne leaned against the wall, eyeing me, posed like a boy band album cover. They'd all showered. *And shaved?* Hard to tell. Their hair was still wet, combed back.

Respectful. At least for the moment. The smell of soap, deodorant, aftershave, cologne, and testosterone was intoxicating.

Where's the mystery man?

"He'll be here," Aaron snickered, reading my mind. "Wouldn't miss this for the world." All three joined in the snickering, a major buzzkill, I had to say.

"Where's my money?" I asked. Suddenly it was like pulling teeth, so shy they were, so nervous and flighty. Was I going to have to take charge and direct the action? Tell them, show them, guide them through the process?

That's not what I want.

The door opened.

I flushed. It was Marvin Heffel, my "best friend" Kayla Smithe's boyfriend, joined at the hip—

What the hell's he doing here?

"Sup? Sorry I'm late," he said brightly, coming right up next to me, kissing me on the cheek, placing his hand in the small of my back, a little too low, something he'd done before, which I'd never thought anything of. He pulled his shirt up, revealing a thick envelope and a well-toned six-pack, the result of varsity basketball, football, tennis, and golf. "I believe this is for you," he winked, showing me the contents of the envelope, fifty one-hundred-dollar bills (I assumed). Stunned, I didn't take the offering.

So that's it, I realized, *how Aaron and his ilk managed to scrounge up five grand . . .*

I snatched the packet from him and stuck it in my handbag. "You might want to count it. You're gonna earn it—"

"I know where you live," I spat back, "and I'm sure you can afford it." I tossed my bag into the corner. "Now let's see the other package you brought for me, huh," I growled, pulling Marv's shirt up with one hand, plunging my hand down into his pants with the other, to the hoots and hollers of the other three. *Might as well break the ice,* I thought at the time. *Full speed ahead, damn the torpedoes.* Skinny Wayne charged, proclaiming, "I got first dibs—it's my house," grabbing me from behind, executing some wrestling move, slamming both Marvin and me to the mattress.

"Game on!" Aaron announced. Eight hours later, it was all over.

Left out of the negotiations, to my surprise, were film and distribution rights to this independent production.

"Don't worry, 'Manda," Aaron assured me when the cell phone cameras came out, as they inevitably did. "We can keep a secret."

I didn't believe him—I'm not that stupid—but by then I was invested in the project, "skin in the game," as they say.

Looking back, I think I should have fired Aaron as my agent. I was blinded by young love, young lust, young trust, youth itself—nature's most precious gift and her cruelest hoax. That night changed everything for me. *Whore.* The word would haunt me. Scar me. Although I never admitted it to anyone but myself, it was a label I deserved, like an esoteric tattoo, visible only to those who knew where to look, decipherable only by those who knew the code. But at the moment of my deepest debasement, I sincerely wished Sister Mary Grace could see me, shaved and bent over, receiving holy *dick* from behind. I wanted Kayla there, too, watching her sweet Marvin's unbridled desire for it, over and over, spitting, spanking, bruising, forced oral, choking orgasms, "hit her again with the belt this time!" And yes, despite the initial agreement (Marv didn't get the memo, apparently), anal. I soaked it up literally and figuratively with every fiber of my being. Taking it. Giving it. Giving in. Just giving.

CHAPTER 43

THE MORNING OF the baby's birth—no, his second birth, his rebirth, his second coming—the morning of the big day, John is still asleep. I watch him for a while. There is something about the way he rests, the way he breathes, that makes me feel as if I have a window into his dreams. He rolls over and smiles serenely, exhaling a soft, satisfied sigh. Perhaps he knows something, or maybe he's content with what he doesn't yet know. Either way, his world, our world, is about to change forever. Despite that fact, or perhaps because of it, I'm totally calm, Zen even. I've been preparing for this moment for thirty-nine weeks and two days! Actually, forever.

Our list is comprehensive, and I will follow it to the letter. At the top of the page I've doodled a blue and white bassinet, a pair of tiny shoes, and a lollipop-shaped pacifier. Seeing my artistic handiwork again fills me with joy. I'm high. Elated. It's finally going to happen for me, for *us*.

My Baby's Birthday - Thursday, September 12 Squash game

Direct-to-voicemail on phone. Messages for John and Mary-Elizabeth Lose driver (if necessary)

Call Uber Bring car seat

Meet that man at agreed-upon location

Hold my baby

Although I'm thoroughly conscious of the indulgence of the last item, I just can't help reading it again and again. I'm ready for the next chapter to unfold, ready to share my life, to give my love, to be complete.

The morning crawls. Nothing's happening when it's supposed to. I'm frantic. My phone rings. A text:

"You need to get here now. The doctor's ready. It's time."

That's all that man wrote.

I check the clock for the hundredth time that morning. It's only a half-hour drive to the squash courts, then add fifteen minutes leeway to do the locker-room thing. John's late, very late, uncharacteristically late when it comes to one of his creepy-competitive, male-bonding sports.

Phone 2 vibrates. I answer.

"You were going to text me when you got in the car." I hear panic in the voice equal to my own.

"I'm not *in* the car," I whisper through clenched teeth.

"Why not?"

"I don't know. He's still here."

"Find out."

He hangs up on me. I make my way to the hallway outside John's home office. He's reading papers, pondering, something he thinks senators do. Fortunately, the door's open and I can make it as casual as can be:

"Sorry to bother you."

"No bother, sweetie—"

"But don't you have a squash game with Steve?"

"Canceled," he says simply, going back to his work, "but thanks for keeping track."

It's a backhanded compliment—"thanks for butting into my business"—and no help to me whatsoever. *Did Steve cancel it or did you cancel it, and why?* I need to ask, but I don't dare. *Are you going to hang around the house all day, for crying out loud?*

I retreat in helpless defeat. I pull out Phone 2.

"Cancelled," I tell that man.

"Stand by, be ready," I hear.

"Be ready for what—"

But he's already hung up. I check the time again. We're running late and I've just revealed myself to John, happy and healthy. Should I start moaning? *I need guidance here.* I hear John's phone in his office. His voice rises; he's irate. I'm still in the hall, looking for escape. It's too late; he's charging from his office. I dive for the bench in the hall—the one nobody ever sits on—next to a tall, stained glass window. I pose like a pregnant saint.

"You okay, pumpkin?" he asks. I give him that much.

"Just a little tired," I say. *And don't call me "pumpkin."* I need to modulate this. He's headed out the door, which I desperately need him to do, but he should also know I'm in some distress, too, I think, for the record. I moan, just slightly.

"Make it till tomorrow?" he asks, returning to me, reaching in the direction of my belly. He knows not to touch, and I'm ready to block his hand if I need to.

"Tomorrow," I assure him.

He retreats. "I'll be back soon. Call if you need anything."

"Where are you going?" I ask before he gets away. "What happened?"

"Somebody's threatening to release my college transcripts," he manages before he whizzes out the door. I wait a few seconds, then jump up to make sure his car leaves the drive and that our chauffeur is driving it. I pull out Phone One to call Uber first, then that man on Phone 2.

The trip feels like a journey. Both the traffic and time itself move even slower than usual. The Uber driver—a foreign student, I think, from Persia, Pakistan or somewhere—wants to call 9-1-1 the moment he sees my over-ripe chassis stumbling out the door, teetering and moaning, carrying an infant's car seat. I tell him "don't even think about fucking with me today," insist we get moving, and downplay the histrionics. The panicked driver, certain he's going to have to deliver the baby himself, perhaps leading off the evening news, maybe inviting scrutiny into his immigration status, is too worried to talk. This is a blessing, actually; I can use the quiet. I wonder what the young Uber-man looked like as a newborn. Was he as dark as he is now?

Darker?

The other random thought crossing my mind concerns the child's name, which we never decided upon. We all agreed that names have power and that the names our parents give us inevitably affect our lives. Beyond that, opinions varied.

"Biblical names fare best," Mary-Elizabeth decided.

"If not too weird," John argued.

"You don't want a name that's too common," his mother warned. "Or too ethnic."

I think about that in the Uber, wishing my parents had named me something less "on the nose," Amanda being Latin for "she who is requiring to be loved"—me all over. Maybe I needed *too* much love, more than my parents could stand. Maybe if they'd named me something different, like Emma ("whole, complete"), they would have been able to tolerate me, perhaps even enough to keep me.

The traffic flows again, and my pulse quickens. I truly feel unwell, shaking and sweating, I consider the gravity of what's about to happen. I can't help contemplating my life and, more broadly, life itself, how the soul morphs from its ethereal construct, grows into flesh and bone, and ultimately becomes human. *And He did breathe into them life, and for good, they were created*, brought forth for a brief sojourn on this terrestrial plane before, inevitably, we all vanish. Gone forever. Buried in the ground. Until, as time passes, we are no longer in the ground, we *are* the ground. Strangely enough, the atheist in me is comforted by these thoughts. My heartbeat returns to normal and I relax. If there is nothing *before* and nothing *after* I won't have to answer for the filthy sins I've done, or the monstrous thing I'm about to do. No purgatory for me, no fire or brimstone, just emptiness. Pure, unblemished nothingness. Paradoxically, if I believed in G-d, this is precisely the end I would pray for.

Seeing that man jolts me out of my philosophical stupor. He's lurking just inside the glass doors to Dr. Prakhid's office building, waiting for me to arrive, careful not to let the driver see him. It occurs to me that ever since we met, I'd always been the one waiting for him.

"You ready?" he asks, taking the child's car seat from me. He grins, the bastard, a broad, genuine, beaming smile that stretches easily between his dimpled cheeks.

"Actually, I thought we could wait a couple more months, so if you could just tell the Doc to postpone everything and take the day off, that would be great." The joke doesn't land (the words sounding so much more hilarious in my head). Nevertheless, it's met with a warm chuckle and knowing nod.

"Come on you, let's go—" But before he finishes his sentence, he pulls me close, wraps his arms around me and squeezes me tightly. He puts his mouth close to my ear and whispers, "Let's go make our miracle happen." We walk down the long hallway together, hand in hand. I feel blissfully at ease, enveloped in love. Everything is going to be all right. I know it.

BOOK 3: MATTHEW

CHAPTER **44**

O DIEM PRAECLARUM! "What a beautiful day!"

Everyone is overjoyed, or, at the very least, *acting* overjoyed. My phone is abuzz. The baby has arrived, a miracle of cosmically synchronized timing. Maybe Jesus is looking out for me after all? I went into sudden, unexpected labor, made it to Dr. Prakhid's office, was whisked away to the hospital and delivered vaginally twenty minutes later, no C-section required, home a few hours after mother and child received a thorough checkup, no overnight stay necessary. I'm back in my bed holding a dear, pinkish-white child, "Matthew," a spur-of-the-moment name choice. In a nutshell: all is good.

"I've never seen such a quick and easy birth!" Dr. Prakhid declares to John in a mutually congratulatory phone call. Then the pair of them go on to bitch about exorbitantly long hospital stays, the cost of medical care, and how "everybody expects to get first-rate treatment for every little ailment but it's us, the top one percent of taxpayers, who inevitably foot the bill!"

Of course, I remember very little of it.

"I must have been in shock," I tell everyone. "I'm just so glad it all came out okay." (So to speak.)

Messages flood my phone, including wildly creative memes and other adulatory platitudes.

John is over the moon (I've always loved that phrase). The staff works like Santa's elves, retrieving all the "bad mojo" things I bought, which they hid away back then, plus a mountain of other items (twice as expensive) "ordered by Nana, and to be paid for after the child was born," to avoid any jinxes floating around. Makes sense—when it comes to outmaneuvering the Devil, bet on Mary-Elizabeth.

"Look, look, the lucky little sonofabitch's got my eyes!"

I wince at John's choice of words before succumbing to a violent, unexpected shudder. The walls close in. I'm looking through a fish-eye lens. Everything's real, but not quite right. The

voices around me bend and twist like an out-of-tune orchestra. My dream takes me somewhere I've never been before, a sparse, pale-green room, a hospital ward maybe, except no one would come to a place like this to get well. Through a broken window frame, a nondescript, snow- covered cityscape quivers in the twilight. As the wind howls, the cold air makes its way inside, creeping over my skin like an icy hand.

Aaron is there, craning his adolescent head around the doorframe, peeking perniciously into the room, teasing me with his eyes. He's cocky and confident, wearing our high school's uniform—crisp white shirt, deep blue jacket, and the standard-issue striped necktie with the square bottom. His lapel is turned outwards so the secret crest (handwoven into every senior's blazer) has been deliberately exposed: two golden eagles facing one another, frozen in stoic silence. One holds a sword, the other a pen. Between them, in broken blue thread, the school's calligraphic motto consummates the design: "With Knowledge Comes Wisdom." I still don't understand what it means.

With a heavy grunt and athletic leap, Aaron catapults himself through the door and into full view. He mimics my shock. From the waist down, he's completely naked, parts dangling, grotesquely large and hideously deformed. Looking makes me sick, but I can't look away. A pale- yellow sign swings precariously over my head, suspended from the industrial ceiling by a thin copper wire. Neon letters hiss and spark: "W-h-o-r-e." The "w" and "r" flicker and fade: whore— hoe—whore—hoe. I throw up violently, purging both my stomach and my soul. The sickly sweet smell of vomit rises from the floor and clouds the tiny space. I scream. Aaron rushes to me, raising a twisted metal coat hanger. I feel it burn, stinging me as it connects savagely with my bulging stomach. I'm cut, ripped open. Distorted and disfigured, I let out a deep, primal moan.

Falling to my knees, broken in flesh and spirit, too terrified to look up, I'm holding a baby in my arms. He looks exactly like Matthew, but I know he's not Matthew. He slides and squirms but makes no sound. For a brief moment everything stops moving except the little pear-shaped tears that flow with excruciating silence over his jaundiced cheeks. I'm instinctively aware that he's hungry, starving in fact. The dark pink nipple peeking out from under my torn shirt presents an obvious target, but he can't latch. My once plump, perky breasts are shriveled and stale. I'm undernourished. Sickly. My skin hangs sallow on my bones. The baby leans to me, opens his wide-set, pale-blue eyes, and whispers, "Help me, Mommy." The pain in my face is unbearable. I'm bleeding, pouring out of myself and onto my child. I need to escape, but I can't. Why is my mother here? My real mother, not the one who picked me out from the orphanage like a rescued dog from the pound.

"Mommy, Mommy, Mommy."

It's all too much. Baby, mother, Aaron, and me. I need it to end. Now. John is shaking me. Violently.

"Wake up, for G-dssake, please wake up!" he screams. "Are you okay?" He's justifiably panicked. *"Are you okay?"* his voice wobbles, desperate and urgent. I nod weakly and he's visibly relieved. I'm reminded again that I've always wanted a man like John—considerate, successful, and objectively handsome. Although we have our ups and downs, he loves me deeply and consistently. I'm certain in the afterlife I will pay a grave debt for what I am doing to him.

And Satan doth recall that which the Lord shall forgive.

"Yes, yes, I'm okay. It's all okay," I stammer. "Is Jason okay?" John stares at me. I've said something wrong, but I can't pinpoint it.

"You won't believe what I—" But just as I'm about to explain, somehow, baby Matthew starts to howl. Baby comes first. We rush to him, close by in our bedroom. After a brief round of out-of-tune lullabies, Matthew closes his eyes and drifts off to sleep. John and I stand over the crib, rocking it gently back and forth, savoring the shallow, peaceful baby snores. We're alone, the three of us—Mary-Elizabeth is gone, I don't care where.

"You called him 'Jason,'" John comments.

"I did?" I reply, genuinely surprised.

"Yes, you said 'Jason.' Just a few minutes ago."

"Um, the dream. It just seemed so real. Must have been a Jason in the dream somewhere." John doesn't speak, but I can see he's not convinced.

"I was thinking of naming him Jason before I picked Matthew," I try, getting the same look. "Damn anesthetic, still messing with my head," I murmur. *Now I'm over-explaining—*

John's skeptical, but he lets it go.

"Leave him sweetheart; he's perfect," John says, taking my hand and pulling me in the direction of our large Satin-and-Silk bed. *Is he serious?* Does he really understand so little about women, or what a woman's body goes through to give birth? If it were anyone else I'd think he was joking, but John . . . "oblivious" would be an understatement.

I hand him a pamphlet from the side table, planted there for just this purpose, a generic thing, my chastity belt. It discretely asks, *"How long should I wait?"* in bold blue letters.

"What's this?" John muses, turning it over to the back where it's stamped with Dr. Prakhid's name, office address, and phone number in the little box designed to "personalize" the mass- produced handout from a pharmaceutical company.

"Six weeks," is the answer. No sex for six weeks, not the "down there" kind anyway, for fear of postpartum hemorrhage or uterine infection.

"But maybe I can help Daddy out," I coo, rubbing my hands, warming them, finding the lubricant in the same side table, also previously stationed. "One rule, though—I get to do all the touching, okay?"

He agrees with a moan as I squeeze him a friendly, free sample. He would agree to anything at this moment. In six weeks, he'll see that I have my body back in shape, and then I'll have no more excuses. The truth is, I don't want any. I just want him. Desperately. His scent is at once comforting and deeply alluring, reminding me of the first time we touched, and how open we once were. I breathe him in, imbibing, thirstily, the tannins of the '73 Bordeaux he's been sipping. His kiss, his smell, makes my heart race. I close my eyes and fantasize. I picture myself on my hands and knees and he's taking me. The sex is rough and hungry and over too quickly, leaving me breathless and satisfied. Then, just when I begin to relax, his body is ready again. He puts one hand over my mouth and the other clasps my neck. He's thrusting. Hard. This time I come. It's familiar and satisfying. Just what Mommy needs.

"Thanks, babes. Looks like we're gonna need a clean-up on aisle five." John's finished and so is my fantasy. My husband's always been a good lover. He knows all my parts. I just wish he knew my soul. Actually, no; he should never know that part of me. No trespassing. For everything to work out as planned he needs to remain precisely how he is now, blissful and ignorant.

CHAPTER 45

I'M BOTH AWESTRUCK and petrified. Amanda has changed, that much is clear. I mean really changed, in the operative sense of the word. Is it possible someone swapped her out for a Manchurian Candidate-type clone when I wasn't paying attention? At this stage, nothing would surprise me. She's a mother now. That's different. Or is it? Maybe I've changed. Maybe she's the same and I see her with different eyes. Certainly, yes. That's true, too. Both things could be true. If you stare into the abyss long enough and all that bullshit. The only thing I'm sure of is that nothing's going to be the same. Ever! I just can't help but wonder how far down the rabbit hole we are all about to go. The stress is getting to her even more than me. I'm not sure what I can do about that. It's not the baby. She loves the baby as much as I do, and everyone else does, too.

That part's clear. That part's clean and pure and innocent and good. The rest of it, that's dark.

CHAPTER 46

FROM THE MOMENT Matt made his debut appearance in our home (swaddled in Loro Piana cashmere), everything changed. Once John *et al.* got over the shock of my emergency delivery, life at The Oaks shifted in a significantly positive fashion. Our formerly austere household was transformed overnight into something oddly reminiscent of an eighties television sitcom. I imagine the title sequence: "The Greedy Speedies: Season 7, episode 2, Baby Booming." A familiar, much-beloved theme song introduces the show. After the obligatory montage (boats, planes, cars, diamonds and surgically sculpted family members) the camera follows baby Matthew, perched in his Porsche car seat in the back of a Rolls Royce limousine (M SPEEDY1) as it makes its way through the gates of number 16 Oak Lane, across the winding driveway, and over the manicured lawns. The director frames our faux-grand three-story residence in a breathtaking establishing shot.

A voiceover narrates our fabled existence in the Queen's English: "The Speedy's newest arrival is here, ready to be welcomed to his palatial residence." A split-screen follows: The Oaks juxtaposed against a toothless, dribbling Matthew. "Master Speedy, this is your new home. Here you will be expected to carry on the proud family tradition of being filthy rich and making everyone around you appear decidedly inferior by comparison." The camera finds John and Mary-Elizabeth beaming with pride (and draped in Armani), front and center in the deliberately imposing entrance. I'm positioned a little behind them, an afterthought, dressed in a dull gray Lagerfeld, like a guest star or maybe just an extra. "With a gummy grin, baby Matthew meets his new family. How lucky he is to have a silver spoon in his little mouth and a veritable entourage kissing his little golden ass. Matthew, you have certainly landed with your bum in the butter.

Hurrah, son, hurrah."

Fade to the real world where Mary-Elizabeth, laden with parcels, charges into the living room flanked by two empty-handed, yet still somehow subservient flunkies.

"Look who brought more gifts for the baby. Am I the best or am I the best?"

"You are the *beast* all right," I mumble.

Confused, not quite trusting her ears, Mum's forced to dismiss my words completely. She displays a grin, hoping it's somehow the correct reaction. Thank you, *Granny,* I think, as I smile back at her. I needed that.

"My little angel has the best granny in the world. Yes, he does," she coos, poking at Matthew in his crib. Her doting, although nauseating, is perfectly understandable. He's truly a beautiful boy, even if I do say so myself. His soft, wispy hair is as blonde as mine. His pale blue eyes mirror John's so closely it's truly unsettling. I seem to recall that early on a baby's eyes will sometimes change color. I pray that doesn't happen. That wouldn't be good. Not for any of us.

His skin is slightly translucent, pinkish white, not dark at all. If anything, he's a little on the pale side. "Who's gonna spoil you? Nana's gonna spoil you." Her sing-song voice makes Matt scrunch his pudgy mouth into a tight, animated pucker. His expression betrays a bodily function brewing inside his miniature frame. I secretly hope he releases something objectionable. But then his grimace gives way to toothless giggles and I'm forced to concede that baby Matthew is genuinely soothed by Mary-Elizabeth's antics.

"Who's Granny's little champion? Who's Granny's little champion?"

I've had enough. I can't stand it. I get up and leave the room. I'll come up with an excuse later if I need one. As I walk away, Mary-Elizabeth's voice fading behind me, I reflect that it was nothing short of a miracle that her sons ever left the nest at all.

Kayla calls. I have to answer. I've put her off seeing our child—"the possibility of infection and all"—but she's clearly intent on acting like she gives a fuck and bolstering her (self- proclaimed) best friend status. To maintain the illusion of concern she abandons the Aaron line of interrogation where we last left off and instead bombards me with a series of questions that might easily have topped Google's *"How do I pretend to care about my friend's new baby?"* search results.

"So, tell me everything. Are you sore? Do you breastfeed? Hah! Of course, you don't! But does *the baby* breastfeed? Ha ha! Sleep through the night? Did you get your appetite back? Is there anything I can do to help? Will you grab a blunt butter knife and stab me repeatedly in the carotid artery until the world is made marginally better with me no longer in it?"

I mumble through the impromptu inquisition. Of all the pain I've been through in the last week, enduring Kayla's contrived enthusiasm is by far the worst.

"You look exhausted dear," Mary-Elizabeth tells me the minute I step back into the room. "Why don't you go upstairs and rest for a bit? Just relax, and let Nana take care of everything." Admittedly, this is one of the rare occasions where I actually agree with one of my mother-in- law's suggestions. Why shouldn't Nana take a shift? Having raised four children of her own, she is certainly qualified. I wonder what Mary-Elizabeth was like as a young mother. Probably very different. Softer perhaps. Or maybe just pretending to be softer.

CHAPTER 47

FOR THE MOMENT, stillness. The staff are nowhere to be seen. I tiptoe downstairs and peek into the living room. Baby Matthew's asleep, rocking gently in Granny's thin, veiny arms, and John is engrossed in the hypnotic catacombs of last week's social media updates on his phone. Now is my chance. I've been waiting all week for an opening like this. Checking to see I have Phone 2, I slip outside.

Looking back at the mansion from the gardens, I appreciate again how far I've come. At Our Lady of Mercy Orphanage, I slept in a single dormitory where eighteen hard, creaky, steel bunk beds accommodated thirty-three fragile, abandoned souls. The deprivation should upset me, but instead I'm proud of what I once was (not *who* but *what*) and what I've become. It always struck me as odd that money was charged with being the root of all evil. In my experience, it was obvious that the *lack* of money was the true culprit.

If that man is angry or apprehensive about my not communicating he certainly knows how to disguise it.

"1-800-Secrets, if you have something to hide, press one now."

The greeting catches me off guard. Instead of offering up some witty retort of my own, I can only manage to stutter, "Um, hi . . . hello? Hello? Where are you?"

"On the Small World After All ride at Disneyland—where do you think I am?"

I fire back: "Listen, while you're working on your stupid jokes, I'm here dealing with everything for both of us, so cut me some slack, okay?"

"Okay, kiddo, I get it. Just relax, leave the baby with you-know-who and bring your pretty little self over here. We have lots to talk about."

"Um, you think?"

"Oh, and bring some photos of Matty. If anyone's entitled to see what the little fella looks like in his new home, it's me, wouldn't you agree?"

I would.

Before I get into the car, I slip off my white, Agent Provocateur panties and put them in my purse, unconcerned with the remote security cameras watching with robotic precision. I savor the brief, "no-briefs," tingling thrill of nakedness between my legs, the tantalizing mix of girly innocence and exposure, reckless abandon and freedom, not unlike the titillation of texting behind the wheel. As I speed along, it occurs to me I *should* be more concerned about Matthew's safety than the junction of my legs. I *should* be monitoring his every move. I do know better. But instead I savor the air against my flesh, which sends my mind drifting naturally back to Aaron and our money game. That's what he called it.

"So, I got the place to myself again, wanna come over and play the money game?"

I'm driving fast, too fast, speeding down the canyon, heading south and thirsting for that man. The vehicle du jour, the Maserati, proves to be the ideal choice for the drive. Its bass-heavy, brain-numbing speaker volume complements my adrenaline-fueled demeanor with uncanny synchronicity. I tap my fingers on the heated, black leather steering wheel, lip-synching, bobbing my head like a carefree teenager. This is it. I'm free again, doing exactly what I want to be doing and being exactly who I want to be.

Pink Floyd's "Comfortably Numb," takes me back to the year I turned fifteen. The summer overflowed with music, and I danced to that particular track a thousand times, mouthing its lyrics about the lost and fearful, old and jaded, the *comfortably numb,* destined to look at life through the wrong end of the telescope, watching everything shrink until—in the ultimate self-fulfilling prophesy—the people, too, disappear into the vanishing point of history.

Not me—that will never be me.

I should have been ashamed. But even now, recalling my adolescent misadventures through the eyes of a battle-worn adult, I wouldn't change a thing. It didn't matter who found out or how many times a classmate faux-coughed "slut" when I walked past, the intoxicating potion of power, control, and unbridled lust were worth the consequences. Truth be told, I crave that feeling again.

Sure, given the opportunity to reverse time, I would do some things differently, be a better version of myself, someone with a *purity of purpose,* the type of woman they write books about, the heroine. Somewhere deep inside of me lives the unblemished soul of an innocent. She's been there since the day I was born. She was with me when I was left, crying, on the steps of the orphanage. She was there when the Staffords picked me out, when I married John and, of course, when I met up with that man. I also know that by my actions, I'm suffocating her, choking her out, mercilessly extracting the last remaining embers of purity from her being, so that once it's all said and done, only darkness will remain.

And He spoke unto the children: who amongst ye that crave for power and lust shall find in them naught, for I have given unto you free will and thy shalt, each one, chose thy path.

The traffic is thick and relentless. It's called physics—a Maserati is no faster than a Honda Civic in LA during the day. I'm inching slowly and breathing fast. Outside, beneath a faded "Psychic Readings & Killer Pastrami Sandwiches" awning, a tall, bony, unkempt girl shouts angrily towards the heavens. I watch, morbidly intrigued, as she unravels. I consider taking the next shift for her.

My arrival at the hotel syncs up with the last verse of Shania Twain's "You're Still the One" as I sail through the lobby. The lyrics, trite as can be, help me to compose myself. That man always gives me butterflies, and I always want more.

"You alone?" His gravelly voice sends shivers up and down my exposed back. What did he expect, that I would bring Matthew? Does he really want to see the baby? I feel sick. That's exactly what he expected. After all, if it weren't for him there would be no Matthew. "Are . . . you . . . alone?" he repeats, and by taking pains to enunciate each word, he makes it clear he means business.

"No, I'm being followed by a band of flute-playing monkeys—what do you think?" Apparently my sarcasm is well-timed; I watch his brow furrow as he breaks into a broad, genuine smile. It's the kind of cornball humor he enjoys, even more so because I picked it up from him.

Man makes plans and G-d laughs, goes the proverb. I, on the other hand, believe *Man makes plans and G-d, for his part, couldn't care less*.

"Tell me everything's gonna work out all right," I insist when it's time for me to leave.

"It will," he nods, and I believe him. He asks if I would like to stay a bit longer to share a rare French cabernet he's been saving especially for me, for *us*. Despite knowing my prolonged absence will most likely garner some unwelcome questions, I acquiesce. By the time I leave, four hours later, the wine is still corked.

CHAPTER 48

I ARRIVE BACK at 16 Oak to find all hell has broken loose.

John's brothers and sister have arrived; the lunatics are in the asylum. Raymond is a couple years older, the eldest, the weight of maintaining appearances on his perpetually hunched shoulders. (John, who you know, is next in age.) Sylvia is a few years younger than John, an emotional mess (hell, they're all emotional messes to one degree or another). Little Mike is last, the dread-locked ne'er-do-well of the family, a cliché of irresponsi-bility, a Trustafarian and professional student with several degrees in a range of subjects, including the hammered dulcimer.

I had spent "quality time" (whatever the fuck that means) with them all, of course, in London. Each took his or her turn popping in, treating our ambassadorial resi-dence like his personal clubhouse—damning the weath-er, directing the staff, draining the booze, and wonder-ing out loud how I could possibly marry their brother, the "weedy Speedy," who clearly garnered no respect whatsoever. This insipid characterization seemed to rub off on their opinion of me as well. Wilt-by-association, so to speak. Of course, they'd never all visited at one time.

"That would be a disaster," John had informed me, the example of which unfolded in front of us now.

Like Mom (Mary-Elizabeth), each needs to be the center of attention, which incites a narcissistic decathlon of Olympic proportions at 16 Oak. John does in fact wilt like an under- watered houseplant under their crushing enthusiasm, and I genuinely feel sorry for him. It's a big family, a large household, overflowing with giant personalities, oversized egos and little substance. It's so opposite to my upbringing it makes me nervous. They dote on Matthew, ganging up on him, surrounding him, poking, which I take personally. None of them have children. Raymond is too "melancholy" (diplo-speak for clinically suicidal) to produce offspring, Sylvia too crazy (as four ex-husbands, none passing the six-month mark, will attest). Mike's various stylish, flamboyant, and handsome traveling companions would indicate a poor candidate for procreation as well, though it doesn't prevent Mike from also being a boastful womanizer, the inheritance being reserved, I think he believes, for heterosexual males. That leaves only John, which means Matthew is the last, best hope for the continued growth of the family tree (presumably a cactus considering the number of pricks involved, ha ha).

It doesn't take Einstein to figure out they need a baby, a real-life breathing baby, all of them, and by handing them one, I am in fact the Messiah.

When the circus is in town, all the clowns pile out of the little car at once. Enter Kayla and Kyle, gracing us with their presence to finally see Matthew, who they're anxious to compare with their own child. Kyle handles the ratings in a number of categories while Kayla swivels her head in a three-way circuit, repeatedly checking out

Matthew's face and comparing it with mine, and with John's, looking for some resemblance, or Third World influence, and when not finding any, taking another lap just to make sure. Kayla and Kyle know Raymond, Sylvia and Mike well, having met at a host of family functions, having bonded "famously," now joined at the hip—golf outings, yacht parties, charity balls (Illuminati meetings?), "part of the family, really," adoption papers not necessary, so deep is their connection. Yes, I'm painfully aware that Kayla Smithe- Beckworth is the sister-in-law they would prefer, not me, and that Kyle is "a stellar example of proper upbringing" in their eyes, who "they're quite privileged to know."

I can't handle it. I run. I find the farthest corner of the garden and dial Phone 2. "What am I going to do?"

"You're not going to do anything except stay calm. We'll work it out." He says "we" like he's there and able to do something, which he's not.

"There are too many people here," I hiss into the phone. I'm having none of his "work it out" crap.

"We delay, that's all," that man says. "It just takes a little longer."

"I'm going to kill someone."

"I suggest adding arsenic to the *crudités*."

"Can you be serious for just once?"

"How long are they staying?"

"I don't know," I tell him, "and I can't ask them, either—it'll just piss them off."

"Ask limp-dick John-boy."

"Don't call him that. Anyway, that'll just piss *him* off."

"Take charge, then," that man commands. "You're the new mother. What you say goes. Use your authority. Boss them around. Make them know what's what."

"I don't know how."

"Just channel your mother-in-law. She's your Yoda. Emulate her bossiness you must."

I burst out laughing. He really is ten years old. Besides, the idea is ridiculous. That's not the way I operate. I'm a sneak-thief, a snake in the grass, a pickpocket and a knife-in-the-back sort of person. But I'm also just smart enough to know he's right.

"They already hate each other, right? Into the stew you must stir some spice, baby." Again, he's right. I guess I had told him more about the Speedy clan than I thought I had.

I charge back inside, footsteps like thunder, but they still don't look up. "Dolores!" I shout, which does get their attention.

Dolores, Georgia's replacement, who smells of disinfectant, and who has been lurking in the hall, hurries out with a double expresso. *Hello, caffeine, my old friend, I get to taste you once again . . .*

"Stick around," I tell her, take a few sips, then hand the cup back. I charge forward, hands out to take my baby from the mob, who have been terrorizing him with a baby bottle of breast- milk, which Matthew is too agitated to even consider.

"That's just for emergencies," I tell them, referring to the bottle, taking the child. "Dolores . . . " She moves smartly forward and whisks the bottle away.

"Of course," Mary-Elizabeth says, as if she knows something about this, though I'm willing to bet no lips have touched those golden nipples in hunger nor in lust.

"I'll feed him," I state firmly, no argument, as I head for the exit. "And turn off the air- conditioner. He's used to ninety-eight point six. He's not an Eskimo, you know."

With that I exit, headed for the bedroom, Dolores in

tow to assist me. Every woman knows a good set of tits is worth its weight in gold, but a mother also understands a good set of tits *with milk* is priceless.

"I'm so glad you are back, Missus," Dolores says when we're alone in the bedroom, as she takes Matthew from me. "The baby, he was sleeping so good today before they came."

"How long have they been here?"

"Seems like they are here forever," Dolores oversteps slightly and I can't help but laugh. "Does Missus think they will all want to be staying for dinner?"

"You'd better be ready, I guess." The worry on Dolores' face is infectious. Suddenly, I feel boiling hot, like I've been placed in a furnace. "Dolores . . . " I try.

"Qué?" she asks, hoping I have the answers.

"Go down there and tell those people that Matthew has had enough excitement for today and needs his sleep. They can see him again tomorrow."

Dolores nods. She approves.

"He will be with me in the baby's room?" she asks. "The nursery," I correct.

"Yes, the nursery."

"Yes. That's perfect. Anywhere away from those . . . from our guests. Anyway, my guess is if there's no baby, they won't stay long. They're probably making reservations already."

Dolores turns sharply and strides off, ready to do battle. I slink into the bathroom to wash off that man, and my new-found family, and my troubles. My naked body looks smaller than usual. Maybe it's the wide bathroom mirror or the harsh white lightbulbs that frame the glass. Whatever the reason, my reflection makes me feel uneasy. I'm wet and shivering. Even after all that washing, scrubbing, loofa-ing and exfoliating, I still don't feel clean.

I hear John bellowing into the phone. Dolores has successfully broken up the family reunion downstairs and now John's upstairs evangelizing, preaching to Leonard Richards (Chief Internal Auditor of Speedy Gas & Paraffin, and campaign manager/advisor and ideological sounding- board to future Senator John Speed (D-CA)).

"It's not just because he's my boy, Rich, I swear, this kid could star in a commercial for beautiful babies."

At the other end of the phone, I picture the tall, bald bean-counter wincing, willing the gushing to stop but compelled by the hand of hierarchy into obedient acquiescence.

"I mean, let's be honest," John drones, "we've all seen some pretty strange-looking babies in our time, no names mentioned, but Rich, I tell ya, my little guy is gonna be a heartbreaker. And he's smart, I can see it in his eyes. He's destined for big things; you mark my words. Maybe he'll finance your quarter-billion dollar leveraged buyout plan. I could put in a good word. Ha. Rich, you gotta have kids, my friend. It's life-changing."

Listening to John speak so passionately reminds me of why I fell in love with him in the first place. I put on a white and gold Versace robe, the one he got me for our anniversary (or Valentine's Day, or my birthday or Arbor Day, who can remember?), breathe deeply and head towards the voice.

"Didn't you have Matthew with you?" John asks, taking the phone from his ear, certain I've flushed Matt down the toilet. "Where is he? Where's our baby?"

Weedy Speedy, the drama-queen.

"With Dolores. In his nursery. She's putting him to sleep." "I thought you were feeding him."

"Done."

John looks dubious, but without any knowledge whatsoever of just how long it might take to breast-feed a healthy infant boy, he says nothing. I'm certain he'll google it later.

"They made reservations, apparently," John tells me. "Madame Y's. You want to come?" "No," I answer, "but you should go."

"You love Madame Y's."

"I love Matthew, I *like* Madame Y's." "Okay, you *like* Madame Y's, so come."

"Next time, I promise, but you really should go. Play the host."

John looks at me, ignoring the phone at his side, the one barking, "Are you there? Are you still there? I can't hear you," in Richards' voice.

"They're quite a handful, aren't they?" John says.

"They're fine," I smile politely. "They don't bother me." *Why is it so easy to lie?*

"They won't stay long," he assures me.

I'm relieved but I don't show it and I certainly don't ask *how* long, not yet. Patience is a virtue, and L-rd knows I could use some virtues.

"Hello, Richards!" I call into John's phone as I pass by, retrieving my clothes. "John says you're doing a hell of a job!" I retreat back into the bathroom, John's eyes boring holes in the back of my head.

CHAPTER 49

A BABY OR a full night's sleep, pick one. A loud, high-pitched wail rips me from my dreams. I read once that a mother, even when under anesthesia, can still recognize her baby when it cries. Baby Matt certainly has a healthy pair of lungs. I've lost track of time. It's the next day already and the Speedies are all in attendance once again. I try to remember—did they say *when* they were leaving? That's right—*never*. When Hell freezes over. Or when Matt gets trundled off to college perhaps, they'll move into the dorm with him, share his drugs, cook noodles on his hot-plate. What am I saying? He'll have a chef, caviar, his own mini-mansion, and snap-the-fuck- out-of-it.

I call that man. We decide to pull the trigger anyway, no matter how many people are around.

"Gotta grab that cheddar before the rat comes back," as Jill Stafford would say.

The baby screams on. Who can blame him? Taking matters (quite literally) into my own hands, I snatch Matthew (a little too aggressively) away from my mother-in-law at the breakfast table, and in the process, elicit evil looks from Silvia, and Mike as well. John continues picking at his whole wheat pancakes, pretending nothing is going on that he's aware of or needs to respond to, a skill which will stand him in good stead in the Senate. Mary-Elizabeth's lingering scowl is tougher to ignore. How is it that even after all this time she still manages to intimidate me? As soon as I break eye contact, I notice her thin upper lip curl, skyward, almost imperceptibly—a subtle and unmistakably vindictive micro-expression. *That's going to cost her,* I think while turning my attention back to Matthew. We will soon see who's actually in control, Mummy Dearest. In the game of life, just like in the game of chess, the unwitting pieces are totally oblivious to the fact that they are not the ones doing battle. Like the ivory queen on the gilded board in the corner, Granny still has no idea who's actually making the moves elsewhere.

With Dolores' help, I attend to diaper duty, cleaning and changing our precious little gift.

Together we dress him in a tiny blue and white sailor suit (Catimini *couture*) and prepare him for yet another photography session. Once the nursery has been sufficiently staged, it's time for photos and more photos. No one can deny that capturing, curating, and editing these digital trophies has redefined parenthood. In a perverse irony, it has become more important to record our baby's moments than to experience them. It's as if modern collective consciousness, burdened with an existential crisis, chose incessant photography as the definitive solution to prove its existence. "I pic, therefore I am." Descartes 2.0. Updated for your selfie world.

Of course, to ensure the Speedies remain at the vanguard of social media proliferation, every digital image of baby Matt is masterfully posed and lit to emphasize that the new heir-apparent is not only unique, but by virtue of his lineage, indisputably superior. Naturally, all of this is lost on Matthew, who, when he finds himself in front of the lens of no less than Handsome Harry

Hudson, "portrait photographer to the stars," expresses his personal distaste for the pomp and ceremony by regurgitating a chunky puree of milk all over Mary-Elizabeth's antique Hermès scarf. Proudly I revel at his innate ability to exact justice on the deserving.

John catches my eye, smiles, and motions towards the photographer, giving me a "thumbs up." If only he knew.

As soon as Handsome Harry leaves, I insist the others do too, indicating "Matthew is tired," a verdict a mother is allowed to make without contradiction, relying on some mysterious extrasensory force she's assumed to possess. Once they're gone, I want nothing more than to be alone with Matthew. I squeeze him tightly to my body and smell his head. The scent envelops me, elevating my senses beyond this terrestrial plane, transporting me back to the day I held him for the first time, an experience nothing short of surreal.

And Jesus blessed her, the mother, the one that doth protect the baby and give forth her milk.

Sending her, singing, on His path.

CHAPTER **50**

PHONE ONE RINGS. I recognize the name. I have no choice but to answer.

"What the hell is going on over there?" a voice demands.

"Dr. Goldman, so nice to hear from you."

"Don't give me that—I heard you had a baby."

"That we did," I tell him.

"How?"

"Not really any of your business, Doc," I fling at him.

"Is he adopted or something?"

"Want me to say it a little slower? M-Y-O-B."

I hear the wheels creaking in Goldman's mind, trying to figure it out whether he's got an angle here or not. Obviously he's surprised. Or overjoyed. Very happy for us both. Who knows with men?

"Boy or girl?" he asks, deciding to play ball, go along, get along.

"A boy, Matthew Luke Speedy," I tell him, "so if you want to send a gift, that would be an appropriate way to address the card. If not, please don't ever call me again."

I hang up on the bastard. I'm going to miss him.

That night I again hear the baby crying. I sneak out of bed and make my way down to the nursery.

The door is locked, of course, but I try it anyway. No luck. I give it my "shave-and-a-haircut" knock.

"Who is it?" I hear Dolores respond ever-so-softly.

"Me, Amanda," I answer.

Dolores opens the door just an inch, suspecting a trap. She looks like she's been awake.

There's a light on in the room.

"I thought I heard the baby crying," I tell her.

She chuckles delightfully and wiggles her finger at my forehead. "I think you go a little *loco*, Mrs. Speedy," she says.

"I think you're right," I agree. "Did I wake you?"

"No," she says. "I read a little, that's all."

"Goodnight then," I tell her, turning back, walking away. I want to see Matthew. I want to watch him sleeping peacefully, off to dreamland, but I can't, not tonight. I've successfully convinced John the child needs to be in another room, so John can "be at his best" and "win that Senate seat." He understands the truth of that, but he also wants only to be a father, which I find endearing and heartbreaking at the same time. *Forgive me father, for I have sinned.*

CHAPTER 51

AFTER *THAT NIGHT*, not surprisingly, things change at the Stafford house. I overhear no more gushing, no "we are so blessed to have kids like these," and certainly no more marital activity to listen in on. Jill does most of the talking, her voice cracking repeatedly and thick with disappointment.

"Oh my G-d Brian, what are we going to do with her? Do you think it's our fault? Um, maybe not fault but, um, responsibility. I mean maybe she didn't know what she was doing. My G-d. She's only 16. Why would she do that? Do you think that, um, maybe they were right? You know, about what they told us. What did Sister Grace say again? Um, 'a bad egg?' I think we need to send her away for a while. Don't we? Do we? I mean, we don't want Devin affected by all this. I mean, can you imagine? Do you think it's true, Brian? What they say she did. I hate to say it but maybe, maybe they're right, maybe she's just a little . . . "

I know what's coming. I've heard it before. But I can't bear to hear it from *her*. The embarrassment. She doesn't deserve it. She deserves something better. Someone better. Better than me. I pull my head out of the vent and push my thumbs into my ears. They no longer love me. I no longer have a home or a family. I hear Jill's tears staining Big Brian's flannel shirt. I grab the razor-sharp scissors from my "Young Fashionista's Designer Kit," stumble to the bathroom and lock the door.

Regardless of what happened after that—the boarding school, the therapy, the being sent away to "find myself," Devin telling me I was his family's biggest regret—*regardless of everything*, I want nothing more than to be back with the Staffords in the warm, post-modern home where we play hide-and-seek, build forts, and spend Christmases laughing at Big Brian's drunken Santa impression. Where, in the brightly tiled kitchen, my mouth waters watching Jill produce tray after tray of steaming-hot gingerbread men, removing them delicately from the wood-fired oven while I beg like a hungry puppy for "just a little nibble, pleeeeeze."

"Um, one day, you know, Amanda, you will make little men of your own, or little women.

Little buns in your little oven." Jill was never at a loss for a clever turn of phrase, one of the many reasons everyone liked her. "You can tell me anything," she'd say. "There's no place for secrets in this house." And my personal favorite: "Jesus is the only one who gets to judge."

Which I actually think she believed until . . . well, until me. If I had a time machine, I'd go back to the chaste and blissful me; I really would. We shared something very precious in the days before my big mistake, something that I deliberately, but not maliciously, destroyed forever. Call it innocence.

Honestly, I loved Jill very much and—more than that—I trusted her. At least as much as an adolescent can trust an adult. In the end, it was because I loved her so dearly that I never spoke to her again.

Return ye not with blood-soaked hands, lest them you touch become unclean.

CHAPTER **52**

JOHN'S LATER THAN usual. I wait at the breakfast table, eyes dead-aimed at the surveillance monitor, the one pointed down the walk to the front gate, beyond which stands the mailbox and Dolores in her apron, smoothing the ground with her foot impatiently. As every person in Los Angeles knows, it's not the smog but the traffic that'll kill you, and this is beginning to look like Judgment Day.

Finally, without explanation, John breezes into the dining room and takes a seat, a glass of orange juice in his hand.

"Where's the g-ddamn staff?" he asks. "Had to squeeze my own," he adds, eyebrows furrowing, as he samples his frothy drink, not offering one to me. "So what's with all the milk in the refrigerator?"

"It's breastmilk."

"Breastmilk?"

"You do know that's what boobs are actually for, right?" I reply, tempted to make some remark about John's memory and ancient history and Mary-Elizabeth's tits—

"I know that—what's it doing in the refrigerator?"

I have an answer for that, too, but I don't remember—

"Why doesn't he suck it right out? Eliminate the middle-man," John declares.

"I have sensitive nipples," I tell him, remembering the excuse.

"You do?" John perks right up, suddenly a subject of great interest to him, it seems. "Well, trust but verify, that's what I always say."

I slap him playfully on the shoulder. "Soon, Daddy, soon."

"Where's Matthew?"

The other question I didn't want to hear. "Still asleep," I say.

"And what's-her-name. Where is she? I'm hungry."

"Getting the mail, I think," at which point I look up and Dolores is indeed holding the mail in one hand and our little bundle of joy in the other, about to open the gates and return to the main house, but the gates open miraculously by themselves and the Mercedes-Maybach sails through and stops cold, window going down. Mary-Elizabeth and Dolores have words, then the chauffeur drives "Liz" on up to the house.

"Are you aware that your cook takes the baby down to the street to pick up the mail?" Mary- Elizabeth crows when she enters.

"She says the fresh air is good for him," I reply casually.

"That's exactly what she said to me," my mother-in-law advises, both surprised and suspicious, as if there was some dark conspiracy going on and Dolores and I had coordinated alibis.

The incident is soon forgotten under the day's mountain of presents. An often overlooked virtue of the moneyed (I love that term—"moneyed") is their consistent propensity for gift- giving. No celebration, wedding, funeral, birthday, breakfast, lunch, dinner, brunch, big or small, is ever undertaken without a corresponding registry. Maybe you can't put a price on friendship, but the well-to-do consider holding-deposits an absolute must.

I sit cross-legged on the floor next to the crib surveying a rainbow of discarded boxes littering the nursery. In what is undoubtedly another worthwhile contender for "First-World Problem of the Year Award," my fingers are numb from repetitive unwrapping. "Tis better to give than to receive" looks good on a greeting card, but after years of barren Christmas mornings in the orphanage, I, for one, still prefer the latter. The gifts range from the sublime to the ridiculous. While I might be able to defend an antique Victorian rattle, it's substantially more challenging to justify a 24 karat-gold Krugerrand tiepin (not exactly childproof, either). A cute and cuddly collectible Steiff teddy bear arrives from none other than Dr. Michael Goldman, OB-GYN, addressed correctly to Matthew Luke Speedy, I notice, no doubt picked out, purchased, wrapped, and mailed by his receptionist, whose name I don't recall. My personal favorite, however, is a first edition of George W. Bush's *Decision Points*. (What baby could survive its first year without one?) A calligraphic note accompanies the memoir: "May your son always vote the *right* way— your friends at the NRC," which is a nasty Republican swipe at John's Senate run. The only surprise is it isn't signed by G.W.B., Number 43 himself. I'm not complaining.

"Babes, are you coming to bed?" John asks. His tone of voice indicates concern. The relatives have gone up the hill to their separate rooms in their separate mansion, Dolores has taken Matthew away to wherever. But I'm still not done—

"Can't you just leave me alone?" I cry out. "You think I'm just sitting here doing nothing.

You know I have to take pictures of all this stuff, write out thank-yous, and post everything before everyone says how ungrateful we are. Let me just finish, okay?" He doesn't reply and I don't blame him. The fact is I'm pushing the definition of "killing time" to the edge of the envelope.

When exhaustion finally gets the better of me, I head upstairs. John is under the covers and fast asleep. Instead of joining him, I opt for the oversize *chaise lounge*. I hold my bulging jewelry box close to my chest and wrap my feet in a yellow Egyptian-silk blanket (intended for a blue- blooded baby boy). In my last wakeful moments I can't help but philosophize how, indisputably, money can indeed buy happiness.

CHAPTER 53

"ANXIETY IS A peculiar emotion, unique in its ability to both provoke action and induce paralysis." In my dream, I'm reading from a term paper I wrote long ago: "Panic and the Cognitive Decision-Making process" (for which I received my standard "A," but which I now consider to be total BS). While at Talbord, I took an elective course in Anthropology, not because I had a deep interest in human behavior, but because it met Thursday mornings, which meant my precious weekends would start a day early. That primary motivation, however, didn't stop me from becoming obsessed with the subject matter. It certainly didn't hurt that Professor

Georgioupolous (our young, tenured lecturer) had both movie star good looks and a way of making the dry coursework seem entirely relevant. And so it followed naturally that I came to fall in love . . . with Anthropology.

Professor ("call me 'G'") Georgioupolous was convinced that people were by and large predictable creatures. This core idea formed the foundation for all his lectures.

"Morning, civilized people . . . and future lawyers . . . today we are going to look into our caveman brains and learn about what happens to us when we're threatened. Thanks to hundreds of years of boring academics like me studying human behavior, we can now predict, with relative certainty, how humans, like some of you in this class, will respond when you are faced with a crisis. The bad news is that we haven't changed much since we crawled out of our caves. Like our Neolithic ancestors, we'll choose either to confront our proverbial mammoths head-on, or more likely, run screaming for the hills." Winking at no one in particular, and flashing an arctic-white smile, he elaborated. "The concept, colloquially known as 'fight or flight,' is hardwired into our primitive brains. We stuffy scholars call this a state of 'hyperarousal' or, to you, 'the shit's gonna hit the fan.'" Chuckles ensued. "You see, in life-threatening situations, your inner caveman, or, to be politically correct, cave-*person*, takes control. Your amygdala springs into action, activating your hypothalamus and flooding your body with adrenaline. Armed with this physiological boost, and infused with cortisol, nature's alarm system, you are now primed and ready to launch into either a ferocious fight or a pretty speedy flight. Are you listening, Amanda?" Amanda. Amanda.

A nightmare intrudes on the dream. I'm no longer in G's class. I'm fifteen years old, back in the orphanage, empty and quiet. I'm uneasy, gravely aware of the perils of solitude. I feel abandoned and vulnerable. I call out: "Hello . . . hello, is anyone there?" The bone-chilling reply echoes from everywhere and nowhere, deep and disharmonious.

"We're here, we're watching you."

I want to run and hide, but I'm frozen in place.

"You know what we want, don't you? We know you

remember us." I close my eyes and shake my head.

"No, I don't. Leave me alone." I squeeze my hands until my sharp, overgrown nails cut into my flesh. I know the voices belong to the cave dwellers lurking in the catacombs of my mind, the haunting memories of that night.

Ice-cold breath drips down the back of my neck. I spin, finding myself face to face with Aaron, close to me, eyes sunken and sallow, torso riddled with lesions. He's shivering and drenched in sweat, an accursed version of the handsome boy I once knew. His smell sickens me. The lacerations that plague his body gape open one by one and fat, headless worms wriggle and writhe out across his jaundiced skin. They're my worms, the silkworms I collected when I was young, housed in an old shoebox with airholes punched into the lid. I watched them spin cocoons, lay eggs and crawl like living concertinas between my fingers. I spent endless hours handling them, delighting in the feeling of their tiny legs as they moved easily over my bare flesh. I don't remember why they were taken from me. "I needed to learn a lesson" is all I recall. Now the worms pierce the transparent membranes holding them in place, and crawl quickly and freely in and out of Aaron's torso, infesting him like the carcass of a rotting animal. I can't look away. I can't run. The putrid smell of decomposing fruit and human feces fills the air. I'd cover my nose, but my hands are shackled together with rusty brass cuffs. I desperately twist and turn to free myself, but my arms are no match for the sharp, metal edges. Blood spills from my wrists, forming dark rivers between my fingers, dripping relentlessly onto a weathered Bible. The bloodstained pages flip furiously, saturating themselves until only a single passage remains: "*Jesus protects young lambs. Let his flock adore him and they will surely be saved.*" I repeat the makeshift prayer over and over in a trembling voice. Asymmetrical blood-flowers blossom around the last legible word, "saved," until it too is overcome. There will be no salvation for me. I look to Aaron and abandon hope.

My body crumbles, disintegrating. I invite the darkness, willing myself to get away, to escape to a dream within a dream. It's no use; the nightmare is unrelenting. In the pit of my subconscious I come face to face with *it*. A fetus. Partially formed. Straddling life and death. His tiny eyes are open, opaque, and squinted. He still breathes, and he's still attached to my body, fastened to me by a clotted umbilical cord. He stares at me, unrelenting. Sobbing, I try to read the blue-plastic hospital tag around his neck, but just as I'm about to decipher the words, my eyes burst open. Aaron grabs me by the hair and pulls me to him. His worms infest my body like a fungus, hissing and burning my flesh. He pushes his tongue into my mouth. I feel it expand. I need oxygen. I have no choice—I bite down. Hard. It's a mistake. The serpentine appendage bursts inside me. Instantly I'm sick, drowning in a thick soup of blood and bile. I feel life slipping away. Everything darkens.

Aaron, fetus, and Bible fade from view, sucked and swallowed by the black hole of regret.

I wake suddenly in total hysteria. John's broad frame hovers over me, eclipsing the light.

With his full weight, he holds me in place. His hands press heavily against my wrists. I'm pinned to the floor, a necessary precaution, I presume, to restrain my flailing limbs and prevent me from injuring myself, like a mental patient. Stiff and drenched in sweat, I stare at John, then *through* him, probing his dark blue eyes, searching, hunting for his soul and failing to find it.

"Get off me!" I scream. "You are hurting me. You're . . . you're smothering me!" I push against his hands violently, throwing him to the floor. We're in the library. It's the middle of the day. I don't know how I got there. Mary-Elizabeth, Raymond, Sylvia, Mike, and a servant (not Dolores) are all there to tell me to relax, the last thing I need to hear. They help John to his feet. "Why is everyone staring at me? I just had a bad dream, okay?" I feign composure. Why *is* everyone staring at me? Did I say something? Did they find out? Have I been discovered? But before I can finish the thought, it becomes obvious: my pants are soaking wet and I've soiled myself. I retreat to the upstairs bathroom. A dozen eyes witness my walk of shame.

"I don't care what you say, Jonathan, she needs a real doctor," I hear Mary-Elizabeth proclaim as she follows John, who follows me. "Someone from America for Heaven's sake, not some Indian quack who bought his degree in the slums of Calcutta. She was never like this with Dr. Goldberger. G-d only knows what kind of voodoo drugs this Indian put her on. I'll be damned if I'm going to put the fate of my first grandchild in the fate of that, that *immigrant*." I hear her outside the master bedroom door while I clean myself up in the bathroom. I can picture it, John wanting to come to me, but also needing to keep his mother at bay, to spare my delicate feelings. My guess is this conversation is only the latest of many I *wasn't* privy to. "I mean this is the mother of your baby we are talking about, not some peasant from Compton. Can't you see she needs real help? You know I'm right. I mean Jesus, John, is *that* really who you want looking after your child?"

By "that" I'm hoping she's still referring to Dr. Prakhid and not me. So far she's managed to couch the argument in the guise of caring about *me*, but it's a backhanded kind of love at best. On second thought, secretly, I'm grateful to Mary-Elizabeth. If she were a more congenial person, or even a more considerate human being, I might feel guilty (maybe). I might even, Heaven forbid, feel actual remorse and decide not to go through with this. Thankfully that sour, twisted misanthrope (still ranting in the wide, art-adorned hallway) has gifted me a "get out of guilt free" card on a silver platter. And not just any silver platter, my dear, a Reed and Barton, of course— only the best for the Speedies.

As the bedlam subsides, and while the entire house staff of 16 Oak Lane buzz around both John's overdramatic mother and me, one tiny detail escapes everyone's attention:

Baby Matthew is gone.

BOOK 4: JUDGES

CHAPTER 54

"SHE'S NEVER AT a loss for words, this one," Jill Stafford would boast. "I think she must have swallowed a dictionary. Well, um, not a dictionary exactly but a thesaurus. No wait, that's a dinosaur, right?"

Ever since I can remember, I've been captivated by the power of words. My high school classmates insisted "books are for geeks," but I read everything I could get my hands on. By the time I was introduced to the science of semantics in my second year of law school, my adolescent flirtations with the nuances of the English language had blossomed into a full-fledged love affair. I reveled in my thriving ability to articulate obscure ideas. My essays won awards and admiration alike. In my final year, when I was invited to address an inaugural jurisprudence class, my hubris was on full display: "In my experience, both explicating and interpreting the subtleties of law can be entirely attributed to nothing more than a combination of comprehension and vocabulary. In short, if you truly understand it, you can explain it. There's a word for everything. Your job, my fellow future lawyers, is simply to pinpoint that word."

Today's events have (beyond a reasonable doubt) proven me wrong. I'm now convinced using words to characterize emotions is the functional equivalent of using a pickax to perform neurosurgery. What word, precisely, should I *pinpoint* now? What word describes a mother's reaction when the baby she held, smelled, kissed and loved is no longer there? That's the word I need—a single word to yell at the top of my lungs. One word that will stop the pain. A word that like Matthew himself, is nowhere to be found.

"C'mon people, this is no time to panic," John takes charge. "Now I want everyone to listen to me and remain calm. Let's not do anything crazy. If we want to find Matthew, we all need to remain positive and alert. I know everyone's very concerned, and I appreciate that, but let's put the emotions aside for now, put our heads together, and figure out what could have happened. Are you with me?" The speech (turned rhetorical question) is delivered solemnly to Mary-Elizabeth, Raymond, Sylvia, Mike, and me with John's signature pre-senatorial inflection. When John and I started dating I teased him mercilessly about "The Voice," the silky smooth tone designed for constituents, news anchors, and on certain memorable nights, foreplay. Years of aspirational posing had equipped future Senator Speedy with a sublime vocal blend of superiority and leadership (with just a dash of condescension mixed in for good measure), volume and pitch honed to perfection. The result was nothing short of auditory sculpture, polished and poised to elicit confidence and endear voters. If I was queen of "the right word," John was king of "saying it well." It was obvious to me, however, that in the shadow of an empty crib, "The Voice" (like a prodigious vocabulary) was not only impotent, but farcical.

"Who else is missing?" Raymond asks.

Sylvia and Mary-Elizabeth hurry off to take a head count of the staff (and the silver, no doubt), although they have no idea who exactly works in our house. Raymond and Mike start their own search, calling far into the rooms, as if a two-week-old could wander off on his own unescorted, or respond to his name for that matter.

I pace relentlessly—back and forth, gripped by fear and paranoia. The deathly silence fallen on The Oaks is disturbed only by distant "Matthew?" calls and my Zanotti pumps tapping out an ominous soundtrack to accompany the mysterious disappearance. I should perfect the sound and dance my way to fame and fortune—

"Jesus, what's the matter with you?" John proclaims. "Would you stop plodding around the house like a Clydesdale with a hernia and sit the fuck down already?" John's outburst serves only to amplify the already unbearable tension.

"I'm sorry, I'm just . . . just . . . " But try as I might, I can't complete the thought. I don't have the word. I'm traumatized, unable to focus, visibly strung out. Even more than his (possibly justified) reprimand, John's "this is no time to panic" speech has left me both marginally confused and absolutely infuriated. The sentiment itself is absurd. *Okay John, let's all remain calm. Why don't we just kick our feet up and enjoy a spot of tea. After all, it's only a missing baby. Perhaps he was misplaced under a sofa cushion or maybe he went for a stroll around the lawns. The landscaping is lovely this time of year. Perhaps someone should check the swimming pool.* I want to punch John, slap his over-primped face, strangle him until he turns blue. Because if there is one thing that he should be doing now, it's panicking (and checking the pool). *Really, will someone go look in the pool?*

Raymond and Mike return first, empty-handed. Mary-Elizabeth and Sylvia follow, announcing that "someone named Dolores" is also missing. They all seem to be able to look calm with terrifying agility, carrying on as if Matthew's absence was nothing more than a speed bump on the road from irritation to normalcy. Of all of us, Mary-Elizabeth's composed demeanor strikes me as particularly incongruent. She sits on the couch by the fireplace and sips sherry as if she expected little Matthew to stroll in at any moment, a girl on his arm, a martini in his hand, and a rip-roaring anecdote to explain his absence. I shudder at various more probable outcomes. It's proving impossible to follow their relaxed example; I'm terrified and it shows. What no one else knows, though, is that (more so than the empty crib) it's actually John and Mary-Elizabeth's apparent absence of *fear* which for good reason scares me senseless.

What anthropology professor "G" left out of his "fight or flight" scenario: shock. Brain- numbing, muscle-freezing, action-killing *shock*. You can't fight, you can't run, you can't breathe. Or maybe I missed that day. Maybe I took off on a Thursday morning for an even earlier weekend and missed the part that's just the opposite of the run-or-gun stuff. Maybe we're possums, bred to roll up in a ball and play dead, hoping the danger goes away.

I can't stand it any longer. I excuse myself to go to the garden, hand in pocket, clutching Phone 2. I check the pool on the way. It's empty. I knew it would be. Once in the garden, sure it's safe, I make the call. We talk. I hang up. I wait. The phone rings again and I read the message.

That's when I scream.

The sound echoes against the house, but it's not an echo. It's John and Mary-Elizabeth and Raymond, Sylvia and Mike, all shrieking to wake the Devil. They, like me, have received the same text.

I hurry back, hoping I haven't been missed (like Dolores). Nobody cares. I'm invisible.

They're all glued to their smartphones, stunned into silence, reading and re-reading the same e- mail sent to each of them, the servants, and to me, too, delivered to our inboxes at 2:07 p.m., opened thirty-some seconds later. In a cruel, ludicrous exhibition of understatement, it's marked "important," like spam. In fact, there is nothing remarkable about the correspondence at all. If it hadn't been for the subject line, it might well have been disregarded, or worse still, deleted.

Context is so important, isn't it? In our heightened awareness, the words jump off the screen. The gravity of the communication is impossible to ignore. One thing is certain: the message is constructed to achieve a single objective: scare the living shit out of us.

From: VDWV4e245@Yandex.ru *To: Johntspeedy@ gmail.com Subject: You baby is with us now*

Today we tooked you child. We do this only for money. Hurting child is not what you want or us want. Us quickly returning child when 32,116 (thirty-two thousand, one hundred and sixteen) bitcoin pay to account #728336406403. Not to contact us - not to contact police - quick to pay.

Two days. Today is count of one.

Before consulting any of us, John replies.

From: Johntspeedy@gmail.com To: VDWV4e245@ Yandex.ru

Please, please don't hurt my baby. Please. We will pay you whatever you want. We just need some time to get the money. Please let us know that he is all right? John Speedy

The auto-response reduces him to tears. *Error Code: #553 Mail undeliverable. The message that you sent could not be delivered to one or more of its recipients.*

Mary-Elizabeth cracks first. I'm not surprised—all that phony serenity—

"Why Jesus? Why?" she screams. "Please G-d, help us get our precious Matthew back. We'll do anything, anything. Please, Jesus, don't let anything happen to him. For Heaven's sake, why? Why would someone do this? Why?"

Um, for money, you overprivileged half-wit. As to your other questions to Jesus and G-d— wrong people to ask, really, unless G-d & Son have started texting ransom notes as part of some new high-tech Biblical wrath. Actually, Mary-Elizabeth's manifestly predictable reaction to the whole ordeal is comforting. If the circumstances themselves weren't so dire, her melodrama would have been laughable. But even though her histrionics grate me, I concede they're both heartfelt and justified. Better than calm and fearless any day.

Choosing to adopt a different tack than his mother, future Senator Speedy (D-CA) stays true to the character he's established, specifically that of the cool and collected superhero. The email has thrust all the rest of us into the Eighth Circle of Hell, but John somehow manages to return to his soap-box to peddle his "it'll turn out all right" routine.

"Don't you worry, babes. Let me handle this. I know exactly what needs to be done. I know how to deal with people like this. They think they have us in a corner, but they forget . . . " He places his manicured hand on my shoulder, " . . . we have G-d on our side."

I freeze, not so sure. His hand and his optimism, both misplaced—

"Remember," he goes on, "no matter how dark things might appear, Jesus is always looking down on us," becoming The Reverend Speedy all of a sudden. "I promise you, He doesn't punish the innocent and He won't let anything happen to our little Matt. Just have faith." I quite literally need to bite my tongue to avoid laughing in his face. *Really John? Jesus will solve this? If I were you, I would leave your Lord out of the negotiations and place your faith in Ben Franklin instead. If I'm interpreting the email correctly, and I'm pretty sure I am, the perpetrators are not coming for redemption. What they want is cold, hard cash. Unless, unbeknownst to me, the Son of G-d owns a savings and loan, please cut the bullshit and start arranging to get the money.*

There's another head count. As before, everybody's there except for Dolores, which everyone finds suspicious.

"She left at four like she always does," one of the other servants offers, which nobody considers much of an alibi.

"That's about when the baby went missing as well," Mike states, stroking his beard thoughtfully. Raymond and Sylvia have also decided they're in an Agatha Christie novel. Their main suspect is, of course, Dolores, though they hesitate to play "the Latinx card."

"It's not racist if she really did it," Mary-Elizabeth tells her children.

Fuck off, Mom, I want to say, but I don't. I can't defend Dolores, not publicly anyway.

Discussion follows, and it's suggested that if she *were* the guilty party, she would never reveal herself so obviously by being the one absent person—

"Unless it's a double switcheroo," John wonders.

He actually uses the word "switcheroo." *What the fuck is the matter with him?*

"The note *does* sound like her," Raymond points out.

"Exactly," Mike argues, "playing on our racial biases. Full of mistakes, the way we *think* someone with her ethnic background would write it."

"Hooking into our inherent Hispanic stereotypes," Sylvia muses.

"What did I just say?" Mike complains.

"You're saying it's a trick?" Mary-Elizabeth asks, clueless.

"I'm saying she's a criminal mastermind," Mike answers.

John, aware of the other servants standing there, whose English is no better than Dolores', worried about a Latin insurrection (long overdue), holds his hand up in truce (*after all, ALL the servants are suspects, not just Dolores*). He turns back to the email itself. Beyond the barely acceptable English-as-a-Second-Language issues, it is in fact neatly cropped and professionally laid out: *sans serif,* double-spaced, size fourteen font. I try to read it again, but the harder I try to concentrate, the more distracted I become. My brain wants to fight, but my imagination is in "flight" mode, skipping to a dark playground where I swing on a faded tire-swing and wonder how kidnappers learn to write ransom notes in the first place.

Word of mouth from generation to generation? Google? Perhaps it's part of the entry-level curriculum at any (dis) reputable, for- profit terrorist school:

"Always use a large, clear font when threatening the violent death of an infant," the professor instructs while the ski-masked students scribble copious notes. "Send both as an attachment and in the body of the email itself. PC *and* Mac-friendly files, please. Now let's turn our attention to this example—world-class, an extortionist on top of his (or her) game, poised for far grander things than simple child abduction. Stopping at infanticide would be a terrible waste of their G-d-given talents. Notice the menacing tone. I'm sure we can all agree the money's as good as in the bank."

Unfortunately, none of the Speedies know what the hell a bitcoin is or how much it's worth.

Precious time is wasted googling the subject to death— "One bitcoin is worth . . . "

"That can't be right . . . can it . . . ?"

"That means . . . "

"300 million dollars," John announces out loud, followed by a hushed reverence for the sheer size of the request. The figures are double-checked. A bitcoin's worth nine grand at the moment. It adds up. But who's counting?

For such a tiny little baby—

"What about someone from the company? Like Richards?" Raymond suggests. "You're always telling us what a greedy little bastard he is."

We wait while John mulls that over, finally shaking his head. "No way. Doesn't have the imagination—"

My phone rings. I shriek, jump, nearly wetting myself. It's not Phone 2, it's One, Kayla calling.

"Hey, 'Manda, you around? Kyle and I were thinking about popping over."

The others hang close to listen in, expecting it's the kidnappers, or news, or some development of some kind which will change things for good. I cover the phone with my hand.

"It's Kayla," I whisper.

The eavesdroppers fall away like leaves off a November maple.

"This actually isn't a good time," I tell Kayla.

"Oh? Why not?" she asks, a perfectly legitimate question if it was *any of her fucking business*.

"Family stuff," I tell her darkly, which effectively shuts her out. As close as she is, she is *not* a Speedy.

Suddenly Mike's got another idea and he's poking his finger at the phone, stabbing it at my ear like a madman.

"Well, if there's anything I can do—" Kayla starts to say.

"There isn't," I interrupt. "Bye." I hang up.

"It's Kayla and Kyle!" Mike nearly screams. "They took the baby."

"Why would they do that?" Sylvia wonders skeptically. "They've got their own baby."

"Did you get a look at that thing of theirs?" Mike challenges.

Gasps of recognition. *When you're right, you're right, Mike.*

"You think they took Matthew out of jealousy?" Mary-Elizabeth queries, rolling the idea around her skull.

"Matthew is obviously a far superior baby," Raymond states, summing up what everyone's thinking.

"True," John agrees without hesitation. "Smarter, better looking, smells better. With my eyes.

Who wouldn't prefer Matthew over that lump they have?"

"And now they have both of the babies?" Izabella from Guatemala chimes in, confused.

We'd all forgotten she was still standing there.

I'd like to jump in and put an end to this speculation. I'd like to remind them all that Kayla and Kyle are solid upstanding citizens, lifelong friends and neighbors, certifiably sane, and not a couple of villains out of a Lifetime thriller movie. I'd like to, but I'm enjoying this too much.

"What about the money?" Mike reminds everyone. "All that money. Isn't that the motive?" "Kyle does spend like crazy," John offers. "Everybody's noticed."

"He's in the newspaper business, right?" Raymond asks.

"We all know where *that's* going," Sylvia chimes in, "what with all the online sources and the loss of ad revenue and all that crap. It's gotta be driving Kyle nuts. He must be feeling a little inadequate, especially with that tiny little dick of his."

All stare at Sylvia, a host of unanswered questions— I double over laughing—*she knows, too!*

To cover my hysteria, I pretend I'm in some kind of delayed postnatal pain. John hurries over to me, to hold and comfort me.

"Okay, let's calm down," he says. "Kayla is Amanda's best friend."

Another spasm of hilarity blasts up my gut to my throat, which I desperately and heroically hold down.

Sylvia? What were you thinking? I had to fuck Kyle, but you?

"It's okay," John whispers, comforting me. "Everybody grieves in a different way."

The others speak more softly now, as if I'm going to shatter into a million pieces, or just not there.

"Doesn't Kyle still have that polo pony?" Mike asks.

"Nobody has a polo pony," Raymond protests. "A chukker only lasts seven minutes and you need six of them for a match to even think about playing polo."

"Oh, aren't we an expert?" Sylvia comments.

"I'm just saying," Raymond answers.

"A 'chukker?' Where'd you come up with that?" "

You need a lot of money, that's all."

"You seem to know an awful lot about polo," Sylvia digs in.

"Not as much as you seem to know about Kyle's dick—" Raymond shoots back.

"Children," Mary-Elizabeth admonishes. "The important thing is Kyle and Kayla are in the newspaper business."

"The buggy whips of our generation," Mike concludes.

"Kyle makes wagers," John states bluntly.

We stare. This *is* news. Plain-wrap Kyle Beckworth is a gambler?

"He's over a hundred grand in debt if the rumors at the club are to be believed," John shrugs. "I know it doesn't sound like much . . . "

Again, I try to hold it back. I guess I'm not there yet, not a total Speedy, and for that I'm grateful. A hundred thousand dollars still sounds like a great deal of money to me. In fact, that very figure is my definition of "real money," even to this day. I know, you can't even buy a decent house in Sheepdip wherever for that, but it still strikes me as more than pocket change.

The family keeps at their speculation and I can't say I'm upset that Kayla and Kyle have been unfairly kicked off Speedy island, at least temporarily.

John stares up at the ceiling, or perhaps the heavens. With an aura of sheer bewilderment, he turns towards me.

"You know if we pay them they won't stop; it will just be the beginning. But if we don't, well, I don't even want to think about what happens if we don't. Jesus. I mean what do you think we should do?"

I'm amazed he's asking me. I've never been consulted before, not on anything important anyway. Is it because I'm "Mom" now? Or is it because I'm such an obvious threat to blow apart like a ticking time bomb? Despite being honored by the request: "What do you think we should do?" I have absolutely no idea. The wide-eyed, idealistic law student, the one who won the big D, the Debutant Debaters Competition, the one with all the words, with all the answers—she would know exactly what to do: "to conclude, ladies and gentlemen, if we, as individuals and as a nation, truly want to remain principled and safe, free in our thoughts and actions, and—dare I say it?—*civilized*, there is only one logical conclusion. We have to commit, in our hearts and minds, that we should never, no matter how dire the circumstances, submit to duress. It is neither hyperbole nor overstatement to argue that our very liberty depends on it. Even at the expense of my own life, or at the expense of the pain or life of a loved one, I would never open the door and negotiate with terrorists. For this is a door that once opened can never again be shut. Say it with me. 'Never.'"

It didn't occur to me at the time that my years of growing up in the suburbs of California hardly qualified me to hold an opinion on the subject of counterterrorism. I was, instead, entirely preoccupied with combining my impressive vocabulary and purposely form-fitting sweater to drive my point home. Basically, I was two tits, full of shit.

I fidget with my phone, pretending to read the ransom note again, wishing that man was there to tell me what to say. The computer-controlled chandelier overhead maintains the ambient light to such an absurd level of contrived perfection that it's virtually impossible to detect how much the world outside has darkened. Because of this technological marvel, we've lost all track of time and are, instead, consumed by the only matter of any consequence at all: the note. But even after analyzing its form, its contents, and its linguistic nuances to the point of absurdity, we are still no closer to reaching a consensus than we were when we started out. Instead we remain tormented by the same two questions: Should we call the police? Should we pay the ransom?

There are no easy answers.

"What if we pay and they just want more?"

"What if we don't and they hurt the baby?"

"How will they know if we call the FBI?"

"Are they watching us right now?"

Yelling. Crying. Glaring. Sulking. Skulking. Anything goes. With our opponents absent or invisible, we have no choice but to turn on each other. Ironically, despite each one of us trying his damndest to make his opinions heard, we all, deep down, wish someone else would make the final call.

Then, as if on cue, the Senator-to-be, in the far corner, weighing in at a lean 180 pounds and wearing a black and gold, hand-embroidered, Givenchy evening blazer, delivers a decisive blow:

"Okay, I want you all to listen and listen good! It's my house, he's my son, and it's my decision. We are not calling the police, and we are not paying the ransom. If they want to deal with the bull, they will get the horns. They can't take him *again*. What good is our baby to them? If they want our money, let them come crawling back. This is basic, straightforward economic theory, people! I'm going to show them who's really in charge here, and I don't want to hear another word on the subject. Is that clear? I'm the one in control here. Understand?"

John's physically primed; his muscles are braced and bulging through his shirt, hair dripping with sweat. He lurches forward and, once again (this time so loudly that Mary-Elizabeth literally jumps out of her seat) screams: "I'm in control!" He is pure testosterone. Primal. And despite the fact that I hate him right then, and don't agree with a single word he's saying . . . I want him.

CHAPTER 55

MY OTHER PHONE has been ringing all day. That man needs an update. My excuse is I couldn't simply wander off without risking seriously unwelcome scrutiny, but truthfully, with all that has happened in the last twenty-four hours, I'm not entirely sure if I'm ready to speak to him yet.

Everything has changed. Like an orchestra without a conductor, 16 Oak has transformed overnight from a symphony of residential harmony to a cacophony of panic and mismanagement. Even the habitually stoic house staff have been found bickering and yelling. No one can escape the pain when a child goes missing.

I grab Phone 2 and make for the garden, only to find John sitting on one of the carved stone benches, his head buried in his hands. The weight of the decisions, the ones that *need* to be made, bear down on him emotionally and physically. He's hunched over. The enormity of the crisis makes him appear small. Although I remain silent, I will him to compromise:

Pay.

John looks up and says something startling: "Stand our ground. If we give an inch, they will take a mile. No

deals, no concessions, no compromise, and no negotiations!" I'm stunned, shocked, gobsmacked. He recites it
verbatim, my debate declaration from the big "D." Does
he recall everything I ever said? Is he some kind of clan-
destine genius with the memory of an elephant and the
recall mechanism of a supercomputer? Maybe John's
a cyborg (that would explain *a lot*)? Or the Rain Man of
Harvard? Maybe he just cares.

Forget what I myself said all those years ago. Forgive
my childish hubris. Tell me to "fuck my stupid principals."
Simply give in. When it comes to money, negotiation is
always an option, and a damn good one. Trust me, I
would know.

I don't push it, though. I leave it "left unsaid." He'll
come around, I'm sure.

"Of course I remember," he states softly, sensing my
shock, "and I would never go against what you said that
day: 'Even at the expense of the life of a loved one, I
would never negotiate with terrorists.'"

My breath won't come; I can't reply. John not only
loves me, but remembers and takes to heart *every*
g-ddamn word I ever said!

"I will never betray your trust, Amanda. If I negotiate
with these animals, you could never love me again . . . I
know that," he says.

My phone's making noise, the second one, the one
I'm not supposed to have. I turn from John and head
back to the house, leaving him devastated, or so I imagine.

"Call me now. I mean NOW!"

The text's curt tone should upset me, but instead I'm
relieved. His urgency reassures me. It reminds me that
even if I feel isolated, I'm not alone. I need to talk to

that man just as much as he needs to hear from me, maybe even more so. I have faith in him that he'll guide me, faith that he always knows exactly what to do. Ironic how that man, of all people, finally turned me into a woman of faith.

"I think I'm going to be sick," I tell the Speedies as I shuffle past, a quick improv, pursing my lips and clutching my stomach. Maybe they'll tell John—"she went to throw up," covering my awkwardness in the garden. I scurry upstairs in the direction of the master bathroom. I double-check no one has followed me, and after a quick pit stop to take off my heels, I make a beeline for the final set of stairs. I crouch, hiding in the cramped walk-space in the attic, obscured from view by a million dollars' worth of art and antiques that don't fit in the house. I fumble with my phone, postponing the inevitable call. *What will I say? How do I even begin?*

"About time you called—"

"I couldn't . . . I mean I dunno what to do now. I think I'm losing my mind. It's all too crazy—"Stop!" he commands, clearly upset. "Breathe."

I try it. It works . . . sort of. To hold it together, I become an actress, reading from a script, no ad-libbing.

"What's wrong?" he asks when he thinks I'm ready.

"Matthew's gone. He's been taken," I tell that man.

"Taken?" he says slowly.

"Kidnapped. My son has been kidnapped."

It sounds flat; I'm not giving it the urgency it deserves.

"Kidnapped?"

"Yes. Taken. Kidnapped. Call it whatever the fuck you want, I don't care. I can't . . . " I don't know what else to say. I suddenly realize I'm terrible at this.

"And you know this because . . . ?" that man coaxes me.

" . . . there's a ransom note on all our phones."

"Okay," he says. He falls silent, breathing deeply into the receiver. He starts to speak, but I can't hold my tongue for even one second longer—

"No one knows what to do next. I mean they're debating the ransom note for fuck's sake, can you believe it? I want to tell them to just pay up, to do anything it takes, to forget about everything else and just get little Matthew back—"

"Slow down."

He's right. I'm talking too fast, but I need to get it all out, share my affliction, *purge*.

"Did they call the cops?" that man asks.

"They've literally done nothing. They haven't called the police, and they haven't agreed to cooperate with the kidnappers. They've just done nothing. What good is all their money if they won't use it to get their baby back? What's wrong with them? What's the matter with these people?"

I picture him listening, judging, waiting to dispense sage, intuitive (and desperately needed) advice. Please help me, I beg, imploring him (albeit telepathically) to guide me, to tell me what to do.

I screwed up, I want to tell him. I need to come clean. There's something I forgot. A fatal mistake. Long ago I said something very, very stupid that John "Total Recall" Speedy remembered and adopted as his personal, life-long credo and is now throwing back in my face as a reason not to rescue his only begotten son from a cruel, untimely death and it's all my fault, all mine. The tears come in great gasps of regret which echo in the attic. All the plans, all the pregnancy, all the gifts and agony and nights with John, not giving him what he wanted, then giving him the child, then this—

"Calm down," that man instructs, undoubtedly the two most infuriating words he could have chosen. I scream and throw the phone violently against the wall where it shatters into expensive e-waste. Sinking to my knees, I cover my eyes, and for the first time since I left the orphanage, I stop crying and pray instead.

Three disjointed and ultimately futile Heavenly F-ther's later, I look around and face the harsh reality of what I've done. I'm all alone in the attic. What's left of Phone 2 lies shattered and splintered on the floor. Like me. I try to breathe normally but my throat is tight. Constricted. My lungs close in on themselves, deflating like a pair of pierced balloons. I take short, sharp gasps— a last, desperate attempt to maintain lucidity. Every inhalation is a battle between biology and will. *How did I sink so low? Was it that night when I was fifteen? Or was it that man again? Or was I simply a victim of my own vices? A g-dless orphan in constant pursuit of an ever-elusive acceptance? Where can I possibly go from here? Only down.*

CHAPTER 56

IT'S GETTING REAL now. More real than I thought possible. Amanda is breaking. I can feel that in my bones. Over time a man develops a certain sense about women. An intuition. I've had my fair share of those feelings. I know them. I know when a woman's about to crack. I wander if it's because of me? Am I the one pushing her over the edge? Can't be. She was crazy when I met her. Come to think of it they all are. Hormonally induced insanity. That entire gender is afflicted.

Maybe that's what I like? Edging slowly up the roller coaster track. Heart pounding. Knuckles white. Waiting. Then gravity takes charge, blowing everything apart. Maybe that's the payoff. Truth be told I'm not exactly a model citizen myself. I've done some stuff I'm not proud of, but that's what keeps it exciting, right? So, whatever happens now I'm going to keep pushing. See just how far everyone is prepared to go. Especially Amanda. If you want an omelet you gotta be willing to break some eggs, right? Yeah, those precious eggs. Crack, crack, crack!

CHAPTER **57**

"I DON'T CARE what the email says, who do they think they are?" Mary-Elizabeth growls in outrage. "The last time I looked this was still America. I'm not going to just stand here while those . . . those . . . sons of you-know-whats try and extort us. I've had it, I'm calling the police." Having overcome her shock-induced inertia, my mother-in-law is now ready to assume control to protect her precious Johnny, her family, and her heir. She's prepared to show the world the Speedies aren't going to be pushed around, especially not, in her exact words: "by some low-life immigrant criminals, the kind that shouldn't have been let into our country in the first place. They ought to be lined up in front of their families and shot!"

I must say that when the designer gloves are off and the chips are down, she really is one tough broad—an impressive sixty-eight-year-old barking orders like a drill sergeant on a cocaine binge. As could be expected from the spineless minions surrounding her, her instructions are obeyed without question or exception.

Until, that is, she suggests calling the police. We all know that's a step too far. With more to lose than anyone, I grab the phone from her hand. At the top of my voice I make my stand.

"Enough! I've had enough!"

They turn to me as if they've never considered the possibility that spouses get a vote.

"Should we have consulted the mother?" is all over their faces.

"Listen, I've had it with all this bullshit. Let's just bury the useless bravado and get real," I tell them. I'm fully aware of my own sudden-onset law school swagger; they're not, but then irony is not their strong suit. "We need to put our heads together and make some impossibly difficult decisions," I press on. "To do this intelligently we need to start by agreeing to one golden rule: that regardless of how infuriated we feel, how vengeful we are, or how reckless we are prepared to be, *no matter what principles we may have expressed in the past . . .* baby Matthew's safe return should be our one and only priority."

The boys at "The D" would have been proud—my most persuasive speech to date, told with confident passion, simple and direct, convincing. *"May I have an 'Amen?'"* I add silently in my head.

CHAPTER 58

GOOD NEWS TRAVELS fast; good scandal, the speed of light. By the time I pulled my panties up, half the school knew about my session with Aaron *et al*. A heartbeat later, when the footage hit the internet, the entire school knew. And when you're fifteen, the entire school is the entire world.

All Hell broke loose.

Kayla Smithe wasn't the first to see it, but she was the angriest. She never confronted her boyfriend Marvin; that scene she saved for me, screaming obscenities at me in front of the lockers in the middle of the hallway in the middle of the school day in the middle of my adolescence. Marvin Heffel was the richest guy in high school, heir to the family hedge fund, lineage back to the May-flower. He was also the most popular and most envied—football captain, student body president, best-looking, best catch, best fucking everything. Every high school has a Marvin Heffel, right? So stupidly perfect it made you wonder if he'd sucked the Devil's dick before being born. Every high school has its Kayla, too. The archetypal princess, an object of sycophantic envy who never ever "put out," as it's so charmingly phrased. "Common knowledge" had it, dear Marvin was too respectful of Kayla to force the issue or go elsewhere. The guys thought he was nuts; the girls swooned, Prince "no-fucking" Charming. Kayla thought the same, I'm sure, the fool. In retrospect, I think it was the revelation of her own stupidity more than Marvin's wayward penis that made Kayla so angry. If Marvin Heffel had any scruples about women, they didn't apply to me. He thought he could fuck me with impunity, in the worst way (an apt description), but he couldn't just ask, could he? (Actually, I might have done it merely to cheese Kayla off—screw him and fuck her at the same time.) Hence, Marv crossed the tracks and joined up with

Aaron, who jumped at the chance to do a favor for the most popular boy on campus. *The best planned lays of mice and men . . .*

So Kayla lights into me in front of everyone, calling me all sorts of things—"skank, slut, whore"—but she doesn't have the vocabulary and runs out of words quickly. By then my head reels and suddenly I'm in a 40s movie, the spinning montage part, and it's all a blur for a minute until the newspaper stops cold with the headline, "Whore-phan!" I drop like a felled oak (I've been told), hitting the over-waxed Formica floor hard, "face-plant" the kids call it.

Kayla's on me in a second, the story goes (I was out cold, remember), giving me mouth-to- mouth while talking to 9-1-1 simultaneously between life-saving puffs of air. The ambulance arrives, Kayla is proclaimed a hero, and I'm whisked to the hospital where they outline in excruciating detail the damage my "lady parts" suffered at the hands of Marvin, Aaron, and the "black-hole-clubhouse" boys. Infection had set in, followed by toxic shock "and if your best friend Kayla hadn't jumped in when she did, young lady (slut), you'd be dead right now (you worthless skank)." *Hail Mary full of Grace, kill me now without a trace.*

Looking back, I think Kayla knew very well that Marvin was acting out for her, attacking *her* when he did those things with me, *to* me, the same way I was putting it to the sisters, especially Sister Mary Grace, rubbing their faces in it across time and space. We've all got a little Judas inside us, don't we? Ready to crush the souls of the "holier than thou" when the time is right. Or the price is right. Or is that just me?

So, bottom line, when all is said and done, at the end of the day (and other hideous old saws), Kayla saved my life and I will never forgive her for that. She dumped her perfect, cheating, two-timing boyfriend (who almost killed me, BTW, with his freaky-big hammer-dick), and ended up with Kyle Beckworth, a tenth as rich, slightly south of attractive, and as enthusiastic in bed as a coma patient (I happen to know). Did I tell her to do that? No. That was *her* choice, *her* cross to bear—like she needed an extra one.

After the hospital stay, with the encouragement (insistence) of the Staffords, I transferred out for a while to somewhere no one knew me. Knew her. Knew *it*. My last two years of high school were served in silent severance at a boarding school, then state college, then Talbord Law. I bore *my* cross with equal measures of pride and shame, alone. In defiant moods I donned revealing outfits designed to flaunt my body and flout convention. In other, darker moments, I cried silently in my room, pillow pulled over my head, wishing I were somewhere else, someone else, repenting and remembering, wondering how I could have been so easily manipulated, so gullible, so in love. I vowed, between muted sobs, that I would never again give my heart away.

And thus were they created, and thus were they destined, each one, the Madonna and the whore . . .

I still have it—the video. Actually, plural, *videos*, since all four of the guys whipped out their phones at some point or another. I watch the (very raw) footage sometimes when I'm alone, to remember that day and remind myself what people are capable of. What *I'm* capable of, for one, but especially what men are capable of. But me too, the poster child for innocence, trust, and naivety.

I also use the videos to orgasm (as have countless others, I'm sure). You can still find the clips on the internet if you know where to look for illegal, underage porn, which most people don't, including the Speedies. It's there on the dark web under "blonde." Or "teen." Or "gangbang." Or "group." Or "interracial." Or simply "Catholic schoolgirl gets railed hard." (The "railed" is accurate, the "Catholic" is not BTW.) A true overachiever, I'm all seven of the top search results. There's nothing that gets you off like it being *you*, with young, healthy guys you once knew, a shared experience, messy and seminal, no pun intended, getting fucked in front of the world.

Sanity and sexuality, love and lust, power and control—not wide roads easy to navigate, but tightropes, fragile and unforgiving. Each of us has a secret box in the attic of our souls where we hide our most intimate desires: wide eyes, bound arms, wet lips, naked bodies, deep kisses, open legs, endless embraces, pleasured moans, and multiple penetrations. It's a box which once unlocked, can never again be sealed. All those years

I managed to relegate the box and its pornographic contents to the depths of my subconscious. Until I found that man.

CHAPTER 59

THE HOUSE IS moving, pacing, fidgeting. Anything to avoid stillness. Despite the contrived motion, no one is talking. The scene unfolds like a screwball farce à la Charlie Chaplin—frantic action without sound, not even a scratchy score played on an upright piano. Up and down stairs, in and out of rooms, movement for movement's sake, as if the continuum of time itself could glean a sense of urgency from the incessant perambulation, so with that in mind, we speed up to relieve the unbearable pain of impotent anticipation.

All conversation is perfunctory: "Are you going outside?" "Would anyone like coffee?" And my own personal favorite, "Everything will be okay." Platitudes, the verbal equivalent of paralysis. *Will* everything be okay? No, I don't believe it will, thank you. In fact, I can't envision any outcome that won't prove, in one way or another, to be completely catastrophic.

I need a reprieve. Like an addict craving her fix, I need to see that man. He's the only one who will know what to say, what to do. My once-balanced temperament is eroding fast, flitting across the invisible line that separates panic from mania.

"I'm going out," I announce to everyone and no one at once. As expected, there are no objections, just a blank stare from John accompanied by a round of zombielike nods from the staff. I grab my keys and escape. I drive fast on the freeway, recklessly, a woman with Astrovan skills behind the wheel of a Maserati. I have nothing to lose. My foot inches closer to the floor. The speedometer climbs. I pop a Xanax and all is better. "Money, Money, Money" blasts from the speakers. ABBA's irresistible harmonizing helps me, once again, to see the light immersed in a hundred decibels of Bose acoustic adrenaline—finger-tapping, blood-pumping, heart-thumping escape. It's exactly what I need.

As the anthem relentlessly chronicles the quintessential American dream, I sing too, loudly and deliberately out of tune, bellowing "Money," strained voice scarcely audible over the combined discord of music and engine. The little white pill puts me into a pharmaceutically induced Zen with remarkable speed. But then an unwanted reinterpretation of the lyrics cuts through me like a scalpel. Are they being ironic? Deriding my prized capitalist ideal? The notion infuriates me. How dare these platinum-selling Swedes pass judgment. They don't know me.

They don't know what I've been through. Have they ever been without? Did they spend their formative years sleeping two to a bed? Childhood mornings shoulder-to-shoulder kneeling on a cold church floor? Eating their meals from tin plates, sharing discarded food with discarded children? Their words tear into my flesh, revealing the soft, vulnerable tissue underneath. My body opens up and my soul bleeds. Is that what this whole thing is really all about? Money? Yes, precisely what I need to end this nightmare. Why won't John just pay up? I slam my fists into the horn. And sob.

"You wanna toke?" That man sits in a red leather chair, rocking slowly, and drawing on a masterfully hand-rolled joint. "Take a hit; it'll chill you out, trust me." His apathy is unbearable; I lose control. The well-appointed vase standing idly near the door makes for a convenient weapon-of-release. I grab it, fresh roses in place, and hurl it across Apartment 307. My target: his smug, smoky head. The projectile is made of thick porcelain, and if it finds its mark, will certainly cause some visually satisfying damage. I will it to hit, cut his face wide open, tear skin from bone. I want to see him bleed and cry and beg. Time stands still as we follow its trajectory with our eyes, pointlessly trying to estimate where it will land. I watch exasperated as it flies past its intended target before colliding with a totally innocent bronze bronco sculpture beyond. For a split second that man is silent, then, "Great shot—I hated that fuckin' horse."

We laugh, bordering on hysteria.

"I'll take that hit now," I tell that man.

The first time I smoked weed was with Aaron the night before our "adventure." Aaron insisted that he, personally, would teach me how to blaze. How benevolent. We took his father's Jeep (moon roof, red leather seats) through the San Fernando Valley to pick up the stuff. With one hand on the wheel, his other hand kneaded my thigh, circling towards my sex. I fixated on his lips, how they separated slightly when he breathed. In that moment he filled my entire world. There was no space for anything else, anything that wasn't Aaron. I was electrified, nervous, and completely amenable—the quintessential fifteen-year-old rebel with "high" expectations.

"Big A . . . "

"Yeah?"

I wasn't really sure how to say it. Ever since I learned how to rub myself, I craved the guilty pleasure of touch. I couldn't say all that, not right then, not to Aaron.

" . . . I need it. Now," I said, simplifying.

Aaron understood. He pulled over. He licked me, the first time I'd ever had a mouth between my legs, although I'd imagined it often. I probably should have been embarrassed, or at the least, modest. I was neither. I spread myself as wide as I could, open and wanting, willing his hungry, darting tongue ever deeper. I pushed myself against his head and held him tightly while I ground my slippery, almost hairless body against his face. The result was even more than I expected.

Afterwards, in an unusual display of tenderness, he kissed me, affording me the sensual pleasure of tasting myself on his lips.

Later, (second) mission accomplished, dope in hand, with the moon rising through the trees and Bob Marley chanting hypnotically in the evening air, I was in adolescent Eden. Paradise found.

"So, what do you think they're gonna do?"

I can't tell if that man is truly concerned. As always, he's a puzzle. However, I realize now that I trust him more than I want to, definitely more than I first intended. As I'm about to answer, my phone (#1) vibrates . . . loudly . . . rattling against the glass table like a poisonous snake, derailing my train of thought. The caller's name, "Mary-Elizabeth Speedy," scrolls across the small screen, too long to remain both static and legible within the allotted space. She used to appear on my phone as "Inheritance-in-law," but John, after a pretty good chuckle, insisted I change it. I thumb the glowing-green answer-button, shut my eyes, frozen, acutely aware of my body, breath, pulse, heartbeat. *Speak, damn you. Say something.*

"Hi, Mary-Elizabeth, I'm just picking up things at the store. Have you heard . . . " but before I can continue, her piercing, incoherent howls tell me something horrifying has happened. I shake violently, uncontrollably. I run to the bathroom to throw up. Without explaining (I don't *have* an explanation), I leave that man alone with his weed and that mysterious grin on his face. It's been thirty-six hours since the note arrived—

I sprint to my car, then back to that man's apartment.

"You know something, don't you?" I demand. "Tell me. Tell me now."

From the same chair, same position, wearing the same smirk, he says, "It'll be all right," exactly what John would say it, which should infuriate me but instead sends me down a long, dark abyss of helplessness. *Passive aggressive and stiff-upper-lipped. I sure know how to pick 'em.*

"Go now." He motions to the door. "Call me later."

"I can't," I admit.

"Why not?"

"My other phone . . . "

"You broke it, didn't you? Like the horse." I won't answer that. *None of your business.*

Besides, the horse is bronze. The horse can't break. The vase, the womanly object, the one with the figure— stacked in fact—it broke into a hundred pieces. That man points to an ornamental *escritoire* on the way to the kitchen. "Top drawer," he says. I follow his finger. A half-dozen phones sit in the drawer—I have no idea why. "Take one."

I grab a phone and get out of there as fast as I can. The drive home is psychological torture of the highest order. With total disregard for my safety I flaunt every traffic law imaginable and arrive back at 16 Oak at breakneck speed. As soon as I walk in I see it.

The box.

They're screaming, every g-ddamn one of them, robbed forever of their privileged-induced naïveté by the severed hand of a two-week-old infant lying silently inside *the box*, shattering the entire world. I'm screaming, too, louder than any of them. *What the fuck?* How someone could do that is inconceivable. The thought devastates like a stray bullet ricocheting around my skull.

"Why, Jesus, why?" John bawls, on his knees, surrounded by his siblings, also wailing, a chorus with Mary-Elizabeth, shoved mercilessly over the edge of sanity by the contents of a slightly beat-up, neon-orange Nike box, size nine.

John passes out, face-forward onto the cold, stone floor.

LAMENTATIONS
CHAPTER 60

WHEN MY CHILDHOOD friend Melissa died, I was there at her bedside. I watched her spirit leave her body. Her eyes emptied before me. The life that once filled her mortal frame escaped. In its place, a thin, gaunt shell of human skin lay where breath and blood once flowed. I recognize that same emptiness in John when he comes to, just barely, no longer able to form words, only sounds, wails of pain. They cut through the night, touching us all. Faced with the stark reality of the package, what could he say? What could anyone say? It was just *there*.

A *tiny hand*.

Severed at the wrist, clutching a rattle, boxed up like an old pair of sneakers, soaked in blood and left to rot in its cardboard coffin. Unthinkable. Unmistakable. Unbearable. Surrounded by screams, I close my eyes, take a handful of white pills from the vial in my pocket and spirit myself away, first to the master bedroom, then to the land of lucid dreaming. I am acutely aware that I'm neither asleep nor awake, and that in the recesses of my mind I have conjured this reality into existence. Theoretically, I should be a goddess reveling in my omnipotence, understanding that everything surrounding me is nothing more than a construct of my imagination. Yet I feel just as powerless to effect outcomes here as I do in the real world. Baby Matthew floats above me, laughing loudly, obnoxiously. His body is plump, puffy, and two-fisted, bobbing around like an overinflated helium balloon threatening to tear open at the seams. With every inhalation his torso distends slightly. I'm terrified he's going to pop, but before I can do anything, my (biological) mother—who I've never met, but who I recognize instantly—appears out of nowhere to save the day. Quickly and decisively, with the help of an invisible cord, she pulls Matthew towards her, to safety, to love.

"I've always been right here with you, you know that, don't you? No matter what, you will always be a part of me," she says. *Now she tells me . . .*

My hands and feet are bare and warm. I begin to glow. My mother is impossibly beautiful. Her skin is pale. She has thick, dark hair and piercing green eyes. When we touch, her hands are as hot as mine. I've never felt so at peace.

"Liar!" baby Matthew screams down at me. "Liar, liar, pants on fire. Slutty, smutty, truth denier." My extremities tighten. My mother gazes at me, into me. Her eyes narrow and darken. I try to explain, to defend myself. It's no use. She turns away and whispers something to her man—my father, I know it. He listens, cringing, behind her, supporting her, waiting patiently. With a nod, he agrees with what she says, her secret revealed. I'm desperate to know, too—to be "in on it"—but when I try asking, the words muddle. I shake my head, trying frantically to spew out questions I've kept inside for so long. It's no use. My voice is lost, drowned in the roar of apathy. Mute and petrified, I cry silent tears and watch as baby Matthew floats away. I shrink into myself. I look at my family one last time. Then it's all over. I know I will never see any of them again. I lurch back into wakefulness, jumping to my feet, rattling my head and shaking my arms fiercely.

"Amanda, Amanda, wake up. It's another one of your nightmares." John's feeble voice does little to comfort me. He, too, has been crying. His eyes are puffy and bloodshot. Tormented.

Tortured. His face betrays his suffering, and a pain no father, no person, should ever know. He's

been ripped open, exposing a gaping, dark, yawning abyss. Words are futile. I wish I were asleep again.

"The hand?" I ask, hoping.

"The hand is real," John tells me. "The box is real. Matthew's hand is inside the box." He says it like a children's book—Bobby and Shelly again, Dick and Jane.

"See Matt's hand. See the rattle. See the box. See Matt's hand bleed. See Matt's hand bleed in the box."

It's a nightmare, but it's also real. We both know it. I claw back to sleep. Paradise lost.

CHAPTER **61**

NOTHING WILL EVER be the same. From this point on, we are, each one of us, shattered mirrors, reflecting only the damage. I feel invisible. Like a ghost. If my life were a movie, I wouldn't have any role at all.

"Cut, cut, what's she doing? Will someone please take her script away. Honey, this isn't a speaking part. Just lay there dead still; we'll tell you when we're done with you."

The camera zooms in. A choker shot. My head lies flat on the table, face obscured, hidden from sight by a tangled mess of platinum blonde hair. As the camera cranes over me, I'm looking upward. Soft, filtered lighting delineates my ruffled silhouette and exposes my wide, hopeless eyes. A bass-baritone voice intones:

"She did this to herself. Believe it or not, she was once our heroine. She had it all. Tragically, she gave it all away. This is her sad story."

The film cuts to Rodeo Drive. I walk, hair perfect, wearing a tailored Gucci suit and heels.

Killer looks. On the bottom of the screen in bold white typeface: "ONE YEAR EARLIER."

Once again my thoughts drift to him. To the night at the bar. That man. Why did I have to pull him back into my life? People, present company included, whether acting deliberately or not, will inevitably seek out ways to complicate their simple lives, constantly searching, seeking something unfamiliar and new, something *more*.

Or something once possessed, now lost—that was me.

Why can't we just be satisfied?

The night Melissa died, we were in her bedroom where we had danced, drank, talked, smoked, and laughed our childhood nights away. The space seemed tight and claustrophobic that night, unlike before. We had both accepted the truth: she was near the end.

"I'll miss you, Mel. I'll think about you every day. I promise," I told her.

She glared at me, the hardened, ice-cold stare of someone who knows, and I shivered. I bowed my head, praying silently that I hadn't crossed an invisible line.

"Don't you dare miss me. You're still gonna be here and I'll be gone. Don't you get it?

Nothing I've done really matters. But you, you can still matter." She took my hand and squeezed it forcefully, punctuating her words with physical pressure. "You can matter to someone." The way she looked at me, I wonder if she meant *her*, that I mattered to *her*—

"Not *me*," she declared, pushing my hand away. "Not *friends*. Forget about friends. Friends are for dumb people and kids. Just grow up and . . . " she started to cry " . . . and love. Just love someone. And let them love you. Trust me, in the end, that's the only thing that'll matter."

CHAPTER **62**

JOHN'S ALONE IN the living room. The others have gone home, or they may be lurking. Now more than ever I need to remain alert and entirely present. No more Xanax, whisky, pot. I sit down next to my husband, take his hand and squeeze it tightly.

"John, listen to me," I say. "You can still save him. You can still save Matthew. You can do it, John; you can be a hero, *my* hero. We both know it's up to you. Do the right thing, please. I'm begging you. Forget about what I said back then at that stupid debate, or what everyone will think, or what they'll say. Who cares? Just think about Matthew. It's only money. What difference does it make?"

"Pay them," he mutters. "That's what you're saying."

"Yes. Exactly."

"Maybe you didn't hear. Maybe you weren't around." The snarky way he says it makes me think he's suspicious of my absences— "Maybe you weren't aware that they doubled the ransom."

I gasp involuntarily. This is no act.

"That's right," John tells me like a knife to my heart.

"Over half a billion dollars. Six hundred million to be exact. Just about the entire Speedy fortune."

"Shit! Shit!" I exclaim. "Damn it!"

John stares at me like he doesn't understand why I'm reacting this way.

"It's our whole future, isn't it?" I stutter. "Your Senate campaign. Everything. It's the money for that."

John looks at me, no indication that he doesn't completely believe my dismay. But there's also a puzzlement there, something off the subject, a side-issue—

"Your father?" I ask. "Maybe he could pitch in?" John spits out a bitter laugh.

"Not a dime. Not if I run for the Senate, which I *will*, damnit! And as a Democrat—it's the only way I have a chance to win."

I stare, not sure I understand.

"'Over my dead body'—that's what he said. Mom, too," John told me. I didn't know. "Just because you're a Democrat?" I ask naively.

He scowls, glaring at me like I've just asked the dumbest question he's ever heard. Who knows, maybe I *have* just asked the dumbest question he's ever heard. I guess I have a lot to learn.

"You think you know everything, don't you?" he accuses in a tone of voice I don't recognize. I don't answer, taking it for a rhetorical question, but maybe I'm mistaken. "You still want me to pay up?"

I confirm it. I do. I still want him to pay. It's too much, way too much, a huge tactical error on the kidnappers' part, but I still want John to pay. He says something but I don't understand it. *I want this over with, once and for all.* John talks again; I can't hear. Maybe it's the pills. *Why did it have to come to this?* Somewhere little Matthew is crying. This isn't what I signed up for. I should just end it. After all, I considered doing that once before, a long time ago, after *that night,* sitting naked in my bathtub, pushing the scissors into my wrist and spilling the first drops of blood, thinking about my parents, the Sisters, Jill Stafford, Melissa, and of course, Aaron—all the while knowing I would never go through with it. Now, crippled by my emotions and watching the hapless entourage dart around 16 Oak like rodents with the plague, a part of me wishes I had finished the job.

"Is it? Answer me, damn you, is it?" John's frantic. Yelling. The question is obviously directed towards me, but I'm somewhere else entirely. Not there with him. Not present. He wants something. He wants me to answer a question, this one not rhetorical, which needs my answer, but I have no idea what it is. *Is it what?* He's proved his point—I *haven't* been paying attention. The voice in my head mimics my debate coach: "Concentrate. Throw yourself into the performance. Be strong. you can do this."

My husband's lips are so close to my face I can taste the breath from his unbrushed teeth.

Once again, louder and now also staccato:

"Answer—the—fucking—question— *Is it?*" The words are hard and cold, launched at me like dull, steel cannonballs. I can't speak. I have no idea what to say. Confused, I let the tears run down my cheeks. "So this whole thing is my fault?" His eyes are volcanic. "Is that what you're saying? That you knew we should have paid them. Before. When it was half as much and Matthew had both hands? Well, you must be happy now. Are you? Are you happy now?" He slaps me. Hard. He's never struck me before, never even come close. It hurts.

More than I imagined it would. Maybe I deserve it. That's what they all say, right? All the abused women. I'm spent, confused, pained, and regretful. I want to apologize, to tell him about that man, the whole damn story. Instead I squeeze my eyes shut and swallow the salty tears. The John I know is lost. The new John, the lesser John, the wife-beater John, drops to his knees. He wraps his arms around my legs and pulls his head towards my thighs. "I'm sorry, I'm so sorry. What have I done? What have we done?" I don't know the answer. It's all a wreck. What have "we" done? Why the "we?"

. . . *And upon the sinner shall I exact My Judgment, a tooth for a tooth, an eye for an eye.*

"Pay them," I tell John, my answer to everything now. "Quickly," I tell him. *Be Speedy, Mr.*

Speedy—for once in your life, be Speedy.

"Pay them, pay them, pay them," John repeats. "Jesus, what kind of a father am I? Matthew, Matthew." He pauses, inhales, and summons the beast inside. "MATTHEW!" he roars. I shudder as the word echoes around me, through me, resounding off the arched ceiling and ricocheting from the walls. Mary-Elizabeth has indeed been lurking, along with Raymond, Sylvia, and Mike. They rush in like little white lab mice.

There are phone calls. Emails. Senator Speedy (D-CA) has spoken. The money machine fires up. 16 Oak transforms from a single-family residence to Fort Bragg. General Jonathan Speedy conscripts the entire household to action. "Operation Recover Matthew" has officially commenced. A DNA lab is contacted. The box is whisked away by private courier for analysis— rush job, spare no expense. Family swabs are taken. On General John's instructions, no police nor any other trained law-enforcement are called. Instead, Harrison James, the family's attorney ($5,000 an hour plus expenses), arrives on the scene. If pacing up and down was the key to remedying the crisis, Harrison's incessant marching would have already fixed it all. Matte-black phone glued to his ear, he barks instructions at his underlings and sweats profusely into his standard issue, pin-striped Brioni suit and Harvard tie. The ransom is both obscene and possibly impossible; even the Speedies don't have that kind of cash on hand. Things need to be sold, accounts liquidated, money borrowed. A legion of bankers, brokers and accountants is mobilized and sworn to secrecy on pain of death.

John's role is suddenly reduced from Commander-in-Chief to pitiful bystander, following Harrison around like a seventh-grade schoolboy with a guy-crush. The staff, for their part, along with me and the rest of the family, perform a delicate balancing act between appearing busy and disappearing altogether. The unmistakable order of chaos.

I'm still crying anyway, processing the extent of the damage. Then, an announcement: "The money's been sent," Harrison states for all to hear. He pulls out a handkerchief and mops his perspiring face in recognition of the staggering amount: $600,000,000. "All we can do now is wait . . . and pray." Harrison delivers the line like he's waiting for the members of the Academy of Arts and Sciences to scurry out from behind a curtain and place a shiny gold Oscar into his puffy pink hands. "Wow, this is heavier than it looks," he beams, shedding his perpetually smug demeanor, donning a phony, child-like humility, thanking "Mom, who always believed in me." (Which isn't true.) Despite his personality (or lack thereof) everyone likes Harrison. More importantly, we trust him. When he says the money's been sent, it has. When he says pray, we probably should.

CHAPTER 63

DOUBLING DOWN ON the ransom is absolutely the craziest thing I have ever done in my life, and I've done some g-ddamn crazy things, trust me! I never thought of myself as a gambler, but that's exactly what I am. I'm looking across the table at the other man's cards. They're face down and I have no idea. What I do know is that there's more than a half billion at stake, and I'm all-in on a stone-cold bluff. Of course, in addition to the cards, I can't see my opponent's face, either. Maybe a good thing. He's already shown himself to be a master of masquerade, predictably unpredictable. I have Amanda to look at, though, if I can manage to keep my eyes up above those spectacular tits, ha ha. Maybe I've been able to read her, maybe not. Who knows anymore? She's good, damn good, but she's also got those same tits in the wringer, which makes her unreliable, untrustworthy, eager, and dangerous. She's played too many cards at too many tables, always for herself, or am I wrong about that, even after all this time? That's the thing about love and gambling—the only real winners are those willing to risk it all.

CHAPTER **64**

16 OAK LANE is broken, awash with anxiety and consumed by a thick tension. We are passengers on a sinking ship, alive but helpless, waiting seated, still and respectful, until we bottom out and drown. Each of us is on trial, charged with crimes we didn't commit, praying the jury rules in our favor.

"Have you reached a verdict?"

"We have, your honor."

"What say you?"

"In the matter of Speedies vs. Anonymous Child Abductors, we find in favor of—"

"Let him in, NOW!" The delicate subtleties of The Voice have abandoned John entirely. His tone is raw, pitched, and pained. We watch, spellbound, as the motion-sensitive monitors pan to a six-foot-four FedEx delivery man (clad in a comically tight khaki uniform) striding up the drive. His carefree gait reminds me of how bright the world can be. As for the neon-orange shoe-box peeking out from under his bulging arm, that reminds us all of something much darker.

John sprints down the drive like the Olympic trails, a heroic effort designed to save both precious seconds and our increasingly precarious sanity at the same time.

"John Poody?"

"Yes, give me that," John snaps, ignoring the mispronunciation, lunging for the package. "You need to sign for it, *sir*," the delivery man tells John, holding the box out of reach with his outrageous wingspan.

John snatches at it—"Give it to me, you idiot—"

But the delivery man is experienced at this sort of thing, relishes it even, making no effort to disguise a delighted smirk. It's been weeks since he's made a rich asshole squirm like this.

"*Sir*, I'm going to have to ask you to sign for this. Otherwise I'm required to take it back to the regional distribution center in Santa Clarita, where you can pick it up Monday morning, window hours posted on our website. No, wait, Monday is a holiday—"

The CRACK is audible, even from inside the mansion, where we watch through double-pane windows. The speed and accuracy of the blow indicate those stories about John's boxing days at Harvard might have had some truth to them after all. John snatches the box from under the sleeping giant and viciously rips it to pieces. Something small and red bounces out and onto the driveway. We try to understand what it is from the expression on John's face, which gives us nothing. Then his brow furrows and his lip curls ever-so-slightly. He's both relieved and slightly confused. Watching from inside the house, the Speedy family and I and the entire staff echo the sentiment. It's not another body part. We'll take that. We'll live with anything else. Anything but *that*.

John reaches down and retrieves a cheap, red, plastic, flash drive and—*Heaven-be-blessed*—nothing else. John turns to the house, while behind, the FedEx man jerks straight up into the air to a violin screech like the not-yet-dead villain of every horror movie ever made—

"Look out, John!" we scream, just enough warning for John to take off running (he lettered in cross-country, too), through the side gate with the angry, growling, bent-on-murder delivery monster at his heels. The FedExinator (ex-linebacker, Marine, UFC heavyweight contender?) closes in, dives forward, and tackles John on the run, propelling them both into the enormous, polyp-shaped swimming pool—34,000 gallons—the flash drive sailing in the direction of the skimmer—

We rush out—

"The basket will catch it!" Raymond declares, a sudden export on all things "swimming pool."

But he's wrong—the blue basket floats up from its receptacle propelled by the churning of the water caused by the continuing melee, John v. FedEx, round 2. The drive dives, like a little red scuba man, under the basket, vacuumed into the underground pipe, headed for the filter pump, 3.0 horsepower of suck in a tight, perfectly engineered package.

"I'll get it!" Raymond assures everyone, running for the pump, hidden behind a row of manicured hedges. We hear a quick grinding sound and a scream—Raymond's. The pump whirring stops and Raymond reappears holding a smaller basket, the one supposed to sit inside the pump, the last safety point ahead of the grinding vanes of the vicious steel impeller. "Somebody forgot to put the basket back . . . " he states miserably.

We don't quite understand, but we know it's not good news, and that somehow Big Jay's Pool and Spa Service (whose stickers are all over everything) is at fault, letting us down horribly.

Meanwhile the battle of the deep end continues in slow motion, both combatants swinging, the water inhibiting any real damage. It's John who realizes first that throwing punches isn't nearly as effective as drowning his opponent. The FedEx man, to his credit, discovers that by moving slightly toward the shallow end he can use both his height and his superior reach to advantage, feet solidly on the bottom while John flails uselessly against the delivery man's straight-arm hold on John Speedy's neck.

We watch, fascinated, more curious than upset, as John's face turns a rather unsettling shade of red, then blue. Sister Sylvia, a strong advocate of non-violence, sighs and shakes her head as she sinks wearily into a nearby lawn chair. Brother Mike cheers John on, pantomiming, shouting "left, right, uppercut, get him!" like a crowd-extra in a 30s boxing film.

Thoroughly disgusted, having seen enough, Mother Mary-Elizabeth pulls out a revolver, old school, a tiny, ivory-handled "ladies model" she's had hidden in a secret pocket of her dress (I learn) ever since I've known her.

"Enough!" she commands, followed by a single deafening blast into the air, which catches everyone's attention.

"Mother . . . " Raymond huffs. He doesn't approve. Mary-Elizabeth turns in his direction. He moves back behind the hedge.

The gunshot, a violation of several local ordinances, nevertheless has the desired effect. The FedEx man, realizing he might have pushed it a little too far this time, climbs the stairs out of the pool like The Creature from the Black Lagoon.

John, from the safety of the deep end (heated to a perfect seventy-seven degrees Fahrenheit, comfortable but still refreshing), yells at the man mercilessly as the soaked driver edges by Mary-Elizabeth and keeps a sharp eye on the pistol at her side. Talking trash like Scottie Pippen, she stays right in the delivery man's face—Anna Wintour meets Rocky Balboa—bobbing and weaving on six-inch stilettos. I'm concurrently gobsmacked by her audacity and genuinely petrified there's going to be more of what is politely referred to as "gunplay."

To everyone's relief, the FedEx man makes it back to his truck safely, older and wiser, therapy in his future.

Raymond and John—after a short confab—decide not to call Big Jay of Big Jay's Pool and Spa Service—"he's done enough damage already, thank you"—opting instead to instruct the chauffeur to tear the pool filter tank apart while Raymond and John (the two least likely people to ever have engaged in manual labor) offer DIY advice. At the bottom of the thing, sifted from the muck of soaked diatomaceous earth, the chauffeur salvages six separate pieces of metal and plastic—what was once the red flash drive, purported to be the precious, sacred instructions to retrieving young one-handed Matthew Speedy, heir to the family fortune, alive.

"Judy," John hops on the phone, calling the office, "it's me. I need you to call that guy . . .

Black . . . Blake . . . you know the guy—from tech support. Send him over to 16 Oak, and for Heaven's sake tell him to drive fast—I will pay the damn speeding tickets. It's an emergency, got it?"

Mary-Elizabeth, John, the staff, the brothers and sister, Harrison James (back again and on the clock) and me—a gallery of morbid, anxious, and useless bystanders—crowd like inquisitive schoolchildren around the computer in John's office. The fact that none of us have the foggiest idea of how a flash drive is supposed to function doesn't stop us from staring in unspoken awe as "Blake," the short, skinny, quick-fingered, Indian-American engineer (name-tag Vihaan Balakrishnan) plies his trade. His dexterity and laser-like focus give me the distinct feeling that if he can't resurrect the fractured data, no one can. He's the epitome of "cool under pressure," sipping lukewarm tea, responding to unrelated texts, entirely unbothered by the breathless audience. He pauses and cracks his knuckles. In the next stage of the delicate operation, Vihaan dares attach the tiny outboard flash drive—hobbled together with Superglue and a prayer—to John's giant, state-of-the-art desktop computer. The mega-screen comes alive and the machine emits a deep, promising whir. But despite Vihaan's relentless cheerleading and attacks on the keyboard, the screen remains unresponsive. He furrows his brow and whispers what I assume to be impolite words in Hindi, then, like all touchy performers, blames the audience.

"Don't all be looking at me at once! You people are making me crazy!" We back away and huddle in the hall.

"Is this guy any good?" Raymond wants to know.

"*He* thinks he is," Sylvia purrs.

"Maybe he's overestimated his skills, or the damage to the data, or both," Mike suggests.

Again, the Speedies say things with no basis in fact. *They'll do fine in Washington,* I can't help thinking. Whatever the case, Vihaan is furiously cursing in the other room, in English and what we guess to be either Hindi or Urdu.

"Or some other Ganges River gibberish," Mary-Elizabeth sneers.

"Are you fucking kidding me?" John bursts out. "I've had it with this." Far behind the rest of us, John has run out of patience. He charges back into his office and yells, "Leave the damn thing alone! I'm calling the FBI!"

The hacker throws his hands in the air, perfectly happy to walk away—

"We'll let the *experts* handle this," John declares, the supreme insult. Vihaan turns to John and delivers his Hollywood blockbuster moment: "You can call fucking Batman if you want, mister, but this thing is completely fucked. You fucked it. All your information—it is now dead." He steps away, mumbles something to Harrison—possibly an address where to send his Oscar— and storms out of the room.

All eyes turn to Harrison James, awaiting a report of what the disgruntled computer expert had to say . . .

"I'm afraid it's broken," Harrison finally notes, reiterating the obvious. "There is nothing we can do now but wait."

Izabella sobs.

"Why they not give the baby back?" she wants to know. "What they want? Mr. John pay them, yes? So why the baby's not back?" No one dares answer. Instead we exchange pathetic glances and pray, silently, for her heart-wrenching tears to end.

"I'll call someone else," John says, taking out his phone. "He's not the only computer genius at the genius bar." John wanders off and Harrison goes with him to speak with him privately. I watch, worried, wishing to be the proverbial fly—

My new phone vibrates. I turn away.

"Phone now," that man is texting.

Then, in the midst of all the chaos, Mrs. Mary-Elizabeth Speedy, heiress, socialite and church-going Protestant, does something particularly unexpected. She tries to connect, touching me, making me jump. I bury the phone message in a pocket. Looking at me dead-on and pressing her palm against my cheek, Liz opens up:

"Listen to me, my dear, I know this is an impossibly difficult time for all of us but . . . " her eyes are dull and moist. "I want you to know something . . . " She strokes me gently. I feel her palm tremble, wet with perspiration. "I want you to know I love you." She's weeping now, visibly vulnerable for the first time since I've known her. In this singular moment, we are family at last. "I need you to be brave now, my darling daughter. To stay strong. We all love you so very much. We always have. No matter what happens, as long as we stay together and put our faith in the Lord and each other we will get through it, I know we will." She's so uncharacteristically candid, I physically recoil. Honestly, I want to reciprocate, to say, "I love you, too," but before I have the chance, *she's* back, the *real* Mary-Elizabeth, the Speedy, with a capital "B." "And if it doesn't go well," she continues, "you can give me another grandson, I know you can," as if Matthew had never existed.

Oh well, too bad about Matthew—time to move on.

It ought to be the final straw, but rather than enraged, I feel vindicated. *Really Mary- Elizabeth? Do you really know for certain I can give you another grandchild? Do you honestly not know anything at all? Did you ever consider you might be wrong? That perhaps all is not what it seems? Remember, even Jesus himself was once mortally betrayed.*

CHAPTER **65**

"YOU THINK I care what happens anymore?" John rants. "I don't! They think I'm a pushover, huh. They're going to see a different side of me now. When I find the sons-of-bitches that did this I'm going to—What the hell are you all looking at? You people. You fucking useless people." John has finally snapped. He roams aimlessly from room to room, his licensed .38 cocked, loaded, and dangling carelessly by his side. It seems all the Speedies are packing firearms today. Slightly cooler heads prevail and John does not, in fact, call the FBI, nor any other law enforcement agency, nor the Army, Navy, Air Force nor Marines, though all are mentioned. I can see Mary-Elizabeth is worried sick for my hubby, John, her second son. The only thing preventing her from calling the psychiatric ward is the possibility of his institutionalization. Safe and sane? They come in a distant second weighed against tarnishing the esteemed family name.

"Here's the thing about becoming a Speedy," Mary-Elizabeth told me the night before my wedding, "there will be those who love you and those who hate you, those who revere you and those who despise you, but no matter what they think, you should pay them no mind. You need to realize that from the moment you say 'I do,' and for the rest of your life, you will always be a Speedy, and they won't. You need to remember that, dear. We, the Speedies, are different, and the family name always comes first."

CHAPTER **66**

THE SUSPENSE IS killing me. I don't understand why she won't just talk to me. We've gone this far down the road together. Don't I deserve better than the cold shoulder? What do the kids call it? "Ghosting?" Why's she ghosting me? We could have worked it out. We could have come up with something agreeable to her and me and the whole fucking Speedy family for that matter. I fear it's the ransom. The double ransom. I worry I'm being punished for that. I need to explain it to her. It was a spur of the moment thing. There was no time to consult. But the decision itself was the correct one, the more I think about it. Unless it drives us apart. I wanted just the opposite. Damn it, that's all I've wanted, for us to be together.

CHAPTER 67

I WANT TO sleep, but I can't. I want to give up, but I won't. Mary-Elizabeth, on the other hand, passes out in a lumpy, wrinkled ball next to the fireplace where she's been dozing restlessly for hours. Her arrhythmic snoring is a rusty metronome, incessant and grating. Fascinated, I watch her ancient body quiver. Every now and then she lets out a protracted groan. Troubled dreams—I know them well. John, near the edge of sanity, augments his gun-toting rants with over-poured single malt Scotches and loud, intermittent wails.

Big brother Raymond has found himself a book to read from the library. I would ask him the title, but he might tell me, and then try to engage me in conversation. I can't risk it. "Bored to death" is a real thing, you know, with astounding fatality rates. How he can read at a time like this, I'll never know. I keep an eye on him, nevertheless, making sure he's moving his eyes and turning pages and not just faking the whole thing, pretending to be literate, which would be a typical Speedy move, as I'm sure you're well aware by now.

John's sister, Sylvia, is missing in action, making phone calls, texting, emailing, Facebooking, Tweeting, Instagramming, whatever the latest format is. I'm surprised she's not podcasting live 24/7. How she does this without revealing that her two-week-old nephew has been kidnapped, had his hand cut off, and may never be heard from again because the flash drive "battle of the deep end" is a puzzle for the ages. I suspect she's leaked things, not enough to jeopardize the child's life, possibly, only enough to impress her various audiences of the seriousness of her own situation. When I suggest maybe she should have a child-heir of her own, she howls laughter.

"Oh, you're a Speedy now, aren't you?" she accuses, knowing full well I never will be, seeing right through me (she thinks). I let that one rest.

Little brother Mike divides his time between solo rounds of hacky sack—which I did not know was still a thing—and crossword puzzles, video games, and sneaking out to the garden to smoke, snort, or partake of whatever makes him an entirely different person each time he returns inside.

I despair of ever speaking to that man again and it's making me crazy. In fact, we've all, in our own ways, left rationality by the roadside. Even the house staff (who have elevated subtle avoidance of eye contact to an art form) appear conspicuously close to complete collapse.

And He doth test his flock, with a hardened hand, lest they will abandon their faith.

I need to stay awake. I must intercept the FedEx man or postman or UPS person. We can't afford to repeat the pool-battle fiasco. DNA results are expected, which will tell us if the hand is in fact "kin" or not—personal information that can't be transmitted electronically for fear of an unintentional HIPAA "personal privacy" violation (aka protecting the company's ass). Battling fatigue and watching the household disintegrate into absurdity, I feel myself falling into the Speedy family malaise, disappearing, descending down the rabbit hole, the one I dug with my own two hands, and wish I hadn't.

To get to my bedroom, I'm forced to pass the nursery, empty, the skylight perfectly illuminating the oversized, eerily lifelike rocking horse (horsehair mane, leather saddle, piercing brown eyes). There's also a built-in changing station and a three-foot gilded mobile along with every conceivable item a baby's room could ever want, except a baby. I hate seeing the crib—white, handcrafted, antique, with a crescent-shaped base, picked out by myself, purchased before the birth, "bad luck" incarnate—how true was that prediction? In a different lifetime, a day ago, I rocked baby Matthew to sleep in that crib. But regardless of how painful it is to see, no one dares shut the door. That would be too much. I wonder how long it needs to stay open? A week, a month, a year? Maybe it would be helpful to circulate a memo. The rich have rules for everything else, why not this?

To Residents and Staff of Sixteen Oak,

In light of the disappearance of Matthew Speedy, kindly leave the nursery door wide open.

In this regard, six months has been deemed to be the correct amount of time to wait for his return. Thereafter, you are more than welcome to abandon hope completely. At that juncture, please feel free to close the matter, and the door, once and for all.

During the first two weeks, we also request you keep the entire ordeal strictly confidential. It would be greatly appreciated if, to the outside world, you would conduct yourself as if everything were totally normal. Give no indication that anything untoward is afoot. This is a person-

al problem, which is better left kept within the confines of the family.

Lastly, if you must cry, please restrict your tears to when you are alone, at night, in your bed.

Yours sincerely,

The Editor-in-Chief @ Kidnapping and The Proper Etiquette

I look around at the Speedy family members in their distinct and separate poses and recognize the scene in the movie, usually before the big battle, when the soldiers take stock of their lives, pull out pictures of their "best girl," "smoke 'em if they got 'em," unfold that crumpled last letter from old Ma (crumpled her own self) while a lowly GI plays a plaintive harmonica in the distance—

"Can I get you anything, Missus?" I jump at the question. "I can see you have not had nothing to eat the whole day." I stare blankly at Izabella from Guatemala, now the most senior of eight employees. True to character, Izabella has been fraught with worry and unafraid to show it. Ever since Matthew disappeared she's barely left the house, electing instead to spend her time preparing meal after (predominantly uneaten) meal. Her station (by default, in Dolores' absence, "head of household"), permits her to defy convention by displaying what I truly believe to be nothing short of heartfelt empathy. "You just wait here and I bring for you some pastry and some tea, yes?"

"Thank you, Izabella, but maybe you should make it a double vodka and a bowl full of Xanax instead."

She stares, innocent, amazed I can joke at a time like this, which is a different time for me than it is for her, a fact which will never, ever be revealed to her. For this, I am sincerely sorry.

CHAPTER 68

WHAT IS "SUSPENSE" anyway? It's like nothing, right? The absence of anything. It's that vast empty space over the teen girl's shoulder where you're pretty sure the movie's nefarious monster is going to jump out because the music is telling you so, refusing to end on a settled note while your fingernails claw the armrest.

What the eyes see and the ears hear, the mind believes. Houdini said that, and he got it on the nose. I know in some ways I'm being deceived and in others ways, deceitful. One thing's for sure, the suspense is killing me.

Nothing is happening, and I don't know how much longer I can take it. Timing is everything. It's all about timing. These things can't be rushed. But wait too long and the crowd gets restless, don't they? Resentful. It's like a magic trick; there needs to be exactly the right proportion of poise, patter, and props for the misdirection to work. In the end, though, it's all misdirection.

Now, for six hundred million reasons, I need the big reveal.

I take a drink. It helps.

CHAPTER **69**

STRAY YE NOT my children, for just as good leadeth to good; sin leadeth to sin. Or is that death? Sin leadeth to death?

I vow not to be this way, not today. I get out of bed to where food has been left for me. I will eat standing, the way a soldier eats before the battle, literally the least I can do. I grab a nauseatingly sweet scone and surrender to the welcome sensation of sugar and sudden energy, washed down with a mouthful of unexpectedly hot coffee. Today's the day. The kidnappers will wait no longer. There's no reason. *Get it done,* I say.

My thoughts are interrupted by Mary-Elizabeth's poorly muted prayers from downstairs. She's started the lamentations and self-pity early this morning: "Please, Jesus, help us. Bring my grandson back, please, Jesus."

I wander downstairs to see her on her knees in the second study, the one with the fireplace. Reverend McMaster is there too, his thick, hirsute hands covering Mary-Elizabeth's head. He encourages her prayers, offering up "amens" and rocking her gently back and forth, the motion unmistakably sexual. Or that's just me and my filthy imagination at work, the Devil on my shoulder—that dude's always there no matter where I go.

Reverend McMaster ("Macky") has never been to our home, though he drops in at The Royal Oaks on occasion to see Mary-Elizabeth if he's "in the neighborhood," usually coinciding with the end of the tax year, culminating in the handing over of a substantial Schedule A deduction and a variety of home-made baked goods (prepared by the kitchen staff, credited to Mary-Elizabeth). Today, though, he's been summoned to place a direct call to Jesus on our behalf, to beseech Him to intervene in a chain of events I can only assume the Son of G-d didn't see coming. I'm trying to be considerate (empathetic even) but I'm still not convinced Macky (or Jesus for that matter) is going to be more help than say, for instance, the FBI, which has still yet to be called. I have to admit, though, watching Big Mack work goes a long way to restoring my faith—specifically, my faith in the church's innate ability to monetize its congregants. I notice that around his permanently sunburned neck he's wearing a thin, wooden crucifix. It reminds me of the one Sister Mary Grace gave me, the one that was purposed to expel my innate malevolence, the one I wore that night. I watch the cross swing back and forth and remember them all, each salty body, each separate slam into me, each squeeze, poke, tickle and spank, each injury and injustice.

All of which I relished at the time as vindication. Exactly what I needed. No, that's not quite right—exactly what I *deserved*.

LAMENTATIONS
CHAPTER 70

STILL NO WORD from the kidnappers. The DNA test results haven't arrived, either, for some reason. The lab claims to have sent them—"we'll send them again"—but they still refuse to email, text, or tell us on the phone. By this point John, Mary-Elizabeth, the siblings and I all agree that despite Harrison's advice to the contrary, it's time to call the police.

"Please, will you call?" John begs, turning to *me*. "I just can't do it. I wouldn't know where to begin." Senator Speedy, captain of the Harvard boxing team and one-quarter-heir to the eighth largest fortune in California, hands me the phone.

"What should I say?" I direct the question towards Mary-Elizabeth (John is no use anymore).

"Just tell them what's happened. They'll understand. Tell them everything."

I stare at the phone. It waits patiently for me to pick it up and take action. It mocks my inertia. I will it to disappear, to dissolve (along with last forty-eight hours) into the glass table. This is it. I know it. There is nothing left to do. The time has come.

Izabella from Guatemala steps in, something on her mind, more coffee perhaps—

"I thought I told you to leave us alone!" John screeches. "For fuck sake, what language do I have to say it in for you people to understand?" Despite his disheveled appearance, John still manages to intimidate. He strides towards Izabella with purpose.

"Mister, you can shout all you want," Izabella barks back, stopping John cold, "but I had to bring this. It's for you." John's frozen stiff, not at the words but at the plain, brown, unstamped, uncreased, unsealed envelope Izabella holds out to him. Even from a distance we can see the envelope has no address, no postmark, not even a name. Instead, in the upper right hand corner, handwritten and underlined . . . the only two words needed: The Baby.

"Maybe it's the DNA results," Raymond suggests.

Fuck. Probably is. Damn it. How'd that happen? I'd been watching like a hawk.

No one moves and then, as if on cue, we all lunge at once. John pulls the envelope away. I have no excuse to tackle him, shred the document, drown it in the pool like the flash drive, so I don't. I'll have to take the consequences whatever they are.

John stares at the single piece of paper. I take a seat, expecting the worst. John reads:

"Money been receive. Too late. Instructions on USB computer device not being followed.

Instruction clear to pick up baby. Not followed. You have more family. Too late for baby. We are not babysitters. You never to contact again."

The note could have been clearer, I admit. I wander off, patrolling the room, not trusting myself. Overcome by nervousness, I stumble into the library where Olfeng,

Vihaan's Czechoslovakian replacement, is hard at work on the pathetic little red flash drive.

"You can stop that now," I tell him. "It's too late for that. No longer relevant."

"Ah. Huh," Olfeng says. I'm not sure of his English. It's not clear he understands. "It doesn't matter anyway," he tells me in perfect English. "The storage drive never had anything on it. It was designed to be defective. It was never any good, even before it got all wet and broken."

I nod, understanding.

"You're sure?" I ask for the record.

"Vihaan was sure, too," he reveals. "He told it to Harrison James, the lawyer."

"Did he tell it to Mr. Speedy?"

"Who?"

"John. My husband. John Speedy."

Olfeng doesn't know. He shrugs and begins gathering his things to go. He hands me the red plastic device, which I pocket. Avoiding the others, I show him out through the side entrance, pausing around front to check for stray DNA results or other hazards.

"Too late for baby," Sylvia is reading again from the note when I come back into the living room. "What does that mean?" She's in denial mode—

"What the fuck do you think it means?!" Raymond screams from his anger stage. "He's dead! Little Matthew is dead!"

We stare at him. There's no need to get so loud about it. *Put it on the internet, why don't you? Tell your friends on Facebook or Instagram or LinkedIn. Make a fucking TikTok.*

But what else could it mean? As for me, I admit it—I look like I've sailed through *all* the stages of grief and am now sitting pretty somewhere in "acceptance" after ten months of this. Time is linear, and there is no going back. What matters now, like always, is what's next.

John's phone, still on the coffee table, lights up, vibrates, and jingles. The text is large, bold, complete confirmation. We can all read it just fine where it sits:

From: VVRT6e226@yandex.ru To: Johntspeedy@gmail.com

Look attachment. Is picture of dead baby. You pay money, but you should have pay more attention. Should have respond to disk drive instructions. More suffer for you and family. Now you delete mail and never to contact again.

Under the thin blue line that separates the footer from the rest of the page, still and ominous:

1 Attachment

No one dares open the jpg file. Total paralysis. A morbid game of Truth or Dare. We silently challenge each other to look at the truth. Finally, Mary-Elizabeth Speedy cracks. She grabs John's phone off the table and thumbs the smooth, glowing screen. Obediently, the pixels arrange themselves. The image is crystal clear: the bruised, bloodied, one-handed corpse of a two-week-old baby boy. Mary-Elizabeth faints. No one goes to her aid. We're fairly sure she's breathing just by looking at her, but none of us considers that important now. John, lost in the crossroads of pain and denial—actually, who knows what he's thinking?—pries his phone from her cold, unconscious hand. Hope exits the house, leaving a vacuum of disbelief. Although we are all together in one room, we are, each one of us, alone with our thoughts. No Hollywood ending this time. I press "delete" on the picture. Matthew is dead. It's over.

REVELATIONS
CHAPTER 71

A YEAR EARLIER, on that fateful date, I laughed myself to tears all the way from Holmsby Boulevard to West Wilshire Lane. The whole delicious scheme, I suddenly realized, could actually work. It was either an epiphany or I was having a nervous breakdown. Perhaps both. I whooped and hollered. Nobody noticed. I was in the Rolls on the way to that man. The windows were up and the AC was on. Do cops stop drivers for vehicular hysteria? I wondered. (Not an issue BTW; my tits always get me off the hook with a stern warning anyway LOL.) I laughed because I finally got it. John was going to be a senator! He could do anything he wanted. He could give me anything I wanted. Anything at all. The fucking Big Rock Candy Mountain! But I wouldn't have to be there with him to enjoy it—no need whatsoever.

"You fucking genius!" I yelled at that man, who couldn't hear me—I was still two miles away. I saw what he was up to then. I got it, sensed it, understood it all clearly. It was brilliant, he was brilliant, and I just couldn't stop laughing.

We made love desperately, like two teenagers in the back of a car. Then we did it all over again. He couldn't get enough of me, and I felt the same way about him.

Then, when the fireworks had all been exploded:

"In other news," he said, "Maria tells me her employers are going to have another baby."

I nodded. I remembered Maria, the young nanny downstairs, already taking care of one toddler, now with another on the way. I knew exactly what that meant. It scared me to death. I shook my head, but I'd already decided. In my mind, I was nodding, not shaking, popping a bottle of imaginary champagne and joining that man in a toast: "To conceiving, both babies and plans."

"This is for you," that man told me, handing me a jewelry box, gold, with a ribbon around it, the size of a bracelet or necklace or watch.

I couldn't help it. I started to cry.

"Now don't get all keyed up," that man warned quickly, seeing the look on my face and the tears down my cheeks. I knew it wasn't more birth control pills. "Open it," he said.

I wiped the tears. I opened it. Inside was a pregnancy test; the little window said "Pregnant." "Oh," I said simply.

"Maria fished this out of their trash. She knew I was in the market."

"They threw this away?" I asked, not sure why, but it sounded like a legitimate question. "People don't save these and frame them, you know."

"You went to a lot of trouble," I said to him.

"It's nothing."

"You know, I hate to burst your balloon, but you can buy these on eBay. Positive tests. They call them 'pranks, gags, jokes.' Five bucks."

He looked horrified. "That's . . . wow . . ."

"Yeah, awful," I agreed.

"But you looked it up on eBay?" he asked. He didn't miss a trick.

"Yeah, just looked. A couple days ago," I confessed.

"So we're thinking the same way."

"Nah, you're way ahead of me," I told him. "Way ahead."

"Flattery will get you everywhere," he whispered.

CHAPTER 72

"A JOURNEY OF a thousand lies begins with a single theft . . ."

Or something like that. At my appointment, I took the liberty of ripping off a few sheets from Dr. Goldman's personalized notepad—probably couldn't fake a pre-scription on there, but good enough for our purposes. Goldman was upset with me, of course, for letting my birth control lapse.

"You know how dangerous it would be for you to get pregnant, right?" he squealed.

"It could kill me."

"Not could, *would* kill you—"

"I'll take the pills, I promise," I told him. "Really, Doctor, you're so kind to worry." That lit up his face (and other regions, I suspect).

"Okay, then, we'll leave things as they are," he said.

The damage Aaron and his friends did, mostly Marvin, the sadist, was permanent. In retrospect, I probably saved Kayla Smithe from the fate I suffered. Who knows what good ol' Marv would have done to Kayla's *hoo-hoo cha-cha* given half a chance. Look what he did to mine, and he only had me for the eight hours.

"Good deeds are quiet; sins shout," Sister Mary Grace used to warn. I didn't need to explain a thing to the Staffords. The doctor on duty did that for me, blurting it all out. He even got the number of guys right—four. What can I say? It was a long night and they were horny teen boys, eager for it, cruelly so, stronger than they knew, and I was a delicate flower, it turned out, a deviant rose on a fragile stem. Plucked. Fucked. Discarded. I heard "hemorrhage, infection, blunt trauma, toxic shock," but it was only pain and humiliation to me, all in a day's work. The bottom line: I was lucky to be alive, I might want to get some counseling, and as to what they figured I *really* wanted to know: I could have all the sex I wanted ("after you become an adult, please") as long as I never got pregnant. "Ticking time-bomb" was the term, I believe. BTW, abortion wasn't ever an option. If there's one thing Sister Mary Grace managed to beat into my "thick little skull," it's that baby-murderers are first in line to Hell. More than dying, I'm afraid of having to decide between my own life, my own soul, or the life and soul of whatever is growing inside me—a tremendous burden to carry, especially for a lifelong atheist like me. Needless to say, my fault. Entirely my fault. So go ahead and judge me; everybody else does.

We took our sweet time with the letter, that man and I, turning it into a game, puzzle, art project. I dug up old paperwork with Dr. Goldman's signature, a nasty scrawl but remarkably consistent. He practiced it over and over again. That man takes pride in making things look authentic, another reason I love him. Between the two of us, we managed the text, appropriately breezy and medically convincing, in Dr. Goldman's "letter-voice," announcing: *"The patient is approximately six weeks pregnant."*

And thus doth He create a man, and on the seventh day He rested from the work which He had done, and it was good.

CHAPTER 73

IT'S TIME. I'VE waited long enough now. Sitting around with my dick in my hand. Hoping that she will come through. I'm not saying that I've given up hope; I'm saying if you want something done right better do it yourself. I know that she thinks she had it all planned out and covered every angle. Maybe that's what I want her to think. Drop some breadcrumbs here and there and watch her follow the trail. It makes me feel better to think of it that way, that I'm the one leading her down the garden path. Watching her stumble and stutter through the maze I've so carefully crafted. Yeah, she's about to learn that this old dog, the one she thought was her obedient pet, still has a few new tricks. And teeth!

CHAPTER 74

THE NIGHT OF Matthew's death, I slip out and go see that man. I have to. A phone call won't do. I'm between Holmsby and West Wilshire again. It's an anniversary of sorts, but this time I'm not laughing. Maybe I should be, but I'm not.

"So we just play hide-the-baby all day and all night?" I asked him when he told me the whole story for the first time, which now seems like forever ago.

"That's right."

"How long do you think we can keep that up?" I wanted to know.

"We only need the baby for a few days—that's all."

Technically, he'd been right. Emotionally, I'm exhausted. We fall into each other's arms at the door and I cry, the tension leaving me in a flood from my eyes. We separate. I sniff.

"You bastard," I tell him.

"What?" he asks.

"You doubled the ransom at the last minute." He looks genuinely puzzled.

"No, I didn't," he tells me. "I don't know what you're talking about." He's telling the truth. I see my horror reflected in his eyes.

KNOCK at the door. I jump and yelp. We freeze, scared to death. *Who could that be? No one knows we're here.*

"Guess who," John Speedy says through the door. The Voice is back—cool, collected, senatorial, sending shivers up and down my spine. "Let me in. Now. We need to talk."

That man and I look at each other in disbelief. We're also terrified and unsure of what to do next. John is not going away. Nothing that easy or simple is going to happen now. I recall the licensed firearm he's been brandishing these last few days. I hope that man has a similar weapon. He hugs me again, soothes me, and whispers, "it's going to be okay."

I want to scream—"it's going to be okay" is exactly what John's been saying. I hate them both.

"Let's see what the senator has to say," that man states out loud, going to the door, opening it.

John stands there, a mischievous smile on his face, hands up in a "don't hurt me" pose.

There's no visible gun, axe, knife, crossbow. That's a good start.

"Mind if I come in?" he asks that man, who backs away from the door to let him pass. "Boo!" he says to me, making me jump like I'd seen a ghost. Nobody moves. We hover around the entrance to the condo's living room.

John and that man square off, eyeing each other, a couple of bulls and only one cow—me. They'll start huffing and puffing and pawing the ground with their hooves in a moment. I like it; it's thrilling; I can smell the blood and spit and semen and my own bodily juices wet for the payoff.

"I don't suppose you have a name," John asks.

"Wouldn't be smart to tell you that, I'm afraid," that man replies.

"No, I suppose not," John nods, understanding. They aren't going to shake hands, but I can see they aren't going to charge each other and maul each other, either.

We take seats in the living room. Drinks are poured and I see we're all going to pretend to a certain level of sophistication, standard practice, I assume, when $600,000,000 and a dead baby are involved.

"So let's get the elephant out of the room—there's no g-ddamn baby, is there?" John asks, just to be sure.

I let that man answer.

"No. There's not. That baby's someone else's. He's back with them now. He's fine and will continue to be well taken care of."

"Is his name Matthew?" John asks, a pathetic plea in his voice. It wasn't his baby; it never will be, but that didn't stop John from falling in love, it seems.

That man shakes his head. The baby's name is Jason, but that man knows better than to reveal it.

"Okay, next question," John begins, painfully, seeming to have aged suddenly. He pulls out a folded sheet of paper. "The DNA test."

That man and I give each other a look. We'd discussed that aspect to death, never locking it down. The best we could manage was "we'll finesse it when the time comes if we have to."

"The hand is not a Speedy hand, of course," John said, waving the paper. "But you already know that, don't you?"

That man nods. I shake my head, indicating the same thing.

"So the hand . . . ?" John asks, swallowing, grabbing courage. He turns to me, an accusatory look, or maybe he thinks the blow will be softer coming from a woman.

"I didn't know about the hand," I tell him honestly, bouncing that same look in that man's direction. "The hand was a surprise." Why John should believe me at this point, I have no idea. Why I care that he believes me, I also don't know.

"Me and Maria—" that man says and stops cold, realizing his mistake. "Me and a colleague," he begins again, "found a crematorium not too far away from here. The night man was shocked, of course. 'You want to give me five hundred dollars for what?' he asked a couple of times before catching on. 'We wanna put someone in the furnace ourselves. A baby, if you've got one in stock,' I told him. He refused. 'C'mon,' I said, 'you get to do it all the time. Spread the fun around a little.

What the hell, let's make it an even grand.' So apparently everything has a price. Ha, look who I'm telling, you two. Anyway, when he was gone, I took the dead baby's hand."

John and I both cringe and turn away. Neither of us consider ourselves squeamish, but the image of that is almost too much to bear.

"Yeah, my colleague had the same reaction," that man comments. "It didn't feel good, trust me, but the baby was *dead*, after all."

I hear him, and there's nothing I can say to convince him that fact doesn't really matter. That he was capable of doing it, dead baby or not, says something about him. The fact that I can still love him despite this says even more about me—

"Shit happens. So what? It's a real hand from a baby who had died. Nobody got hurt," that man protests, annoyed at our dainty sensibilities.

"Thank God for that, anyway," John says. "So there never was a Speedy baby?" John tries again though he knows better. It doesn't matter how many times he asks, it's always going to be the same answer, but there's still hope there, the dying embers of a desperate flame of faith.

I shake my head. That man shakes his head. I have no heart to speak; neither does that man.

I don't want to hurt John; that man (amazingly) doesn't seem to want to either.

"So again, who was Matthew? Or Jason, or whatever his name was?" John wants to know.

That man looks at me, accusing. I wave my hand in irritation—*no, I did not give it away! I didn't!* But I did. I remember it well. Blamed it on a dream. The irony that a dream might have led to this nightmare is not lost on me.

"The baby lives not far away," that man explains, "with his parents. We borrowed him.

That's the baby you know."

"Dolores?" John asks. "Did she do the borrowing?"

I shake my head. I won't say. That man seems proud of my silence. *John's not as stupid as he looks*, I want to warn that man, but I don't, because then violence might break out, John against me, that man against him.

"So enlighten me. How exactly did the whole bullshit birth thing go down, anyway?" John wants to know.

"You were supposed to have your squash game—" I say.

"—and instead I got that call, the blackmail about my grades—"

"His idea," I state, pointing to that man.

"What made you think my grades were so horrible?" John asks.

"I knew rich kids growing up," that man smiles.

John smiles back. He doesn't pursue it.

"It got you out of the way," that man points out.

"And since you used the chauffeur," I continue, "I could use Uber, moan and groan a lot, and give the driver a tip large enough for him to remember me if it ever came to that."

"So no scheduled cesarean?"

That man and I shake our heads. I don't mention that man's willingness to cut me open to create a convincing scar—

"Emergency vaginal delivery," that man explains. "Her idea," he adds, pointing to me.

"So the Uber driver dropped you off at the doctor's office . . ." John guesses, suddenly anxious to move on, squeamish maybe.

". . . and we walked out the doctor's office back door," that man finishes.

For lunch, right over there at that table, I'm tempted to add, but I don't. John has been cooperative so far (in fact, downright co-conspiratorial) but who knows how many times you can kick a dog before he bites your foot clean off? He doesn't need to know about that man's friend, a movie costumer who supplied us with a foam-rubber "bump-suit" for the whole range of the pregnancy, or be reminded of how I kept him from seeing me naked all those months. And John certainly doesn't need to know the details of Matthew's miraculous birth—how four hours after being summoned into action, I held a wriggling, crying, healthy, eight-pound, three-ounce baby boy. He doesn't need to know that the three of us—me, *that man*, and baby—cuddled naked together on the bed, a picture-perfect moment. Or what that man said when he first laid eyes on Jason, aka Matthew:

"He's just about as perfect as he can be. All ten fingers, all ten toes, and a wonderful good pair of loud lungs. He even looks like you. I wish he was ours."

John doesn't need to know I was startled, overcome, and how in remarkable solidarity with baby Matthew, I started to cry.

"What about Prakhid?" John asks. "Is he even a real doctor?"

"An actor," that man answers. "Not too much to show for it yet."

"Well, he's very good," John says in his own defense. That man shrugs.

"He has a tendency to go off-script, I'm afraid, but he can be convincing when he drills into the part."

"He'll be well compensated, I imagine," John mutters. That man nods.

"So about *our* money," John says, getting down to business. "The amount you asked for wasn't enough."

"So you doubled it," I complete the thought.

"Don't worry, you got the same amount, but then so

did I. We split the six-hundred million right down the mid-dle. It's already done. You got your Bitcoin account; I got mine."

"But it's your own money . . . " that man says. John's shaking his head.

"Mother's money. Mary-Elizabeth Speedy's money. Liz's money. Trust money. Family money. She's generous to a point but that's it. I knew from the beginning this one was up to something," John said, shaking a finger at me (not the middle one). "I just wasn't sure what it was. If I'm ever going to be a senator, I need to get hold of *all* of my mother's assets, which, between us, I think we've just about done. She would never contribute to my campaign, not really, not enough—a token at most. She thinks the whole thing's just a waste of resources and senators are all crooks anyway." John pauses. "So, fuck, what can I say? When she's right, she's right, but I still want to be a senator, in the worst way or not. Anyway, all beside the point because it's not just the money. She's worried about investigations into the Speedy fortune, es-pecially if I give that oval office a run, which I definite-ly plan on doing. There are gas-soaked skeletons in the family closet ready to burst into flame, see? Reporters will dig, books will be written, a Speedy demise will fol-low. What's that thing you say?" John asks, turning to me: "Behind every great fortune lies a great crime?"

I'm shocked. He really does remember everything I ever said.

"Mother has never apologized for her wealth, or for *anything* for that matter, so the fact that she never got specific about what crime exactly—never even *hinted* at it—can only mean one thing: it's *unspeakable*."

John lets the word linger for a moment before he

emits a guilty, hollow laugh, followed by a shiver.

That man and I look at each other. We're too surprised to be upset. John waits.

"Let me get this straight," that man manages, "we asked for three-hundred-million dollars, you raised six-hundred-million instead, then put half of that in our account and the other half in yours?"

"Uh huh."

"To run for the Senate."

"Yeah," John declares enthusiastically. "I'm counting on your votes."

That man and I check each other again. Our long con becomes John's con as well. *"Why not?"* we communicate with our eyes. *The more the merrier.* When I look back at John, I see with certainty that he *will* be President someday, and a damn good one at that.

"So I guess we're all in it together," I smile, pretending we have any other choice.

John shares the smile before he turns to that man and asks him, "Do you think my wife and I could talk for a few minutes? Alone."

That man is alarmed at the idea, but he sees I'm willing, if only out of curiosity about what John could possibly have to say. I sense that man trusts me maybe, just that far.

"Please, be my guest," he says, putting down his drink and picking up a light jacket. "I'll just take a little walk around the block. I have my phone. If you slit her throat, Senator, you will be next, understand?"

By the way John laughs, you can tell he likes being called "Senator."

"Why would I do that?"

We all know why—anybody else probably would.

"Later," that man says, and backs out of the condo. As soon as he's gone, John turns to me.

"I know you can't have children," he tells me. "I've known that for a long, long time."

I'm stunned.

"When did you know?"

"Before we were married."

"Jesus fuck!" I exclaim, more amazed than angry.

"Now that you're rich yourself, there are things you should know. In a way it's my fault, really. I should have told you."

"What are you talking about?"

"When you're this rich, you make it a point to find out about the people around you," John states rather matter-of-factly, not something he's particularly proud of. "And before you ask, Mother does *not* know you can't have children, and I trust you to keep it that way. She can deal with a murdered grandson, and she'll have to deal with not having much money, but what she can't deal with is being shown to be foolish."

I'm not sure I can be that generous—

"Me?" John interrupts the thought. "I've always been foolish. Foolish and gullible." He grins that boyish grin that once made me want to fuck him every time he flashed it. "Fool me once, fool me twice, I don't care. Incidentally, Dr. Goldman doesn't know that I know, either. He didn't betray you."

"Why didn't you *say* something?" I ask, exasperated. "All those hints, all that prodding? 'Give us a baby, give us a baby.' That was just cruel."

"I was waiting for you to tell me," John counters. "All

those years I was hoping you'd be honest with me. It hurt me a great deal that you couldn't do that, couldn't trust me. I loved you. I still love you."

I'm mortified. At least that man isn't hearing this. What's the expression? *"Awkward."* I'm also intrigued— John seems to have finally grown a pair. That's why he wanted that man to go for a walk—not to kill me, but to show me his shiny new balls in private. Does he really think I care? Okay, I do, a little.

"I know about the stuff on the internet, too," he continues. I gasp, more surprised than ashamed.

All those times I could have told Kyle to go fuck himself (instead of me). "Who told you?" I ask.

"The detectives," he answers. "Wait. Why? Who else knows?" he adds, alarmed.

"Nobody," I answer, which I see he doesn't believe. "Maybe Kayla," I mention, leaving out Kyle. I've taken John's money and busted his balls, there's no need to break his heart, too. The fact was I succumbed to Kyle's blackmail for a good cause: to protect John's political image and give him a shot at the Senate—

Which probably wouldn't make John feel any better.

"I watch sometimes," he admits, and I can tell by his face what he's talking about.

"You do?" I blush, really blush, bright red.

"When you're not . . . you know . . . when you're not available in person."

"Oh Jesus," I mutter.

"Yeah, Jesus."

"You knew I could still get pregnant, though," I suddenly realize, getting angry again. "What?" he asks, surprised.

"You knew I could still get pregnant."

"No."

"You knew that it would *kill me* if I got pregnant."

"I did not know that—" John protested.

"Yet you fucked me anyway," I hiss at him.

"I was told you *couldn't* get pregnant—"

"Because it would kill me."

"So . . . birth control?" he asks helplessly.

I snicker in disgust. I'm tired of this conversation. We lied to each other. Maybe we had a good thing going, maybe not, but we killed it with lies—that much was true.

And Jesus reached towards the Heavens and spoke: "What profiteth them that sin against their fellow man, for in the end are they not all but dust?"

CHAPTER **75**

BEING RIGHT—IT can sting like a motherfucker. So yeah, I knew Amanda was playing me all along. I didn't know exactly how or what, but I knew. That's what kept me in it. Pure masochism. Even when I knew she wasn't ever going to be mine. I needed to solve the puzzle, no matter how perilous. No matter what the cost. I married her despite Mum's misgivings, and Raymond's and Sylvia's and Mike's and hell, everybody who met her. Maybe I stuck with her just to find out what she was up to. Seriously, have you ever seen anybody get up and walk out in the middle of a magic trick? So I watched, mesmerized, until the (bitter) end, playing the deuce but palming the ace.

Well, who's laughing now? Just seeing the look on her face was worth the ride. Worth more than the three hundred million. Priceless, actually. I bet Mr. Anonymous thinks she betrayed him somehow. That's a hoot. Maybe it'll eat at the two of them, gnaw at them, eroding whatever special bond they think they share, until it tears them apart. Ha! I'd enjoy that. Maybe she'll come back. I can only hope. I will hope. After the wringer she's put me through, I should care about my own pride and self-es-

teem, but what do I give a fuck? If she was the one with all the money, I would have screwed her over to get it, I'm sure. After all, I did it to my own mother, for

Godsakes. Outrageous fortunes beget outrageous misfortunes. I know that. You can't put a price on love? Bullshit. Everything's for sale. That's why I'd take her back and she doesn't even have to beg . . . not much.

But I'm not an idiot. Just a dreamer. She's not coming back. If they were going to go at each other, they would have done it in the nine months they had under the pressure of the scam. They didn't. Their bond is forever most likely. Screw me with a ten-foot pole.

The blackmail about my grades—that hurt more than anything, I must say. I've maintained a 4.0 GPA since I was a fetus. Amanda should have known that. I'm pissed she thought otherwise, and bought into that guy's fucked-up stereotype of a rich kid. I'm not a genius, maybe, but I'm close, damn it. And all that baloney about not attending the birth. Infections? "Has to be a cesarean, yadda yadda—" I wasn't born yesterday. But the dead giveaway, actually, was the sex. Twenty times in fourteen days (but who's counting?). That's when I knew that bitch was up to something. Despite what she thinks, she wasn't my first (or last) and I know how to spot a fake when I feel one. What the mouth not sayeth, the body doth betrayeth. Or some bullshit like that.

And the baby, the fucking baby. Not my fault to begin with, either. I had no idea Mother was going to act the way she did, holding Amanda solely accountable for the proliferation of the Speedy species. She never pressured Raymond that way, or Sylvia, or Mike. I didn't care that Amanda couldn't have kids. Frankly, her sordid background was a turn-on, a real kick. I wanted a *wife for Poke 'er Night; I didn't give a holy fuck about the other nights of the week. I know, I know—senator's wives have to hit some mark above skank, but it's a low bar, and it didn't take much to get Amanda going, I have to say. Best of all, she loved any and all of it. At least that's what it felt like to me. Ask any man; he'll tell you he'll take enthusiasm over looks or skill, any of it, any day (though Amanda has it all—no tradeoff required—check the tapes). Thank you, Jesus! And yes, I know how that sounds. I'm shallow. Guess what? I don't care. Speedies are different. Entitlement is an inherited trait, after all. Her stuff on the internet was a big help, I gotta say. You know how many beautiful women throw themselves at me every day? It kept me faithful to her (mostly), though her youth on those tapes did creep me out a little, I swear to God. But without the visual aids always a double-click away, I'm not sure what kind of husband I would have been.*

Honest though, it's not all about making love. My deepest sexual fantasy: Amanda tells me the truth, the whole truth, so help her g-ddamnit. All about Aaron, the injuries, the gangbang, the videos, getting kicked out of the house, school, the whole deal. Damn, I wanted to hear that from her, not from three oily detectives submitting extensive, single-spaced reports and ridiculously padded expense accounts. In this fantasy, she tells me the whole truth just so I know, just because she loves me and wants me to know: "There's something I've got to tell you, something from my past. I don't want us to have any secrets, ever. I know you love me enough not to judge me. No matter what, I'll always love you."

Fuck, I'm getting hard just thinking about it.

But I guess that wasn't going to happen in real life, like a lot of sex fantasies. I knew something was up, just not exactly what, and I sure as hell didn't know the old boy-friend would reappear like the Second Coming, not at the beginning anyway. I hope it was all worth it for them. The money will help, but take it from someone who's had money, it's not everything.

Take my mother, for instance. Please. Her willingness to invest her fortune on her grandson, but never me, her son, hurt me a great deal. The kind of pain only money can buy.

CHAPTER 76

A LOT HAS happened in the six months since the final email. John and I are divorced. The police, FBI, and tabloids have, each one, taken turns at dissecting the horrific story. Each and every one of us has been examined and cross-examined, interviewed, praised, vilified, and sensationalized (though my long-ago night with Aaron and the boys hasn't surfaced. Yet). We have been the subject *de jour* at dinner tables across America. We are even—based solely on the notoriety— asked to dinner at The White House, an invitation senatorial candidate John Speedy eagerly accepts, to be attended with his grieving ex-wife (me).

The FBI knows about my past, prefers not to pursue it, and intends to keep it secret. "We think you've suffered enough," is their unofficial position.

They question me about an anonymous letter they receive that claims: "there never was a baby." I recognize Dr. Goldman's scrawl immediately; so do they. To his credit, Goldman refuses to violate doctor-patient confidentiality, or confirm he wrote the note. The feds aren't buying the "no baby" idea anyway.

"Who does this guy think we are, the Federal Bureau of Imbeciles?"

The documentation on baby Matthew is overwhelming: hundreds of videos and thousands of photos masterfully staged, including one special image (among the teeming memes) taken by none other than Handsome Harry Hudson, "portrait photographer to the stars."

"Shit, there's gotta be more photos of that kid than Prince Archie fucking Windsor," one of the agents observes, noting the sheer size of the collection.

"I pic, therefore I am," the other agent states, swear to G-d, *my thoughts exactly.*

"The kid's got his father's eyes," the first agent points out, and his partner agrees, confirming the absurdity of the allegation.

"Never was a baby, my ass."

The tip is discarded, filed under "nonsense" along with approximately 800 others, most suggesting alien abduction.

Other, more down-to-Earth conspiracy theories circulate, but the conventional wisdom prevails that Matthew Speedy was kidnapped and mutilated, and even though 600 million was paid in ransom, the child was killed anyway, and the perpetrators are still at large. Due mainly to overwhelming sympathy for John's suffering (always *his* suffering, never mine), the election was what you'd expect—John won easily. His newfound fame and public persona as a caring father who'd sustained unparalleled loss went a long way; 300 million in cash from "special interests" pouring in at precisely the right moment (John's share of the ransom) took him the rest of the way. Mary-Elizabeth put up her own $100 contribution to the campaign and received a baseball cap and a tote bag in exchange.

"It's the least I could do," she said.

With the money gone, most of the staff of 16 Oak have sought alternative employment.

Attorney Harrison James retired from his law practice to write his memoirs. Maria and Dolores still work as nannies, but Dolores also volunteers as a grief counselor at a local church. They're working together on a tell-all book about the Speedy kidnapping, which, because of their criminal liability in the scheme, will not only *not* tell all, but will tell *nothing*.

Kyle and Kayla expect another child, or so I read in the society pages. I never spoke to them again. The couple reached out to John, inquiring about me, apparently, so John says. Kayla tried to describe the entire Aaron/Marvin episode to him until he told her to "shut her trap or he'd shut it for her." John cut off all communications after that. Very chivalrous. That man never defended me that way when he had the chance. That's just not his style. But he has other charms.

I'm holding his hand now. That man. Squeezing it. We are living in his condo temporarily, a facebrick studio with an oversized bed and a bronze horse statue (stolen, I learn). It's perfect.

With our newfound wealth, our options are limitless, but for the time being we're just thrilled to death to be together again without all the sneaking around, though to be honest, that was fun, too.

"When were you going to tell me about the hand?" I finally ask him.

"I wasn't. Your reaction to the bloody hand in the box

and the dead baby in the photograph needed to be spontaneous."

"You didn't trust my acting."

"Should I have?"

I think about that. I'm not an actress, I guess. Being a two-faced liar's not the same, I suppose.

"Why didn't you use Matthew for the dead baby?" I ask, another question on my mind.

"It's amazing nobody noticed it was a different kid, isn't it?" that man remarks.

"*I* noticed."

"And I'm so happy you didn't say anything," that man laughs, and I have to admit, I find it funny, too. "No," he goes on. "Even asleep, little Matthew—aka Jason—looked very much alive. It just didn't work the way I thought it would. So I took a picture of the dead kid at the morgue."

"Before you chopped his hand off."

"Yeah," that man says. "Pretty stupid of me, actually. Do the hand, *then* shoot the picture, for crying out loud. I had to pay someone to Photoshop it off. I won't make *that* mistake again," he laughs uncomfortably. I can see he wants to drop the subject. So I do, but he also needs to say: "I'm sorry I didn't tell you. It wasn't your acting. It's because I knew you wouldn't approve."

"I don't."

"You had your secrets; I had mine," he says.

"Secrets?"

He doesn't answer, hinting he knows all, which is like him. The only secret I have is how much I loved John through the entire thing, and love him still, something I only tell here.

The couple downstairs, Doug and Taylor, who do indeed work for Pixar, have become our good friends. They're far too busy to pay attention to the news, and have no idea who I am (or they are very good actors). We've become close to them and adore their two children, Janice and Jason. Janice is two years old, Jason is seven months now. The two nannies, Maria and her cousin Dolores, have become our close friends as well. They've both come into a great deal of money, and along with their book deal, no longer need to work as nannies, but continue out of love for the children and devotion to Doug and Taylor. I'm Aunty Amanda, which fills me with delight; that man is "Batman" in the kids' pronunciation, which pleases him as well. In the evening, we often sit out on the back lawn and play with the children and talk.

"So . . . there's something we want to ask you," Taylor says one night.

I hope it's not group sex, though I have to admit I've thought about it.

"We'd like you to be godparents to our son," Taylor announces.

"Oh," I answer, genuinely surprised. That man is equally stunned, flattered, and delighted. I cry. He holds me, explaining to Doug and Taylor that I'd "come from a strong religious background—she takes these things very seriously."

"But I'm not Catholic," I explain. "You'll want a Catholic godmother for little Matthew." "Matthew?" Taylor asks.

"What?" I respond, confused.

"You called Jason 'Matthew.'"

I gasp and hold my hand over my mouth, appalled at the mistake. "I . . . " I don't know what to say. I laugh it off.

That man watches me, amused, curious. "Long story," I tell them.

"We've got time," Doug remarks. "We'd love to hear it."

No, you wouldn't, I start to say. "Someday," I lie instead.

In the end, after extensive discussion, that man and I agree we're not really "godparent material" and politely decline the honor.

CHAPTER 77

I FOUND THE note in the car, right about the time Aman-
da announced her pregnancy. In my egotism, narcis-
sism, delusion, whatever you want to call it, I assumed
the note was for me. I know now it was written for him,
that man. Nobody will ever feel this way about me, I'm
afraid. Power, money—I can have those, but not the
note. That's valuable. That's priceless. That's what I want.
Hell, that's what we all want, somebody to love us this
completely:

"To you, my man—I have no idea why I'm doing this.
The risk is great, but then so is the reward, and not the
one you're thinking of. My reward is you, and your ad-
miration and respect. Maybe I've been loved and just
didn't recognize it, but it feels more like that has never
happened. Except from you. From the very first. We've
come a long way you and I. Remember? I remember it
all. Every minute. All the other stuff doesn't matter to me.
You know I'm risking my life for one reason and one rea-
son only—for you. I understand that's a terrible burden
to shoulder, but no less than my load, is it? There's noth-
ing I would love so much as to have your baby. Maybe

you don't know that. Maybe I need to say that out loud, but I don't have the power or the courage to either say it or do it. Hence this note. You are my everything, forever. All my love, Amanda."

CHAPTER 78

BIRTH AND DEATH. They have always been related. The day my innocence died, my love was born. A love that would haunt me and hurt me, soothe me and slave me. A love that would, ultimately, save me. A love that would be my first and my last. My alpha and my omega. G-d knows, it was all I ever wanted.

It took me years of looking, but I finally found him in a bar in London, a place for expats and refugees, American, Canadian, European, South African, Australian and Asian. Not a pub— definitely not—a *bar*. Our faux-accidental meeting was a work of art. I told the bartender I was surprising my husband by pretending to be a stranger. For his twenty-pound tip his task was simple.

"'Ey guv, that girl over there—the one with the tits you could hang the king's crown on— she's checking you out. What say you buy her a drink?"

As soon as he saw me, he knew. His grin looked like it might just break his face into a dozen little pieces. My own face flushed red, burning like the hottest room in Hell. He composed himself; I tried to do the same.

"That's kind of a strong drink for a girl," he said as he

sat next to me at the table without asking, a little too close, too familiar.

"That's kind of jerk thing to say."

"Hey, what can I say? I'm kind of a jerk," he said. He finished his drink and ordered another one—double vodka, rocks, no lime, no lemon, no mixer, no original- ity—an accountant's drink, the beverage of someone unimaginative, someone who'd be bad in bed. I knew better.

"You gonna buy me one?" I asked.

"That depends. You gonna tell me about your life now, or you gonna make me guess?"

"I'm a rocket scientist," I joked.

"It wouldn't surprise me, but it would be a real waste of those perfect tits."

I blushed all over again. Anyone else I would have been offended, slap him maybe, or a knee to the groin. But that man. His confidence. His cologne. The way he walked. It's very important how a man holds himself. Not many men know how to enter a room, grab control, take what they want. But every woman, whether she admits it or not, wants a man like that.

"I'm married," I told him, offering him my left hand, flashing a flawless 10-carat, round-cut, Ideal, H, VVS2 di- amond ring mounted on my finger.

"Anybody can put on a ring," he noted.

"I'm married," I assured him.

"And I really don't care what your fingers say," he said, taking a large mouthful of vodka. I smelled it on his breath as he leaned forward. He was drunker than I'd originally thought, drunker than I wanted him. "What I want to know is, are you happy?"

"Aaron . . . " I breathed—

"Shhh," he admonished, holding a finger up to his lips. "That's not me anymore."

"No?" I asked, curious, desperate to know the story.

"The name's Duke now. Duke Zattman . . . but you can call me That Man . . . everybody does."

"I could use that drink now, 'Duke,'" I told him.

He laughed. "Bartender," he called.

Why'd I do it? Why'd I take that kind of chance? Why risk everything I had? You can probably guess. I had no choice. First kiss. First touch. One more round of truth-or-dare, pinky-swear, "your hand/my thing" double-dare. Love me. My love. Aaron and the boys. Teen lust. So raw. Passion. Power. A certain borrowed Jeep. "The money game," which had nothing to do with money. Our days and nights dance in my head like ghosts. I should evict them, but how? I should be shamed, apologetic, traumatized. Nah. I'm the opposite. Proud. *That night* changed me, opened me, defined me. No longer the abandoned orphan, no longer the girl, I became the woman. The goddess. There's my religion: I worship the goddess who is me, not the me before, but the different me after—reborn, empowered, resurrected, entirely and unashamedly *turned on*, infused with carnal flames and ignited by reckless abandon. The me who is worthy of love.

I have no regrets. The memories are my drug. Sexual serotonin. I shoot up by shooting my hand down my pants. I'm there again, lying naked on the bed. They are all there. Aaron and the boys, watching me, wanting me, taking me. Why shouldn't I seek it out again and again and relive it over and over? I begged for that night of euphoric debauchery, a total surrender, free. Finally free.

Free from expectations, pain, abandonment, inhibitions, identity, society, and disguise. Just me—raw, uninhibited, authentic. Me.

"The videos are still up on the internet," I mention at some point.

"I know," he answers. "I watch them. Often."

"Ha!" I laugh. I don't tell him I watch them too.

That man, aka Aaron, aka "Duke," figured it out. Figured me out. Figured us out. I knew he would. Seeing me in that bar "gave birth to an idea"—that's what he said. But it was more than an idea. It was a detailed plan. A long con. A magic trick. An illusion that left the crowd gasping and the magician's assistant with everything she'd ever wanted: freedom, money, power, and most precious of all, *him*.

In our little Garden of Eden, she is Eve, but I am not Adam, I am the serpent. That's the way our story unfolded, and it suited me fine.

THE END

Believe it or not, I was born long before The Baby. Without my parents, Len and Evelyn Levy, neither I, nor Mathew Speedy (The Baby) would have ever existed. So, mom and dad, thank you, for bringing me into this world and giving me wings. You are my hero's and inspiration.

Dave Eisenstark, calling you an editor would be like calling Michelangelo a roof painter. You are an artist, a word-wizard and one of the most talented humans I've ever met. Without you there would be no Baby. I can't wait to work on the screenplay together.

To all my friends and loved ones, thank you for a lifetime of involuntary contributions to my art. There is a little piece of each of you in the Speedy family. So, in no particular order, Gila, Howard, Yaakov Dov, Yehuda Zev, Gazza, Lizy A, Debs R, Dr. Bailey, Turtle, Taryn L, Jeff (the funniest guy I know), Party Todd, Brando, Heather L, L.T., Dave V and "the one-in-a-billion Dudu". Each of you holds a special place in my mind, heart and life.

To Devin K and the team at Harnix Publishing. Thank you for giving birth to The Baby.

Lastly, to Brian L, for watching over me. Always.

Made in the USA
Middletown, DE
24 October 2021